Me and Mrs. Jones

Me and Mrs. Jones

a novel by
k. m. Thompson

The characters and events in this book are fictitious. Any resemblance to actual persons, living or dead, is purely coincidental.

RJ Publications
rjeantay@yahoo.com
www.rjpublications.com

Copyright © 2005 by K. M. Thompson
All Rights Reserved
ISBN 0-9769277-3-X

Without limiting the rights under copyright reserved above, no part of this book may be reproduced in any form whatsoever without the prior consent of both the copyright owner and the above publisher of this book.

Printed in the United States of America
March 2006

Visit K. M. Thompson at www.kmthompsonbooks.com

11 12 13 14 15 16 17 18 19 20

For comments email K. M. Thompson at
kmthomp1@yahoo.com

To the Love of my Life –

Acknowledgements

First and foremost, I must thank the Almighty for blessing me with the gift to write. He has walked beside me every step of the way, and has even carried me through when I thought I couldn't make it.

A very special thank you to my parents, my brother and his family. I love you with all my heart – thanks for always believing. And of course, I gotta give love to my extended family – The Regulars. Sorry about all the unreturned phone calls, but now you understand what I've been working on. We all have to live our dreams, or else, what's the point!

To those who won't stop supporting me: Iris & Steven Williams, Mahalia & Eddie Thompson, Michelle Jones (no relation to Faith), Lisa Graham, Rakara, Romani Morris, Esmirna Soto, Ryan Toal, Amanda McCormick, Delali & Bethany Bonuedi, Alemayehu Gared, Jacqueline Williams, Eyoda Williams and Michael Medina. Thanks for continuing to believe in me and for allowing me to use a little bit of all of you in these characters. I can't forget J and the City Slickers. Good luck on your tour. And to all of my creative writing students who couldn't wait for this book to be released. I told you all that it was possible.

I definitely have to give a shout-out to my publisher, Richard Jeanty and RJ Publications for having enough faith in me to take a chance on my work. And to Treasure E. Blue for your confidence in this book.

To the bookstores around the way: Multicultural Bookworld and the Black Library Booksellers for getting the word out about my debut novel. It's already paying off. A big shout out to all the street vendors for pushing urban literature. And to A Nubian Notion bookstores, Amazon.com and Barnes & Noble.

A big shout out to Bob's Bistro in Boston. Thanks for looking out.

And last but not least, a special thanks to Soko my publicist who has been working by my side since I started this manuscript. Thanks for making me known before my time. We are definitely putting Boston back on the map!

... of a Woman

I have felt the love of a woman, and
I don't know if I can explain the
sensations that flow throughout my body.

I have felt the warmth of her breasts, run
my fingers through her hair;
tongue trickling down the small of her back.

Have you inhaled the scent of a woman, that
reminds you of a gardens medley
filled with roses, African orchids, and lilies?

Did you touch the flesh of a woman, causing
an arousal between your
thighs, making you flow like the white waters?

I have sipped the lips of a woman. Kiwi licking
lips of a woman. Putting
a shame to the desire of passion fruit.

I have tasted the love of a woman, sweet juicy
gumdrops of her soul,
more luscious in my mouth than in my hands.

I have heard the sounds of a woman, as I am
lulled into a dream,
tickling my ears and relaxing my night.

I have felt the love of a woman, the tender
love of a woman,
that I would have never felt without her.

- K. M. Thompson

Bag Lady

"**Come** to think of it, when was the last time you got a piece of ass?" Cynthia asked me as if this were the most appropriate time.

My fork landed on my plate as I almost choked on the grains of shrimp fried rice I just sat on my tongue. It was only the two of us, but my brown skin was already turning dark red, and under my armpits were about to get drenched. What gave her the nerve to come at me like that?

"Excuse me," I said reaching for my water bottle. We were in the food court at the South Shore Plaza in Braintree. And after spending about three hours searching through the *Pink Room* at Victoria's Secret, we came here to munch, debrief about our workweek, and discuss our findings in our favorite store. Our sex life was not supposed to be on that menu.

We had just gone from a discussion of how one of our colleagues, who is not even two years younger than we were, had just gone through her third divorce and was already dating her ex man's best friend. *Hoe!* Was the only thought that came to mind. She had been sleeping with that guy for about a year now, and her husband just recently found out. Can you believe she was the one who asked for the divorce... and alimony? Now that poor sucker is paying for his ex-wife and her new beau.

Then we discussed how my so-called racist boss was developing a thing for Cynthia. She had no problem with the fact that he was German. Her only concern was the size of his package. "He is a cutie," she said. "But I've already heard that he doesn't have much to work with. I would turn that Nazi out if I was sure he had the tools – but I am not about to waste a few minutes of my time."

"A few minutes?"

"Yeah. From what I heard, it took this girl a few minutes to find it, and by the time she got it in her, he was done."

"Where do you get this stuff?" I was intrigued and disgusted all at the same time.

"You know I don't reveal my sources. But girl, I believe her. Look at the way he walks. He may act like a hard ass, but his insecurity is in his walk. He knows his shit is small. And then the other day when he sat across from us in the cafeteria, I took a good look... and nothing. Not a damn thing and it's not like his pants were loose fitting. His pants are always tight where his pee-pee is supposed to be."

"Pee-pee?"

"Pee-pee indeed. His shit so small he can piss on his own—"

"Cynthia!"

Neither one of us could resist laughing. Cynthia was always spitting some nonsense out of her mouth. She had me laughing so hard that tears were pouring out of my eyes.

And I kept on laughing until my sex-life became the next topic of discussion.

"You mean to tell me that you bought five pairs of underwear and you have no one to show them to... do you?" She lowered her eyes, sucked her teeth and then frowned. "You *have* been getting some haven't you? And you're keeping me in the dark. I can't believe you."

I swallowed hard, cleared my throat and then told her that she was crazy. It didn't make any sense where this was coming from. Just because I bought myself a few pairs of panties and a pink teddy didn't have to mean that I'm getting some... did it? Well, either way, in my case I wasn't getting any – at all. I was just buying stuff that looks and feels good on me.

"How did sex become the topic of the day?" I finally asked. "I thought we were coming out here to do some shopping, have lunch and maybe catch a movie. Woman's Day, isn't that what you called it?"

"Yes," she started. "But what do women talk about more than anything else? Sex and men. I'm just getting the ball rolling. So tell me, has a man been taking up that vacancy in your bed or not? Don't leave me in suspense, because you of all people should know that I *will* start filling in the blanks."

Cynthia was not lying about that, this sister could not get through a day without hearing or making up some gossip. And if I didn't fill her in, she would formulate something in that head of hers and the next thing you know - it is fact.

"I am not sleeping with anyone. I haven't had a date since Stan was sent to prison."

"It's been two years since that damn, no good ex-husband of yours got locked up. I can't believe you're still waiting for him after what he did to you." Cynthia's finger was swaying back and forth in front of my face. It was an annoying habit and I wished she would grow out of it. If you didn't know any better, you would think that this woman was telling me off.

"Stan's not my ex... yet," I said. "And I told you about

waving your finger in front of me."

She apologized after dipping back into her food. "He should be. I mean, that bastard held a gun to your skull and then almost shot you in the leg. Attempted murder! Stan's lucky they gave him life. I can't wait until Massachusetts reinstates the death penalty."

"Let's not go there. I know what he did to me, I was there, remember. I still have damn nightmares about that shit. I don't even know if I should be happy that Corey was there. He's been temperamental ever since."

"If he hadn't been there, you could be dead right now."

She was right. Period! If my son hadn't been there then Stan would have probably killed me.

After slurping down the rest of her soda, Cynthia said, "Speaking of Corey, has he heard anything from Morehouse yet?"

Finishing off my last piece of chicken, I shook my head letting her know that we were still waiting to hear something.

"Woman, I don't know how you ended up with a son so smart. I don't think Corey took after you or Stan, he's damn near a genius. I know he still has all those girls crank-calling the house, doesn't he? How many times have you changed your number now?"

"At least three times since last year. It slowed down after I got him that cell phone, but he went and lost it. Now those little hoochies are starting to call again."

"I can't wait to have a few kids of my own. All my girls got gang loads, and I'm still single and child-less. I'm about to go to a sperm bank and find me a nice lawyer or better yet a physician."

"Why not get both and end up with twins. One can take the other one to court for malpractice suits. Talk about sibling rivalry."

She rolled her eyes and almost had to fight from

waving her finger again. "Don't be stupid."

"Me?" I laughed. "You're the one talking about going to a sperm bank. You have a new man every few days. At least one of them had some sort of potential, but you just don't give them enough time to prove themselves."

"The last guy I dated lasted two weeks. I finally brought him home after we went bowling, of all places. We got back to my apartment, and the next thing I know he's in the bathroom butt-naked."

Cynthia grabbed her bags, so I figured it was about time to go. Before I could put my belongings together, she was on her feet and fuming.

"I mean, I was all down for a night full of passion, but this fella had man-titties. Can you believe that? Man-titties. Aargh."

That was nasty, but instead of making either of us feel worse I simply frowned and kept all comments to myself.

Cynthia and I had been hanging out like this for a few years now. Every couple of days we hit up a mall or two. Usually on the weekends, but a new bra just came out so we decided to make a special trip. We'd been working together for the last eight years and we were tighter than tight. She knew almost every move I made or was going to make, and vice versa. Shoot, the girl even knew when I had to use the bathroom. She said it was in the way I walk. If you ask me, I'd say she's just crazy.

My apartment was empty when I got there. It was Thursday evening and Corey was probably out with his best friend, Darius. Like Cynthia said, Corey was smart and I sure as hell didn't know where it came from. Stan and I were both mediocre students and no one in either side of our families went straight to college after high school. I didn't even apply to college my senior year, and as far as I know, Stan didn't either. Back then the most important thing was that we both had our high school diplomas. Years later, after Corey was born, I got an Associate's Degree and eventually earned my Bachelor's Degree in business administration.

I brought the mail, catalogues and magazines in and laid everything on the kitchen island. For some reason, even though I just ate all that Chinese Food at the mall, I was still hungry. There were a few pieces of fried chicken in the refrigerator from last night, so I took out a drumstick and heated it in the microwave. Damn, if I didn't watch myself I was gonna get fat and never find a real man.

Stan's picture was still taped to the refrigerator door. I hated thinking about that bastard, and I'm sure that as long as he was a part of my son's life, I would have to deal with him. Why in the hell did *I* have to keep laying my eyes on him? I thought about it for a second and then balled the picture up and tossed it into the trash. Corey wouldn't miss it, would he? It didn't really matter much because he had a picture of his father somewhere in his bedroom.

As soon as the photo hit the bottom of the trash barrel, a tear fell behind it. I wasn't gonna let him get to me. No matter how much it hurt, I was not going to let Stan bring me back down. Shoot, I was too strong of a woman to let that happen again. Before you know it, I'd be a single woman again and the right man would come strolling into my life. I believed that and I had faith that it was going to happen.

I let myself get those damn tears out so I could hurry up and move on.

(Just to) Get By

After finishing my after-school detention for cursing in class, I headed down to Dudley Square to meet Corey at Stash's restaurant. Damn, I was starving. Lucky for me, when I got there he had already ordered my favorite: a steak, onion and cheese sub. The greedy bastard was sitting in our regular seats chomping down on his grilled-chicken sub before I even got inside. Right next to him was an open Boston Herald newspaper.

"Darius, what you think about that Ms. Jackson?" He said swallowing a big chunk of chicken.

I laughed, "You know I just finished bagging that."

"Man, please," he said. "You ain't never gonna get a piece of that ass."

After I picked up my order, Corey started questioning me about something he read in the newspaper. This brother was always on top of what was happening in the news, which impressed me. Corey read the Boston Herald front to back everyday, and skimmed through the New York Times every once and a while. He was addicted to the six o'clock and the eleven o'clock news. Sometimes I wondered if he would choose MSNBC over a fine-ass sistah.

Corey was a smart dude, which is why he did so well

on the Massachusetts Comprehensive Assessment System test. While all of us were struggling to pass MCAS so that we could graduate, on exam day Corey just walked in, took the test without even a ball of sweat forming across his forehead, and exited the room.

That happened two years ago, back in the tenth grade, and the shit still pisses me off. And being one of the few students in our class to pass on the first try, Corey was the only senior who got accepted to more than four colleges that year. A bunch of us were waiting to do our second or third retest – still trying to graduate on time, while Corey was only waiting to take his finals.

"You heard about the teachers down south, sleeping with those thirteen year-old boys?" He asked as I poured hot sauce over my sub. "Yep. Down in South Carolina and one in Florida." Taking a fry from my plate, he said, "How come we never got blessed with teachers like Mary Kay Letourneau?"

"Man, what I wouldn't give to be a thirteen year-old boy sleeping with my teacher."

"What I wouldn't give to be an eighteen year-old boy sleeping with my teacher. Now, I would wear those teachers out. Back then I didn't know what I was doing."

"Shit, Corey. You still don't know what the hell you doing."

Corey said, "Ask that baby momma of yours if I know what I'm doing, son?"

"You should be calling me *daddy*. But I guess your momma never told you about us, huh?" I said with a serious face. "You know your head is shaped just like the tip of my..."

"Forget you." Corey threw up his middle finger with the quickness.

We both cracked up. Corey had been down with me since middle school and he was still my boy to the end.

He had my back that day when bitch-ass Marcel tried to jump me in Dudley Square, it had something to do with me disrespecting his ho-ass sister. That mofo was determined to believe her lying ass was a virgin. Marcel had two dudes with him and I was by myself. The odds were in their favor, but to their surprise, I held my own for a while. When Corey showed up, it was pretty much over. Corey was carrying a knife, as usual, so Marcel and his boys scattered. The next time we saw Marcel in school, Corey was there to make sure that we had an up and up fight. No one got seriously hurt and it was squashed after that.

We hopped on the city bus and headed by his house to check for a financial aid packet. It wasn't there, and Corey was getting pissed. He'd been waiting three weeks to hear something back from Morehouse. Corey may have been intelligent, but he wasn't paid. Well, not well paid. His mother, by herself, took care of most of his financial needs. She was an administrator at a community college – so he had a free ride there. But Corey wanted to go to one of the many universities that accepted him. Especially Morehouse. Although he said that his mother made pretty decent money, there was no way he could afford any of the schools. But because of his grades, he figured he could get some type of grants or possibly a scholarship.

"The letter from Morehouse should have been here since Monday," he said tossing his bag beside his bed. "I was online the other day and it was being processed still. And with those whack-ass computers at our school, I couldn't get online today."

"You're the smartest kid I know," I said, picking up a two year-old picture of us. Corey was a little lighter than I was, and he always kept his hair cut really low. "Probably the smartest kid in the school. Aren't you ranked in the top-ten? The top-three even?"

"I don't know. The Vice Principal didn't have time to figure it out," he said as he went to change into his new Air Force Ones. As he walked passed me, I noticed that I was still a little taller than him, and a little thicker.

"Mr. Gray is a straight dumb-ass. I don't know how he got the job as Vice Principal. What does that say about the school?"

"He probably slept his way to the top."

We tried to laugh, but it didn't help much. Corey deserved the best. He and his moms had gone through so much already. His father had been in and out of prison most of Corey's life. Domestic abuse, drug possession, and weapons possession were just a few of the charges. The last time he went in, it was for attempted murder of Corey's mom.

Instead of hanging down at our boy Ricardo's house like we had planned, we ended up sitting around battling on his PlayStation system. I was tearing Corey's ass up in Madden when Mrs. Jones came home from work. She had groceries in her car and yelled for Corey to help bring them in. They were like family to me, so it was automatic that I help out. When Mrs. Jones saw me, she just smiled. An extra hand to help with the groceries.

Mrs. Jones was different from most mothers. Although she spoiled her son like any mother would, she was more like a friend and confidant to Corey and his boys. I can't count the number of times when she stayed up late into the night with us, playing PlayStation or watching movies. My own mother couldn't recall the name of the last girl I dated outside of my baby's mamma. But Mrs. Jones knew the name of almost every girl Corey brought around. She may not have liked the majority of them, but at least she had an idea who they were.

"How's your son?" She asked as I placed the bag on the table. As Mrs. Jones leaned to put something into the fridge, my eyes drifted to her tight waist, down towards her curvaceous hips and perfectly sculpted legs. Aargh! What the hell was I doing? I shook the vision from my head and thought of how this woman treated me like her own son. It would be like looking at my own mother. Aargh!

"He's good. Big as hell," I coughed. "Umm, excuse me."

She smirked as her striking cat eyes warned me not to curse again. "I can imagine. A year-old already," she said staring deep into my eyes. "You know fatherhood is not all fun and games. It's not just about spending weekends with your kids. Or babysitting. You have to be a man and take care of your responsibility."

I knew she was talking more at me, than about me. She was talking about Mr. Jones, Corey's father. I never really got to know him, but when I did see him he used to tell me to call him by his first name.

"I know Mrs. Jones," I said. "I see Lil' Darius almost everyday. Even though me and Nina aren't together, we still share custody. My moms ain't hearing that nonsense and I'm not trying to be no weekend dad."

Corey came in just in time to rescue me from the conversation. He must have been listening from outside.

"Come on," he said. "If you want to eat here tonight, you can't just stand around lollygagging."

When we got back to the car, he told me that his father had called from prison late the other night and his mom was still upset. Corey spoke to him for a little while and said that Stan wanted him to come by the prison to visit him. Although Corey was dead-set against going, he ended up telling Stan that he would try to find a ride up there.

"What'd your mom say?" I asked.

"She's pissed about it," he whispered. "She said that I should let him die in there alone. So, I'm not going up there."

"But you told him that you were going to find a way up to see him," I said.

I took the last two grocery bags out of the trunk and followed Corey to the porch.

"So what? I lied to get him off the phone. You know what he tried to do to my mother. Fuck him."

Mrs. Jones looked at her son in frustration. "I told you to stop all that swearing." She knew that he got his foul mouth from her and Stan. Back in the day, Mrs. Jones had a mouth like a sailor. Not to mention the language his father used to use. Mrs. Jones just recently slowed down on all of that swearing after Stan held that gun to her head. She used to smoke a lot of weed too, but gave all that up a couple of years ago.

Corey didn't say anything to her about the conversation, but I could tell that he really wanted to see his father, despite what the old man did. He would never let his mother know that because there was no telling what it would do to her if she knew how he really felt.

Corey usually kept his emotions inside, let stuff build up, and then exploded all over people. I wasn't sure how he felt half the time. I learned to just go by what he told me, because whenever I tried to figure out what he was feeling, I was always wrong.

During dinner, Mrs. Jones brought up Nina's name again. She was wondering if I was going to invite her to the graduation party she was throwing for me and Corey. More so for Corey, because we still weren't sure if I was graduating.

"Damn, Mom. It's only February. Can we get through finals and shi... stuff first?" He asked playfully. Mrs. Jones was overly excited because Corey was going to be the first member of the family to graduate from high school with honors, and go straight to college.

"I just can't wait, Corey. Can't a mother be proud of her son? I've already invited some of my colleagues."

Corey dropped his fork onto his plate. "I don't want any of those chumps coming to my barbeque. People might think I'm going to school there."

"Well, if you don't get that scholarship from Morehouse, then..." Mrs. Jones started.

"I'll get it. Don't worry about that," Corey said balling up his face. "I'll get enough money to get away from this city. I'm not just depending on Morehouse. I'll go to Virginia, D.C., somewhere. I'm sure as hell not staying here." Throwing his hands up, Corey forced his chair back and stomped off to his room.

Mrs. Jones didn't bother calling him back this time. It was the normal fit that Corey took when they discussed his future. We both knew how much Corey hated being in Boston. He wanted big things and he felt that the city was too small for him. Plus, there were just too many haters trying to keep a brother down. Mrs. Jones got it, and I think that that was why she let him walk away. There were times when they would battle it out for hours, while I would sit and play PlayStation games by myself.

"Are you almost done?" I asked Mrs. Jones as I swallowed the last bit of my fried chicken. "I can wash the dishes for you."

"Can we just sit here for a little while?" She asked.

I nodded. Usually, just the mention of Stan's name would cause her to steam up. I could only imagine what was going on inside her mind after speaking to him. She watched me as I took a sip of my Kool-Aid, and wouldn't lower her eyes until I put the glass down.

She said, "I hear that you may not be getting your diploma."

"Yeah, it's that stupid-ass MCAS," I said. "Sorry about swearing, but it sucks. The English section was no problem at all. My reading skills and vocab are on point. It's the damn math."

"Believe me, I understand." She grabbed my plate as she stood from the table. "The test was specifically created to keep a few people from getting ahead. I'm sure I don't have to give you a heads up on who those people are."

"You got that right. I mean, the kids in Milton are complaining because they are not getting the highest scores. But shit... can a brother from Roxbury even pass the damn thing. Every time I take it, I miss by one. I've spent four years in high school and didn't miss more than five days in all of those years. Now I can't get a diploma because I don't know the area of an isosceles triangle. They say MCAS is a way to test the teachers. Well, damn give me my diploma and fire my geometry teacher."

"Do you need some help studying for it?"

"I've been going to tutoring sessions since November. They want me out of that school as much as I want to be out."

"Sorry to say, but half of the teachers in your school wouldn't have passed MCAS if they offered it back when they were students."

"Corey passed that test the first time he took it. What did you do to get him to be so smart?"

Mrs. Jones started to say something, but then paused. I wondered if she was going to tell me to ask Corey to tutor me. We tried it before, but it turned into a wrestling match, and then a conversation about girls. We ended our first tutoring session smoking a blizz. That was the last time we tried the tutoring thing.

15   Me and Mrs. Jones

She emptied the dishes into the sink and started running the water. I stood up and walked to her. There was no way I was going to let her wash those dishes after she spent all evening cooking.

"Let me do it. I need to work off some of this bomb-ass chicken, anyway."

Mrs. Jones looked at me again and I apologized for my mouth. As I took the dish-soap from the side of the sink, she rubbed her fingers through my braids. A tingling sensation ran down my back. Its not that I haven't had older women touch my hair. My aunts used to braid my hair all the time. But the way she touched me was different. It reminded of the way Nina touches my head.

"You guys and your braids. When are you going to cut these?" She asked as I washed the dishes.

"My mother is always telling me to cut my hair before I start going to college interviews. She said that no one would take me if I look like a thug. But I see a lot of brothers over at Northeastern University wearing braids all the time."

"Well, you're right. But it may be a good idea to..." her voice faded off. "Never mind, it's not important. Thank you for washing those things. I've always hated washing dishes."

Corey used his mother's car to drive me home about an hour later. My mother was already in bed when I got there. My father was wide-awake, just getting home from his shift at work. He had been a project manager at Nstar Electric way before I was born, while my mom was a senior program director at a women's shelter. I don't really know what she does there, and I guess she's not allowed to talk about it. Sometimes she would come home all stressed out, and would have to wait patiently for one of my father's southern massages.

"Hey, Darius," my dad said. He sat in the living room untying his boots. My father was reaching his mid-fifties and he looked worn out. Working the same three-to-eleven shift for twenty years was wearing on him and we all knew it. The pay was good but he was getting too old for it.

I said, "Sup, Pops. Just getting in from work?"

"Same thing every night." It was clear by his distraught expression that he hated his job. "Your mother told me that she got a call from your school today. You had detention again for using profanity?"

"It wasn't my fault, Pops," I begged. "This girl was talking trash to me, but the teacher didn't hear when she swore."

"I don't want to hear anything about what somebody *made* you do. It's getting tired, Darius. When are you going to man-up and be your own person?"

I assumed the question was rhetorical.

"You gotta stop letting these people get to you, son. You always seem to be the one who ends up in trouble. You hear me?"

"Yeah, but..."

"I don't want the buts. I want you to get your act together. You're eighteen and still getting in trouble over nonsense."

There was nothing I could say to that and he knew it. Sometimes I thought my father had the agility to be assistant district attorney like McCoy was on Law and Order. If it wasn't for my older half-brother Deon, Pops would have probably gone on to college after high school. But he got his girlfriend pregnant and he gave up a football scholarship from Florida A&M to stay here and raise his son. They got married, and after two months they realized that it wasn't meant to be. They're still cool though, and my dad is always there for Deon. Me and Deon grew up like full-blood brothers. His mother treats me like her own son, and my mom treats Deon the same.

After getting out of his shoes, Pops asked me about the MCAS. "When is the retest?"

"In a few weeks."

Pops stood up and grabbed his shoes. "This whole thing sucks. I have the mind to go down to your school tomorrow and start cursing myself. With all that detention you've gotten this year, they should have given you extra tutoring for that shit." He caught himself, but didn't apologize. He headed to the staircase and told me that I needed to get ready for bed.

I Used to Love Him

I couldn't believe that son of a bitch called here the other night. Once in a while is fine, but two nights in a row was overstepping his boundaries. I tossed and turned in my bed for two nights straight after that.

Me and Stan had already been through too much, and I was ready for it to stop. We were lovers in middle school. Lost contact when we went to separate high schools, but then bumped into each other at a club when we were seventeen. He was still looking as good as he did when we messed around in seventh-grade English class. Those light green eyes, and the light brown lips. Back then he was being chased by all those little nasty heifers because he was light-skinned. Light skin brothers were "in" back in the day. It was all about the complexion and the hair.

And Stan still had it going on. He had that silky Indian hair when we were in middle school. That was the reason that I chased after him. I have always had a weakness for a man's hair. If Stan had a low-cut that night at the club, then I probably wouldn't have approached him. But the brother was sporting a high top fade, with the S-curl. The Al B. Sure style. His hair was naturally curly, so I couldn't understand why he went and put all those chemicals in there.

Regardless, a few nights later, he took me to his mom's house where I washed his hair and gave him a touch up. Then we had long, steaming-hot, back-scratching, sex in the same room where I lost my virginity four years earlier.

Stan had me thinking that he was a good man. An exceptional man who was on his way to the top of the music industry. Although he had just lost his father to cancer, he was still dedicated to his career as a producer. Stan didn't talk much about college, but he did discuss settling down one day, and said that he would spend a couple of years perfecting his music and production skills. I supported my man all the way. He was going to be the next Jimmy Jam and his partner was going to be Terry Lewis. They even laid my voice down on a couple of tracks. Mostly background. I wasn't into singing, but he kept telling me how sweet my voice was.

When I got pregnant a few months before graduation, Stan didn't hesitate with the proposal. It was like he'd been carrying that ring around for months, waiting for the right moment to pop the question. He said we were soul mates and he was already planning to ask for my hand in marriage. With the baby coming along, there was "no better time than right now." Stan wanted to be the kind of father that his father never was. Take care of his family so that they would not be ashamed of him. And he was what he promised... in the beginning.

By the time Corey was two, Stan's music career was suffering like the life of Ed-OG and da Bull Dogs. Our dream world had started to crumble. Stan was out drinking, smoking and doing anything else late into the night. And when he finally did come home, the fights would start. In the beginning the fights were all verbal. Later they became physical. I may have spent many nights in the emergency room getting stitches, but I am not a wimp. Stan would sit right next to me in the ER with his own share of bruises.

Our life was somewhat normal after Stan spent his first month in jail for domestic abuse. After he got out, with his completely shaved head, he stayed clean for about a year. Corey was around six years old. Stan would read him bedtime stories every night, taught him how to play basketball and how to ride a bike. Stan was every bit of the father he set out to be, but the one thing that was missing from the big picture was me. He left me out of all of the football games and the trips to New York. It was like he never forgave me for having him locked up. What the hell was I supposed to do? The bastard was banging on me like I was a damn punching bag!

We didn't talk much that year; we didn't make love at all. He screwed me a couple of times like I was some whore he met on the corner, but he didn't make love to me. It didn't take long before he started creeping and bringing home strands of bleached blond hair. He even had the nerve to have blond pubic hair all around his genitals. He wore that shit like it was a trophy. I didn't care though. I was creeping my damn self. Can't no man hold a good woman down. No, I wasn't sleeping around. I was always faithful to him. But I did creep my way into college and eventually got a job at the same community college where I got my Associate's Degree. The pay was good, and his envious attitude was another reason why things went sour between us.

By the second year, we were no longer sleeping together at all. We were still living under the same roof and remained somewhat friends, but the sex was off limits. During that year, I started dating one of my former professors. A young, handsome brother. Philip was in his early thirties, I believe. We went out a few times and he helped me get a job at the school. When Stan found out, he went ape-shit and threatened to have the guy fired. So I ended the relationship. Philip never understood why and he eventually transferred to another school. I haven't spoken to him since.

Time passed and the fights gradually started up again. Then the drugs snuck back into the house and the next thing you know, the police were raiding our home, I was placed in handcuffs in front of my twelve-year-old son and I almost lost my job.

Stan was messing my life up, and was working on destroying Corey's as well. I couldn't have it. A year later, I had him arrested for slapping me after a Christmas party at work. I came home late, and I have to be honest, I'd been blazing with Cynthia and a few other colleagues. Stan had been doing coke and was strung out. It was a good thing I let Corey stay the night with his friend Darius that night. He didn't have to witness his parents acting like a bunch of crack-heads.

But being the lonely-fool that I was, I let Stan come back home. We went back and forth for a couple of years, until I caught him in my bed with some Puerto Rican bitch. After that he had to go. And it all went down hill from there, *like it wasn't bad enough before*. Then there was that night two years ago. I hate thinking about it. But like Cynthia constantly reminded me, if it hadn't been for Corey wrestling the gun out of his father's hand, I honestly believe that Stan would have killed me. Before the gun hit the floor, it went off and the bullet missed my right leg by about an inch.

That bastard was not going to see my son, I didn't care how much pleading he did. The only reason I let Corey speak to Stan is because Corey still seemed to have some sort of relationship with him. Instead of me being the one to pull him away from his father, Corey had to make that decision on his own. I couldn't read Corey's mind, and he never really talked to me about it but my guess was that he had mixed feelings about his father. Part of him must have hated Stan, the other probably missed him.

So, until Corey was ready to cut ties with the man who tried to kill his mother, I was going to have to let the calls through. I was going to have to give Stan the telephone number whenever I changed it. It seemed like I was going to end up dealing with Stan's BS until the day Corey moved out and got his own place. Those inevitable conversations between me and Stan will be limited to a simple greeting and a *hold-on, here's your son.*

Still, that bastard needs to limit his calls to once a month.

The Seed (2.0)

Nina came by early as hell that morning because something was wrong with Lil' Darius. She said he had been crying for hours and she didn't know what to do. My mom woke me up when Nina got to the house with my son. It was only a little after four and I had a Pre-Calculus exam first period. Needless to say, I wasn't trying to get up.

"Take him to the hospital," I said trying to roll back into bed.

"Oh, no you don't," my mom demanded. She pulled the covers completely off of me and it was cold as hell. "You helped create this baby, you're gonna help take care of him."

"Dammit!" I shouted. I hopped out of bed, while my mother coddled my crying son.

"Get your clothes on and take my car to the emergency room at Boston Medical Center. No offense Nina, but your mother's car is in no condition to be driving this baby around. Mine is more reliable", my mom said. As I got dressed, Mom turned to Nina. "You have your medical insurance card with you, right Nina? You don't want anything holding you all up."

"Yes Mami, I have everything. I keep stuff like that in

my purse just in case anything happens while we're out."

"Smart girl. I don't know why none of your commonsense rubbed off on my son." Lil' Darius' cries were calmer than before. "What's taking you so long? This boy is running a fever."

"I can't find my other shoe," I said looking underneath my bed.

"Oh, Lord!" Mom handed Lil' Darius back to Nina, reached down beside me, and pulled my sneaker from underneath the shirt I had on earlier.

"Here," she said giving it to me. "Now go. The keys are on the kitchen counter. I left you a cup of coffee down there too."

Nina and I were halfway out of the driveway when Mom came to the porch and shouted for us to be careful.

It turned out that my one-year-old son was suffering from an ear infection. We were in the hospital until about seven-thirty. I called Mom as soon as we checked in, then again after we met with the nurse, and after the doctor gave us the results. Doctor James said that he'd had the infection for three days now.

When I found out how long my son had been suffering like that, I was pissed. If she hadn't spent most of her time at the nail salon and at the clubs, then she would have known that my son was in pain. Nina wasn't a bad mother, but sometimes I wished I would have gotten full custody of Lil' Darius.

"Three days and you're just finding out?" I said to her when we got inside the car.

She immediately shouted back, "Like *you* knew."

"He doesn't live with me. What kind of mother are you? I bet he was crying all night until you got back from the club, huh? Your stank-ass Momma didn't even do anything. If he was crying she should have called my cell phone. She didn't have a problem calling me when I was sleeping with you. Always trying to find out where you were."

"For your information, my mom didn't have him. My little sister did. And I wasn't at the club, I went to a funeral."

"This late? Whose funeral?"

"You don't know her."

"You're lying, because I can still smell the smoke in your hair. I can't believe you. And I told you I didn't want your sister babysitting him. The last time she did, you caught her giving head to some dude while Lil' Darius was in the other room."

"Just drop me off so I can get my mother's car. I need some sleep and you need to go to school."

"Forget school. I'm taking little man home with me. You can get some sleep. I'm staying home with him today."

"Fine. Just drop me off at the bus stop and I'll find a way to get the car later."

"What sense would that make, Nina? I can take you home and you can just go to sleep. Then I'll drive your car when I bring Lil' Darius home."

I pulled onto her street and stopped in front of her apartment complex. Before she got out, she kissed Lil' Darius on the forehead. He was knocked out in his car seat. Nina looked at me and without saying a word she ran her fingers through my braids.

"You know they need to be redone," she said softly. "And since you're not going to school today, maybe you should come on up let me do them for you."

How was I going to resist that? She was running her fingers through my hair like she used to do. That was my spot and when Mrs. Jones ran her fingers through it the other night, it got me turned on. Damn, not again. I had to get her out of my head.

The best way to get a woman out of your mind is to boink another one. At least that's what Corey used to tell me. So that's exactly what I did. I took Nina upstairs, said what's up to her stank-ass mom, put Lil' Darius in his bedroom and then boned the hell out of Nina. Just like old times. It was better than it used to be though. There were no strings attached. No 'I love you's'. Nothing but a quick piece and a thank you, call me later.

After I got dressed, Nina asked me if I still wanted her to braid my hair. Not that I needed it redone, but I didn't want to treat her like some chick from the block. Nina didn't want to be by herself and I could understand that. So I let her take each braid a loose slowly. She was playing Fantasia's CD, singing along and massaging my temples at the same time. I felt like I was being set up. What happened to the wham, bam, thank you Ma'am?

I asked, "What are you doing?"

"You used to love it when I massaged your head like this," she said. "Is it bothering you?"

It wasn't and I did not want her to stop, but I didn't want her to be falling for me again.

"No, it's cool. But I just need to get home with Lil' Darius, My moms stayed home from work because she wanted to make sure everything was all right. How much longer is this going to take?"

"Damn, nigga," she said softly slapping the back of my head. "You lucky I'm doing this for you." She took the comb and parted my hair from the middle. "Lemme hurry this shit up."

"I'm just saying I don't want to get him there too late. He's not staying with me tonight so I want to make sure he gets back home at a decent hour."

Nina ignored me, and went back to singing along with Fantasia. About an hour later, she was almost done with only two braids left. She started to part my hair, and then dropped the comb into my lap. As if by instinct, she reached down for it. But she grabbed the wrong thing.

I looked up at her. We were both ready for round two. She kissed me and then undid my pants to expose my erection. Her hands pulled up my shirts, as she massaged my stomach all the way down to my boxers. Nina climbed over me, brought her mouth down to my manhood and went to work.

She was working me hard. Harder than usual, like she was going to war on a brother. But just before I ejaculated, her mother walked in carrying Lil' Darius.

A Woman's Worth

The last thing I wanted to do after work was to drag my body down to the gym. I was so pissed about Stan's phone call that I hardly got any sleep last night either. Now, there I was with my Nike gym bag, sitting on the passenger side of Cynthia's car. I had pre-packed my Nike gym shorts, t-shirt and sneakers. Even though I wasn't in the mood, I still had to look my best in case a decent brother came in to do a workout.

If it wasn't for Cynthia and Karen, I would have rushed home right after work, but these sisters knew my game plan. They had a plan of their own. They met me outside of my office trying to sneak out a few minutes early, and practically hemmed me up and dragged me out to Cynthia's car. I protested that I had my ride, but Karen reminded me that we had parking permits, and could leave our cars in the lot up until midnight.

Cynthia marched me to my car to get my bag from the trunk, and then we were off to do a three hour workout.

"I hear there's a cute new Hip-Hop aerobics instructor," Karen said making sure I caught her eye. That meant that he was off limits to the rest of us. "Rita told me about him. She took his class the other night."

I put on my seatbelt as soon as Cynthia's crazy-ass pulled out of the parking lot. If I *had* to go to the gym, I wanted to get there in one piece.

"Why isn't Rita riding with us today?" Not that I missed her.

"She's doing a job for her supervisor," Cynthia said matter-of-factly. "She's been *doing* a lot of jobs for her new supervisor."

"Isn't he married to the Vice President of Finance's daughter?" I asked. "Rita could lose her job over some mess like this."

"You think that hoochie really cares? She's just looking for another piece of ass, and a raise."

"Cynthia, you always got something to say about somebody," Karen laughed. "You need to leave poor Rita alone. She's just like the rest of us, trying to find a decent man."

"Finding a decent man and finding a married man are two totally different things. It's not *decent* to get with a married man," Cynthia said.

I had to add my two cents in. "It's hard enough to find a man, but some of us are lucky enough to do so. Then to have another sistah come along and give him some on the side is... is..."

"Tell it like it is" Cynthia said, pulling into the parking garage. "It's fucked up."

"Thanks for putting it so bluntly," I said. "But it is. It makes you want to give up on relationships, and give up on the brothahs all together."

"White men ain't no different. They have the highest infidelity rates in the country."

This conversation continued as we made our way from the car, to the elevator, and into the locker room.

"Where'd you get your stats, girl?" Karen asked Cynthia as she changed into her New Balance workout gear. "As far as I know, brothers' cheating is at an all time high."

"Cynthia, I think you went and threw something out there that you can't back. Whites have a higher divorce rate for damn sure, because they're the only ones getting married. I was reading that only fifty percent of sistahs get married, compared to like eighty percent of white women."

My girl hated getting shut down, but I had to go there. And if I knew Cynthia, she would pull out something else that would blow us away.

Before we were completely dressed for our workout, Cynthia brought up the fact that as Black women, we needed to stop giving away the milk for free.

"Why should they marry us if they can get the cow for free?" She said slipping into a black sports bra. "I know I'm just as guilty as the next woman, but we need to teach these brothers how to respect us, take care of us, and treat us like the Nubian queens that we are." She started gyrating her hips, and massaging her thighs. "This body is a temple. God blessed these thighs with his own fingertips, and it would be a sign of disrespect to let some low-life brother contaminate any part of this."

Clearing my throat, I had one last question to ask. "So you're going to practice celibacy?"

"Hell no!"

We all burst out laughing and headed out to the aerobics studio.

Karen was right, the aerobics instructor was cute. Although aerobics classes were usually filled with women, this one in particular was actually *filled* with women. The three of us had to fight our way to find a spot. Cynthia and Karen found two empty spots near each other, while I ended up on the opposite side of the room. And more women were still spilling in after that.

The room was filled to capacity and the instructor had to send a few of the late arrivals out. If he hadn't promised them space up front during his next session, he would have definitely lost some points.

Twenty minutes into the workout, I was hovering in the corner next to Cynthia and half the other women in the room. We sat, sweating, panting and practically hyperventilating as we watched Karen and the others try to keep up with the instructor. Apparently, Adam, the instructor did some work with Usher, Omarion, and Britney Spears. So when he combined the Box with another Hip Hop dance, I impressed myself by keeping up. It wasn't until he wanted us to combine the first six dance moves together, that I lost my way. I could hardly remember the Box, the only step I had down, when he got to the Shake. So, I had to sit my ass down. At least I had more endurance and coordination than Cynthia. She sat down after only five minutes – before he even got to the Box.

But Karen was moving. I bet she had been practicing all last night. I knew she owned the Grind's Hip Hop Aerobics video, but to my knowledge she never even opened it. Well, at least not until the night before class. If this guy was as cute as Rita said he was, Karen had to be well prepared. And like I said, he was.

Adam had an intense smile with pearly whites, was a little lighter than I'd prefer, and had light green eyes. He immediately grabbed my attention, and if it hadn't been for Karen being my girl, and his eyes being too similar to Stan's, I would have actually made a move on him. So, with Karen being one of three women who remained standing at the end of the session, Cynthia and I decided to leave her with the opportunity to introduce herself to Adam. As we made our exit, I overheard Adam telling her how impressed he was with her movements. And what did she do? What all women do. She lied and then stroked his ego.

"I've never done Hip Hop aerobics before. You must just be an excellent teacher, would you be willing to give private sessions?"

With that, Cynthia and I knew that we had just lost our friend for the day.

"I guess I'm happy for her," I said when I mounted the exercise bike. "She just met him so I hope she doesn't give it up to him."

"You know Karen," Cynthia said. She was already into the groove, while I was still deciding on which program to use. Uphill incline, low-effort valley, or combinations.

"Exactly, that's why I'm worried. After that conversation we had earlier, I can still tell that she's desperate for a man- married or not. Gay or straight. And I'll tell you something, Adam looked a little too flamboyant for my taste..."

"I know you're not jealous, girl," she said.

"Jealous?"

"Yeah, you sound the same way I did when my sister married that doctor. I was hating like a mofo, but I had to get over it. So, Faith... get over it."

Before I could curse her out, she said, "A good man will come along before you know it. One for the both of us. Just be ready for him, okay. Promise me that you won't chase the next good one away. This time you can't blame Stan. He's out of the picture. The next time you mess up, like you did with Prof, then you mess up on your own."

I finally started my program and rode up that hill as fast as I could. There wasn't much I could say to Cynthia after that. I wouldn't even promise her anything. I did promise myself though. If I was ever blessed with a real man, I would hold on to him for dear life. Fat, ugly. Tall, short. Light, dark. Didn't matter. The next man that I let into my life and into my bed was going to have to be the *one*.

cool Like That

"**You's** a busta, man," Corey laughed. "So what if her moms walked in. Did she finish?"

"Shut the hell up. Of course she didn't finish. I had to finish it off when I got home. Joint was hurting like a bitch."

We were pulling into the gas station in Egleston Square when Corey made a comment that I'll never forget. "You should've asked her moms to join in. You know how she's been checking you."

"I ain't messing with nobody's momma."

"Ain't nothing wrong with it, mothers are human too. They need to get bagged just like the rest of us." After a brief silence, Corey started cracking up. He got out of the car and then asked me if I wanted something from the store.

"Just a box of Black and Milds." As he walked away, I called for him to get a Pepsi.

After filling up the tank, we rolled over to Ricardo's. Ricardo was the type of Latino who thought he was Black. It was cool, sometimes, but I had a problem when he tried to call me nigga. Same with Nina. When she calls me that, I always have to hold back from illin' on her. I let it slide with both of them because they just didn't know any better, and I was not in the mood to teach anybody about the history of that word.

"Sup nigga," Ricardo said. He was already high. His bedroom was cloudy and there was a half-naked Spanish girl lying on the bed. She was rolling a blunt, and I'm sure she wasn't gonna share.

We dapped each other up and sat on the floor. I pulled out a Black and Mild and lit it with the Latina's lighter. She was pretty fly. Long curly hair, light-skinned with a full-size ass. I accidentally touched her thigh when I gave her back the lighter.

"Didn't see you in school today," Ricardo said taking the blunt from the Latina. He lit it with the same lighter and took a toke.

I said, "My son was sick. I had to take him and Nina to the hospital this morning."

"He a'ight?" Ricardo passed his joint back to the girl. She was sitting up now, and her voluptuous breasts looked like they were about to fall out of her halter-top.

"Yeah," I said trying to keep from staring. "Just an ear infection. We got him some medicine."

Ricardo said, "Hope you're keeping him indoors, you don't want that shit to get worse."

"Yeah, I was supposed to have him with me, but I ran into a few complications and had to leave him home with his mother."

Corey took the Black and Mild from me. "What new movies do you have?" Corey asked.

Ricardo went over to his DVD collection and tossed one to Corey. "I got that new Denzel flick."

Checking out the cover, Corey was impressed. "This isn't even in the theaters yet."

"I told you my video-guy is good," Ricardo said. He blew smoke into his girl's mouth and she accepted it.

"Let me use this," Corey said still admiring the DVD.

"Nigga's always want to borrow shit and don't ever bring it back."

Ricardo was definitely going to let him borrow it. He used that same line every time we wanted to borrow one of his DVDs. And we always gave the same response. "Then let us know who your man is and we can get our own."

Thing is, Ricardo always wanted to be the center of attention. The man. The person who everyone needed to come to for everything. But we never inflated his ego when it came to stuff like that. He was cool as hell though, and Ricardo had the best movies, the best CDs, and the best weed around. So even though we didn't show him the respect he wanted, everyone did come to him and he was cool with it.

Corey handed Ricardo a couple of ten-dollar bills, and Ricardo pulled a bag of weed out of his pocket.

"Is this shit as good as the last batch?" I asked him.

"I only talk to my *customers*," Ricardo laughed. "When are you gonna start buying your own weed and stop depending on your boy's allowance? You're the only one of us with a real job, and you're broker than all of us."

Corey snickered as I flipped him the finger. Forget that Puerto Rican spic. Unlike the two of them, I had a son to help support. Besides, I was only working like five hours a week at a fast food restaurant. I was lucky I could afford to buy diapers and still have enough to buy minutes for my cell phone.

"My shit is always good," he said. "Money back guarantee."

Me and Corey smoked the entire bag before we left Ricardo's house. He was right, his product was good. I could hardly move when I was done and ended up falling asleep right there on his floor. If my phone hadn't rung, I probably would have slept through the night, because

Corey was knocked out too.

"Hello," I said into the phone.

"Darius?"

"Mrs. Jones?" I was surprised. It had to be a dream because I was imagining her fingers running through my hair.

"You sound funny," she said. "Is Corey with you?"

"Huh-uh," I said clearing my throat. "We fell asleep watching a movie."

"I can't believe he lost that cell phone I bought him. Can I speak to him please?"

I nudged Corey until he woke up cursing. Passing him the phone, I forgot to tell him who it was.

"Who the fuck is this?"

All I could hear was Mrs. Jones' yelling. I stood up and saw a nasty, hairy-assed, naked Puerto Rican man, and a beautifully enticing naked Puerto-Rican female. They were both knocked out. I just walked to the bathroom and took a piss.

When I came back, Corey was on his feet, wide-awake and ready to go.

"Moms is wildin'," he said. "I gotta go home. You coming with me or you going to your house?"

"I might as well come with you. If my mother smells this on me, she'll beat the hell out of me. Your mother is a little more understanding."

It was almost seven when we got to his house. Corey's mother was standing in the doorway when we pulled up and she started yelling as soon as we got out of the car.

"Where the hell were you? First you take my car from my job. And now it's almost seven o'clock. You're just lucky Cynthia drove me home. You had me here worried about you. You didn't call..."

"Mom," he cut in when we reached her. "Ease up."

"You've been smoking that stuff again?" She slapped

him in the back of the head and followed us into the house. "He has you doing it too?" She asked me.

She already knew that we smoked weed. Not that she liked the idea, but since she had spent most of Corey's young life smoking marijuana, there was hardly anything she could say.

"What was so urgent?" Corey asked pulling his jacket off. He tossed the Denzel DVD on the couch. "I was knocked out."

Mrs. Jones looked at Corey for a short while, and then hugged him. "You got it."

It took a second for it to click. But it finally did. "Morehouse?" Me and Corey both shouted.

"You got the two-year scholarship, and they say it's renewable for the last two years. And you know you already have grants and loans as a back up."

"Are you serious?" He hugged his mom back.

She pulled Corey away from her. "Would I play about something like this? My only son leaving me. Would I make a joke about that? I'm still trying to get you to enroll at my job."

Hugging him again, tears formed in Mrs. Jones' eyes. I could sense the sadness as well as the excitement in their embrace. And from a distance, I had the exact same reaction. I was going to be losing my best friend, but my best friend was going away to become a man. I was proud of him, but I was going to miss him.

"Congratulations," I said patting him on the back.

After they released, he turned around and gave me a quick half-hug.

"So, you want to celebrate?" I asked looking over at his mom. I had a feeling that she already planned something for him.

And I wasn't wrong. Mrs. Jones already put together a small party, with a bunch of Corey's relatives. She ordered pizza and Chinese Food and had it delivered. Everyone showed up about an hour after we arrived. One of Corey's cousins was a deejay and he kept playing stuff like Kanye West, Jay-Z and 50 Cent. After a while, Mrs. Jones told him to play some old school so that she could dance with her son. The deejay threw on Billy Paul's famous tune as Mrs. Jones made Corey get off the couch and dance with her in the center of the room. The rest of us stood around watching and cheering them on.

It was cool. A few of his aunts and their husbands got on the dance floor and congratulated Corey. Honestly, I don't think anyone was surprised that Corey achieved as much as he did, and we all had the confidence that Corey was going to reach the top. He was the president of our class, running neck and neck for valedictorian and was going to one of the most prestigious colleges in the country. Nothing could go wrong at this point. So, what if I was going to miss having him around? As I looked at the faces of all of his supporters, I knew that everything was going to be fine.

When the song ended, Corey slipped away from his mother before she could get a grip. Corey always hated dancing and Mrs. Jones loved to embarrass him. But this time Corey was out and she let him go. I was about to go and grab a wine cooler from the kitchen, when Mrs. Jones took my arm.

"I want to dance with my other son, now," she said.

By this time, more people were on the dance floor so I wasn't as uncomfortable dancing with her. In the past, me and Mrs. Jones always got down and boogied. I used to teach her the newest street moves, and then she would show me how to do some old school dances. There was this one dance I made up by accident. I called it the Roxbury Shuffle. It was something like the Harlem Shake mixed with the running man. I tried to teach her the steps a few months back.

We eased into the next two songs as her nephew mixed some old school beats with some new Hip Hop. Mrs. Jones and I were getting down on that dance floor, and with the moves we were doing we could have won a dance contest. The next song slowed us down a bit. I wished the deejay had kept it moving because halfway through that Shirley Murdock song, instead of gyrating my shoulders, I was rubbing up on my best friend's mother. When I realized what I was doing, I pulled away from her.

"Sorry," I mumbled, more to myself than to anyone else.

Her nails grazed my braids again, and I was shaken. "It's okay."

I got a stiff one, harder than hard. *Shit*, was all I could think to myself. I had to get out of there. Mrs. Jones moved in closer to me and rubbed against my dong. I jerked and excused myself. It was time to go home.

Corey dropped me off around eleven. My parent's bedroom light was still on and I knew that I was in for a good pep talk.

"I don't know why you didn't just stay the night," Corey said. "We could have left for school together like we always do."

"I didn't have any clothes."

"Man, we wear the same shit. Why is tonight so different?"

"Damn, you starting to sound like Nina," I joked. "How long has it been since you had a girl?"

"I had your moms this afternoon," he laughed. "Does that count?"

I smiled uncomfortably and then got out of the car. "I'll talk to you in the morning, all right."

Corey threw up the peace sign and I went inside to

face the music. My mom was on the couch, rocking her leg like she always does when she's pissed. As soon as I walked in, she started yelling at me.

"Where have you been?" It was rhetorical. "You dropped the car off earlier and I haven't seen you since. How is Lil' Darius? I can't believe you had me worried like this..."

"Be easy, Ma," I said. "I was with Corey. Mrs. Jones threw him a little get-together because he got a scholarship to go to Morehouse."

"Well, congratulations to Corey. Now back to you. You cannot be staying out like this. I understand that Corey is your friend and all, but you have your own life. Your own family. I would love to have a party for you, celebrating your high school graduation and being accepted to college. Don't you want to make Lil' Darius proud by seeing his father walk across the stage to receive his diploma?"

"I'm trying, Mom. It's this damn MCAS."

"Watch your mouth," she spat.

I apologized. "But you know what I mean. The test is just too hard. It's not made for..."

"I don't want to hear another person say that the test isn't geared towards Black people. If you study as much as your *Black* friend Corey then you would do as well as he did. Stop making excuses for yourself."

I couldn't deal with her talking much longer. Instead of going to the kitchen to grab a bite to eat like I usually do, I went straight to my room and slammed the door. She didn't say anything else after I left.

Killing Me Softly

What was I doing to myself? I let that little boy rub up on me like that, and in front of everyone. I'm just glad that my guests were too wasted to recognize what was happening, and I was too wasted to stop it. Poor guy got in over his head and it was a good thing he caught himself. Shit, I'm old enough to be his Mama!

But I have to admit it felt good. Feeling his body up on mine like that...

This shit can't be happening. I am not one of those teachers from Down South, looking to get a quickie from one of my students. I am a grown-ass woman with a grown-ass son and I am trying to get my life in order.

Still, the images wouldn't leave.

Darius walking into my bedroom, his long mane in need of a feminine touch. The innocent look in his eyes, the bright lonesome smile. Dripping wet from the shower, Darius walks in bare chest, lean and athletic, wearing silk boxer shorts. His dimples shine with his pearly white teeth.

He asks me if Corey's coming home for the night, but I tell him that Corey is in Atlanta visiting Morehouse. Darius tells me that he forgot. Then there was no more talk of Corey. It was all about Darius and Faith Jones.

Sitting on the edge of my bed, I spread my legs and wave for Darius to come and make himself comfortable on the floor beneath me. I rest a pillow between my ankles and he sits down. Before touching his hair, I rub his shoulders the way I used to do to Stan. I press on the nape of his neck, let my finger tips run down his spine, and then across his chest. His nipples are still damp – hard but damp.

Darius brings me in for a kiss. His tongue parting my lips and finding its way to my own resistant tongue. Moments pass and we release.

I graze my fingers through his hair, parting it down the middle, at the same time running them along the tip of his ear. His spot, just like Stan. The more braids I complete, the wetter my panties get, and the wetter I get, the bigger he gets. Darius rubs my toes, massages my ankles.

When I am halfway done, I give in to my emotions. I tilt Darius' head to the side and bring his mouth to mine. He lifts himself from the floor and we make our way to the top of the bed. Darius strips me of my thong and thrusts himself inside of me. He is in full control, knowing my body better than I know it myself. This young man knows how to please me and I will not stop him...

And then I woke up, horny as hell and ready for some real life pleasure. There were only two ways to get over this feeling. I could use my little blue battery-operated friend, or I could call the real thing on over. There was no way I was going to call Darius. So, I reached in between the mattress and box spring and pulled out trusty-ol-Blue.

At work the next morning, I sat in my office staring at a picture of Corey from first grade. He had grown up so fast and he was about to be leaving me. There were days when I would sit back and think about Corey and Stan. When I got pregnant and moved in with Stan, I never figured that I would one day be alone. But it was happening right before my eyes. My husband was locked up and my only son was going away to meet some Spelman girl who would sweep him off his feet and he would forget about his mother.

And then he entered. Tall, as dark as Wesley, and as fine as Denzel. His chest was busting through his pinstripe suit and his smile was lighting up my office. I crossed my legs underneath my desk, hoping to keep myself from getting too excited.

"Hi, can I help you?" I said trying to hide my attraction.

His smile got even brighter. "I'm looking for someone, but I think she gave me the wrong directions to her department," he said looking over the sheet of paper in his hands. "Do you know where I can find the hospitality department?"

I pointed to the sign outside my door. "As you probably saw, you're in Student Accounts, right now." Bringing my hand back, I accidentally knocked over Corey's picture. It fell off the desk and hit the floor.

Being a gentleman, he picked up the unbroken frame and I thanked him.

"Is this your son?" He asked placing it on my desk.

"Yeah, but it's an old picture. Very old. He's seventeen now, and about to go to Morehouse College in…"

"In Atlanta, right? I have a niece who goes to Spelman. Maybe I can introduce them."

"No, that's okay," I said abruptly. I needed to let Corey go but it was just too hard. "I mean, he already has a bunch of friends going down with him. Besides, I don't even know you."

"Well, I'm Kael." He reached over the picture and

offered me a handshake. I accepted as he continued. "And if you don't mind me saying, you are very attractive. I didn't expect to see anyone as beautiful as you, in a school like this."

"I don't know if that's a compliment or not, but I *know* I don't like you talking down about my colleagues."

He lowered his eyes apologetically, and then stuffed the paper into his pocket as he turned to walk away. Before he was out of the office, I gave him quick instructions on how to get to hospitality. He thanked me and left.

When I went to meet Cynthia for lunch, she was busy talking to Karen and Rita about Kael. I was wondering if he had been looking for one of them but I was not trying to get pulled in to the conversation. I was hungry and I wanted to hurry over to Bob's Bistro, our favorite restaurant, which was a few blocks from the college. The girls were talking about how gorgeous Kael was, and how good-looking their children would be if they had any.

Then there was the hater. There is always a hater.

"He's probably on the Down Low," Rita said taking a bite of her home-made garden salad. "A man that handsome..."

"Shit, girl," Cynthia laughed. "Even if he was ugly, you'd still say he was on the DL. That's why you can't get a real man now. Thinking every man you meet is gay." I guess Cynthia didn't want to pull her card about the vice president.

Rita said," No. I'm *single* because I am looking for a quality man. I ain't trying to catch no gay man's HIV just because he likes to be poked."

"Not every gay man has AIDS," I added in. I had a cousin who was gay *and* AIDS-free and I wanted to make sure I got that message across.

"True that, Faith. But still, if I had to I'd take a man and poke him myself. I'm tired of being without a man," Karen added. "Plus them gay men know how to shop. It'd be like marrying myself with the extra bonus." Apparently, it didn't work out with the aerobics instructor. She wouldn't admit to it, but I still thought he was gay.

I sucked my teeth. "You need to cut it out, Karen."

"Oh come on, Faith," Karen said. "You know as well as any of us that a good man is hard to find. A good dick walks past us every ten minutes, but a good solid man does not come that easily. We sistahs gotta take what we can get."

Cynthia started up, "I don't know about that, girlfriend. I am not trying to mess with just any man. I'm with Rita about that AIDS shit. No, I don't think every Black man I see is gay either, and Faith, I know that all gay men don't have AIDS. I'm just extra cautious. Anyway, all this talk started up with those E. Lynn Harris books..."

"Oh girl, tell it. Those books are so enlightening," Rita said.

"But I think it's exaggerating. E. Lynn Harris is an excellent writer, and there is a lot of truth to his works. It's just that he is writing about a certain group of people. Gay and bi-sexual men. If we start claiming that ALL of our men are gay, then who do we have left? Are all of our men thugs and gangstas like they portray them in films? Are us sistahs all whores and prostitutes like they show us in videos?"

"Preach on, girl," Karen said.

Cynthia said, "I'm serious. And it's not fair. I had a good man for a long time, but I messed up. Ya'll remember Jason." All of us nodded. "Well, I messed around on him because I thought he was too good. After reading *Invisible Life*, I started questioning Jason every time he went out with his boys. Now look at me, manless. And look at Jason. Happily married to this white girl from his job, got three beautiful kids and just got his master's degree in criminology."

She had a point. Cynthia always had a point, which is why she was my girl. Rita and Karen are both cool sistahs, but Cynthia is my heart. Of us all, she is the one that we lean to for advice, support and the one we turn to in confidence. Although Cynthia is younger than both Rita and I, she is still like the big sister in the group. She's been working at the college longer than the rest of us, and she taught all of us the ropes as soon as we got there.

I reminded Cynthia that our time was running short, and she reminded me that she was Dean of her department and that her lunch hour didn't start until she reached the restaurant. The ladies laughed as me and Cynthia headed off to her car.

She asked, "Who is he?"

"What are you talking about?" I asked waiting for her to open the doors.

Cynthia unlocked the doors and we got inside.

"You got that look in your eyes again. Like when you were messing around with that professor. Is he back around? Is he the one you've been sexing?"

"I don't know what you're talking about. I haven't seen Philip in years."

"Then you got somebody new."

I sighed as I sat my purse on the floor, thinking that my behavior would prove to her that she was heading down the wrong path. It was irritating me that she could see right through me. Hopefully, Corey couldn't tell because if he found out what I'd been thinking about his best friend I couldn't imagine what he would do.

"There is no *one* and no*thing* going on."

"Then it must be Kael. I heard that he met an attractive woman in Student Accounts and I assumed it was you. I have a gift for these things, and you know it. You can't hide those blushing cheeks of yours. Come on, fill a sistah in."

I had to get her off the path. Actually, I had to make sure that she didn't go down the right one. I had to place a detour sign.

"Okay, I give in. I just thought that the guy was cute. That's it," I said. It wasn't an all-out lie. I did think that he was cute.

"I knew it, I'm never wrong. So... did you get his number?"

When was this going to end? "No, I don't think he is my type and anyways..."

"I hope you're not letting what those girls were saying out there, get to you. Rita thinks that any guy who doesn't want to eat her out is gay. And Karen. Well, Karen is just a little confused right now since she found out that Adam was bi-sexual. Once she gets laid, she'll be fine."

I told her that it just wasn't the right time to get involved with a guy. With Corey making arrangements to move to Atlanta, I needed to start getting my priorities in order.

"Then this is just the right time to meet a man. You don't want to be alone when Corey leaves. So, you know what I'll do? I'll call Kael tonight and invite him over for dinner. Be there at seven."

"I can't... how do you know his number? Were you the *someone* that he was looking for?"

"He's my cousin and I directed him to your department on purpose. After that spiel at the gym, I figured it was time to pull out the ammo. And Kael is the one. So I'll set it up for seven." She pulled into a parking spot outside of Bob's Bistro and that was the end of the conversation.

That bitch! I thought to myself as she turned off the ignition. How was she going to just set me up on a date with this guy? What was I going to do about Corey's dinner? What was I going to wear?

Stick Up Kid

Oh, it was about that time. School was out and we needed some weed badly. Corey had some ideas and I was down with almost anything he wanted to do. We were planning to celebrate his acceptance to Morehouse and his financial package. But there was one problem. We had no money and Ricardo wasn't about to hook us up with an IOU.

We got with two more of our boys and decided that there was only one thing left to do. We couldn't ask our parents for money to buy herb, and since we all lied to our parents a week ago about borrowing money for sneakers, clothes and whatever else we could think of, our parents had decided to close the bank on us.

Corey suggested that we head out to an upscale suburb outside of Boston and rob some people. He heard it was pretty easy to do, especially if we had some extra hands to help out. For some reason, I wasn't surprised when he told me about the plan, and then showed me his gun.

"Where the hell did you get that?"

"My cousin Tony," he said, admiring the piece. "You remember the deejay from my party, don't you?"

"Just be careful with that," I said keeping my composure. "I don't want it accidently going off and shooting my fine-ass."

He laughed as he put it away.

Without hesitation, we called our boys Wilson and Nathan. Wilson grew up with me and Corey. The three of us were inseparable back in the day. But about a year ago, Wilson moved to Quincy and became a hotshot quarterback at East Quincy High School. Me and Corey checked out a few games. The brother had skills.

We met Nathan right around the time that Wilson was leaving. He was more Corey's friend than mine, but he was all right. He'd do any kind of dirt - just ask once. We don't hang out with Nathan too much because he gets into a lot of trouble. He's been locked up a few times, spent the summer in a juvenile detention center. But now that he's eighteen, the next time he goes in, he'll be tried as an adult. Nathan knew this, and he still did dirt.

We decided to meet at Corey's house right after last period. There was no way I was going to go through with this thing without a plan. By the time we got to Corey's, Nathan was already waiting outside the front door. Instead of bringing his car, Nathan had ridden his black and red Kawasaki Ninja and left it parked on the side of the house.

"Why'd you park it way over there?" Corey asked him.

"I don't want those hating-ass neighbors of yours trying to mess with my ride. They may not pay too much attention to it if it's around the corner."

Both Corey and I shook our heads in disbelief.

"You park that up in Franklin Field Projects everyday, and you're scared of parking it in front of this three-family house?" I asked him.

Nathan ignored me and followed us into the house. I started reminiscing about the previous night, as we passed into the living room where me and Mrs. Jones had danced in the center of the floor. I wondered why she didn't push me away, or excuse herself from the dance floor. If Corey had danced with my mom like that, she would have probably slapped him in the head. But Mrs. Jones didn't. Maybe she liked it... Maybe I was reading too much into it.

Nathan asked, "Not that I'm knocking the idea, Corey, but what makes you think that a bunch of joggers are going to be carrying around the kind of bills you've been talking about?"

"My cousin told me," Corey said. "He did the same thing last week and he made out big time. As long as you do what I tell you, we'll get paid."

"I still can't believe it, but hey I'm down for whatever," Nathan said. "So, how long before Wilson gets here?"

"He's driving down from Quincy. It'll take a little while," Corey answered.

"Damn, won't it be too late?"

"Look, Nathan," I said. "As long as we're out there before dark, it's all good. It's at night that they expect to get robbed. They don't expect brothers to creep up on them at gunpoint and take their wallets and purses in the middle of the day. Those suburbanites will be too scared to scream. We'll get what we need, and be out before you know it."

I was talking like I was a professional and I have never robbed anyone in my life. Corey had. He and a few of his cousins used to ride through the suburbs and rob unexpected mothers and joggers with a 9mm. The last time they'd gone, Corey asked me to come along for the ride, but I was too chicken-hearted. This time I wasn't going to back out, although I was having second thoughts. I hoped that Wilson wouldn't show up and that Corey would decide not to go. But it was very unlikely that something like that would happen. Wilson was not going to pass up a chance to get some money and spend the night smoking weed with his old friends.

When a car pulled into the driveway, Corey rushed over to the living room window.

"Damn, it's my mother. What the hell is she doing home so early?"

Mrs. Jones opened the door and walked straight into the living room. She was looking as good as she did the night before. As good as she always looked. She had a light cocoa complexion with naturally long, soft hair.

"Hi fellas," she said. "Hey Nathan, long time no see. How's your mother?"

Nathan put on a tough front. "Fine," he said sharply.

Corey's mom looked at him strangely. She knew something was up, but seemed too preoccupied to care. For some reason, Mrs. Jones didn't look at me or greet me the way she usually did.

"Was your mom upset when you got home last night?" She finally asked without even looking at me.

"She'll be fine," I said. 'You know how she...'"

Before I could finish my sentence, Mrs. Jones was already talking to Corey.

"I have a date tonight, okay," she said. She glanced at me and then turned her attention back to Corey. "So you'll have to scrape up something to eat. There are leftovers in the fridge from last night and we have some microwaveable food in the freezer."

This seemed like a blessing in disguise. Now, all Corey had to do was ask his mother for a few dollars for food and then we could buy some weed without having to jump anyone. I waited anxiously for Corey to pop the question.

"So what do you three have planned for the evening?"

"Chillin'," Corey said. "Just chillin'"

Just then, the doorbell rang. Corey went to answer it, while his mom stayed in the room with us.

"Nathan!" Corey called from the other room. "Wilson needs some help out here, come on."

Nathan asked me why Corey didn't ask me to help. I told him that Corey knew that I would say 'no'.

When Nathan left, Mrs. Jones went to look out of the window.

"I haven't seen Wilson since he moved to Quincy with his father. How are they doing?" She asked me.

Reluctantly, I walked over to her. Her frame was delicious and I wanted to sink my teeth into her. I brushed past her, with my jones sliding against her side. I apologized, but she didn't accept it. She turned around and looked at me for a long while. Grabbing my neck, Mrs. Jones pulled my lips to hers and slid her tongue into my mouth.

"Well?" Mrs. Jones asked, snatching me out of my daydream.

"Oh," I said. "Fine I guess. Corey speaks to him more than I do."

Mrs. Jones looked at me, lowered her eyes to the floor, bit her lip and then walked out of the room. When I looked myself over, I recognized the bulge in my pants. The odd thing is I didn't even realize that I had a hard-on.

"Trouble with the stick," Corey said when he came into the room.

"What?" I asked him.

"Wilson was having trouble changing gears," Corey said. "Nathan works at his father's auto-body shop so he's out there helping him repair it. You all right?"

"Yeah, yeah," I said. "I'm fine." I was starting to sound a little nervous. "Why'd you ask?"

"Never mind," he said. "Where's my mother?"

"I don't know. She must have gone into the kitchen."

Corey yelled to his mother that we were leaving, and

told her not to stay out too late with that nigga. She told him to watch his mouth and said to have a good time. I yelled goodbye to her, and she returned the farewell with little emotion.

We were almost at our destination when Wilson started up with Nathan. The two of them were cool, but had never really got to know each other. I don't think that Wilson liked the idea of someone taking his "place" after he left.

"You still ain't getting no ass, Nathan?" Wilson asked him.

"What the hell are you talking about?" Nathan asked. "I get ass almost everyday. You the one out there in Quincy messing with that virgin."

"Kid please," Wilson shot back. "She's not the only chick out there. I get mine. If not from her, then from the cheerleaders."

"I can't believe you're messing around on Damita," Corey said. "That sistah is gorgeous. She's a junior too, right?"

Wilson was a year behind us. So while we were preparing for *graduation*, he was preparing for his senior year. Like Corey, Wilson was just waiting for the colleges to start offering him scholarships. It shouldn't have been any question because he was an excellent quarterback and we were all sure that he would get a free ride to almost any university.

"That girl is my heart," Wilson said. "But a brother can only wait for so long. And I've been waiting since we started going out back in October."

"Still," I added. "She's good people. Why won't you let somebody else have her?"

"Who?" Wilson asked. "Like you. Man please. I will

not lose my Princess. I love her too much and I'll kill any mofo that tries to step between me and Damita."

"We get it," Corey said. "We don't want the girl. We were just saying she seems like good people. None of us even know her like that."

The car was parked near Hemlock Gorge and the four of us got out and entered the park. The plan was to stand, incognito, near the runners' path. First, two of us would wait a quarter of a mile away from the others. We were supposed to wait for a jogger, and when we were sure that it was safe, Nathan would jump out at them, pull out the 9mm and demand their cash. If there were any hesitation, someone from the other group would jump out, to let the person know that they were surrounded.

This all had to be done in enough time so that another jogger wouldn't happen to come along the same path. It seemed like a fool-proof plan.

We stood behind the trees for about ten minutes before the first runner came by. Before Nathan could jump out behind him, another jogger came along the path. The thought that crossed my mind was that the second jogger could have been stalking the first one. If anything happened, I wondered if Corey would want to rescue the person. We could be heroes or perpetrators. I'd rather be a hero.

The joggers disappeared down the path along with my chance of being a superman.

Moments later, a man came jogging down the path all by himself. He tripped on a rock and then cursed to himself. The man, who looked to be in his twenties or so, sat down on a boulder not too far from Nathan. He took his shoe off and started massaging his foot.

I didn't know what was going to happen. Nathan had the opportunity to handle this guy. He was alone and injured. But since me and Corey were further up, we couldn't tell Nathan to make his move. We looked at each other, hoping that Wilson would make Nathan go out there.

We were stuck in our spots, waiting anxiously for someone to make a move. I was sweating bullets as I moved a little and accidently made some noise in the bushes. The man looked in our direction but could not spot us. He must have figured that we were squirrels, because he eventually went back to massaging his feet.

Before another thought entered my mind, Nathan jumped out of the bushes and yelled for the man to give up all of his money. Corey looked directly at me. He was looking just as nervous as I was. Although he had done this before, it was hitting him as though it was the first time. It seemed like he was regretting his decision to come.

The man threw his shoe at Nathan and ran towards me and Corey. One of us had to get out there. Corey didn't move. He was the one carrying a gun, but he wouldn't budge.

Nathan yelled for the man to stop and then we heard the gun go off. The man stopped right beside where we were hiding. Nathan walked up on him with Wilson not too far behind. But me and Corey did not move out of those bushes. Nathan put his gun to the man's head and demanded that he empty out his pockets.

He reached into the pockets of his sweatpants and pulled out a bunch of lint.

"See, nothing," he said in shock. "I have nothing."

"Stop lying you prick," Wilson shouted. "I'll have him blow your head off, now reach inside those shoes and pull out some Benjamin's."

The man refused and Nathan slapped him with his gun, knocking the man down to his knees. He pulled back the clip and was about to pull the trigger.

Corey wouldn't move. He was just sitting there watching. This couldn't be happening. I was not a murderer or an accomplice. If I let that happen we were all going to go down, not just the man who pulled the trigger. Four Black dudes and a dead white man. Yeah, we were all going to get the hot chair.

I ran out of the bushes, startling everyone, and told the man to take off his shoes. Nathan pulled his gun back from his head. The man finally took off one of his shoes and three fifty-dollar bills were stuck to his sock.

Wilson frowned as he took them off. Corey came out slowly zipping up his pants.

"What were you two doing in there?" Wilson asked putting the money in his pocket. "Humping?"

Corey threw up his middle finger.

"Shit," Corey said. "I was taking a piss. I don't know what took *him* so long to get out here."

Corey was saving face, as usual. It was all-good. At least all of us were out there together. Nathan put the gun away, and as soon as we heard footsteps coming along the path, we bolted back into the bushes and ran to the car. The man was screaming for help, but by the time someone got to him, we were already at the car. The only description that he would have would be: Four average-height black men who looked to be in their late teens. We weren't worried. We were going to get high.

Say Yes

Kael was nice and all, and although I did what I could to keep him from getting to me, he slipped his way in. He wore a navy Sean Jean button-up shirt and a pair of jeans. His entire outfit was loose fitting, unlike the suit I saw him in early. The suit must have been tailor made to fit his bulging physique. To me, he looked good either way.

Cynthia forced him to tell me that he was studying for his certificate of public accounting, why he decided to wait before he had kids, and about how he is still taking care of his sick momma. It was a little ridiculous, but at the same time it was a turn on. Kael was a year younger than me, a financial analyst, and was going to business school part-time at night. He received his undergraduate degree in accounting from Northeastern University.

It was almost too good to be true, and if it wasn't for Cynthia badgering it out of him, I don't think I would have believed any of it. But he was too resistant to share, meaning that he wasn't trying to sell himself.

"Faith here is going back to school to become a business-lawyer," Cynthia said taking the last bite of her salmon.

I said, "I was only thinking about it. I never said I was going. Besides, it's a little late for me to be thinking about law school."

"You should do it," Kael said. "Don't let anything hold you back from what you really want. Look at your son, he's going to pursue his dreams at Morehouse."

"So, you two already did some talking, huh," Cynthia beamed.

"Just a little," Kael said. "I was telling her about my niece at Spelman."

Cynthia laughed. "Oh please, Corey would not be interested in that chicken-head."

"Cynthia," I said almost choking on my wine. "That's his niece."

"That's his goddaughter," she revealed. "It might be his real daughter. Her mother slept with so many men before she was born that she didn't know who that daddy was. And since Kael is the only respectable guy she knew, she asked him to be the godfather."

Kael said that his niece/goddaughter was a sweet girl and was nothing like her mother. Cynthia sucked her teeth and then took the plates to the kitchen.

"I'm really sorry for what I said earlier," Kael whispered after Cynthia was out of earshot. "I was trying to compliment you."

"I already forgot about it. There's no need to let it linger." I took another sip of wine. "And thank you."

He fidgeted with his napkin, trying to hold himself back from something. I had a feeling I knew what it was. Kael's soft, almost shy eyes avoiding mine as if he were trying to keep his true feelings a secret.

Kael finally asked, "Are you free anytime this weekend?"

"I don't know," I started. "Corey has...."

"She's free," Cynthia called from the kitchen.

Kael and I looked at each other. I was free, but I was still a little uncomfortable going out with a guy that I just met. Well, he was Cynthia's cousin and I knew she wouldn't set me up with a psychopath. So, eventually I agreed.

It was only seconds later that Cynthia joined us with slices of brownies topped with whip cream.

"Damn, girl," I said. "You really know how to hook it up in the kitchen."

She thanked me and told Kael that she had been showing me the way around the kitchen as well. He seemed impressed. Then she said, "I've been cooking since I was a kid. You know I want to open up my own restaurant in a couple of years, right here in the hood."

"Weren't you going to name it La' Vida or something like that?" Kael asked. "She's been talking about having her own restaurant since fifth grade."

"Why La' Vida?" I asked.

"It's *the life*. Girl, don't you listen to Ricky Martin. Livin..." She started singing the tunes to the former Menudo star's solo classic.

Lucky for me, Kael cut her off. "She's been crazy about that man for far too long. She claims that on opening night she's gonna spend the whole night shaking her buns."

We all burst into laughter. It felt good to be around some adults for a change. I spent so much time with Corey and his friends playing video games and watching BET, that sometimes I forgot that I wasn't a teenager. But sitting with some folks my own age made for mature conversations, not just about the best PlayStation games, but about the future and goals. The more I thought about it, the more I was looking forward to my date with Kael.

I dropped Kael off at his condo after dinner, because as Cynthia explained it, his Infiniti was getting detailed. It was a smooth ride. And to top it off, we had the same taste in music. Neosoul to the heart. Jill Scott, Floetry, and oh my boo, John Legend. We bumped John all the

way to his place.
    When we got there, he invited me up for coffee, but I told him that I'd take a rain check. There was no need for us to rush into anything too soon. Saturday was only a few days away and the *coffee* could wait until then. Before he got out of the car, we sat in front of the entrance of his condominium, talking about our dreams. He was more intelligent than I thought. Back in high school, Kael had actually considered going into business with Cynthia. I asked him why they never partnered up.
    "Because, she's the type that doesn't always follow through. She has a lot of potential, but Cynthia doesn't always do what she is supposed to do."
    "Well, she finished college and worked her way up to dean. That should prove something."
    "Yeah, but she didn't get into a culinary arts program. Her degree is in hospitality and she just happened to take a few cooking classes. She could have her certificate in culinary arts by now, but she decided not to go back to school."
    Kael seemed to be going down that path of dogging out my friends like he did back at the job, but he caught himself.
    "Not that I don't have faith in her, but I do expect a lot from her," he said. "Cynthia is too smart to be content working at a community college." Before I could butt in, he continued. "Now, there is nothing wrong with having those types of jobs, but there is something wrong when you don't strive for more. If this is the dream, hey, go for it, but if you aspire to be something else- like the chef at your own restaurant- then you shouldn't let your job hinder you. Take what experience you can from it, but don't settle."
    He had a point, and I had to agree.
    Since midnight was creeping up on us, I bid Kael

farewell and promised to accept his call if he tried to reach me the following day. There was a brief hug, and I was on my way back home. I thought about Kael all the way to the house.

When I got into the house, the kitchen light was still on, and there was a note from Corey sitting on top of the microwave. He hoped that I had a good time and wished me a goodnight's sleep. I folded it up and made plans to add it to my 'Boo Boo Collection'. Boo Boo was a nickname he always hated. But it stuck with me, just like the very first Mother's Day card he made me when he was four. Years ago, Corey told me that keeping all of that stuff would eventually cause a fire. So I started putting everything into a fire-resistant box-anything to keep from tossing it out.

I opened the fridge and pulled out the carton of orange juice. It was down to its last drip. All I could think was that I had just gone shopping and now the OJ was almost empty. Corey and his friends. They can be so young and immature at times. It was probably Darius who drank most of it because he was always looking for something to eat and drink. Well, after Corey left for school I wouldn't have to see his friends that often. Probably not at all.

Shutting the fridge, I felt something sliding along my fingers. I jumped, dropped the orange juice on the floor and looked at the body standing beside me. His bare, but hair-covered legs, cotton boxers and tank top. Then the braids, those long braids that needed a touch-up.

"Sorry, Mrs. Jones," Darius said. "I didn't mean to scare you." He rushed over to get some paper towels. "I was looking for something to drink."

"Well, the orange juice is all gone now. Thanks to you," I said.

"I'm really sorry." He got on the floor and tried to

wipe it up but I reached for the paper towels.

"I can do it myself."

"No, let me do it." He set the carton up right and then started to spread the fluid over the floor.

I was a little annoyed because he was invading my quiet time. At least, that's what I led myself to believe. "You're making a mess," I said.

I placed my hand on top of his to stop him. His hand slowed to a halt and he looked at me with those soft eyes. Darius' lips were so tender that I had a hard time resisting. I couldn't though. He was *my other son* and sixteen years younger than me. Even if he was eighteen, wouldn't I still end up in jail? Damn, I said to myself. Just let go of his hand, escape to my bedroom- alone. But I couldn't leave. I couldn't let go. I couldn't resist.

His eyes searched mine, and before I knew what hit me, my lips were all over his. My tongue massaging his tongue, my fingers running through his cornrows. Darius wasn't resisting either. Why didn't he stop me? Why didn't I stop myself? But suddenly I did stop. Minutes later, I did get up and I did leave the kitchen. What had I done? And how could I undo it?

(My Mind's Gone) Half Crazy

It had to be a dream. I must have been sleepwalking or something. I lied down on the futon and tried to chase everything that happened out of my mind. What the hell happened in that kitchen? Mrs. Jones and me? Me and Corey's mom? It was a dream, and the sooner I took myself to bed, the better. I would wake up the next morning and this would all be behind me.

"Was my mother home?" Corey asked sleepily.

I jumped back, realizing that Corey was still awake, all the while hoping that it was a part of my dream too. It had to be, because there was no way I'd kissed Corey's mother. "Huh?" I asked. "Oh, yeah. She just came in. I'm going back to sleep."

"Did she say how her date went?"

"Damn, no. Now can I get some sleep?"

"I should go and find out."

If he got out of his bed then this would all seem too real, but as long as we were both asleep then none of this was real. So he just needed to take his ass back to sleep. A dream is a dream, right?

"Let her sleep, man," I said. "She looked tired, so just talk to her in the morning."

He paused for a few seconds and then finally agreed. He said that he would make her spill the beans in the morning. Minutes later he was snoring and I was still staring at the dark ceiling.

I refused to go downstairs for breakfast, but Corey made me get up. He wanted to talk to his mom before she left for work, and he wanted me to be there when he did it. Of course I didn't want to go, but I had no choice. Not that I owed him anything, but we were boys and I knew he would have done the same for me.

When we got down to the kitchen, only one plate of food was prepared. Eggs, bacon and waffles. Corey looked at me apologetically and then offered to share his food. I decided to get a bowl of cereal.

"Ma," he called. "Hey Ma."

Mrs. Jones came into the kitchen fully dressed with her briefcase ready for work. She asked Corey what he wanted, but never looked at me.

"Why didn't you make enough for Darius?" he asked her.

She said, "I didn't know he was here. But I'm running late for work, so I need to go. He can have some cereal." She glanced at me and then dropped her eyes to my shirt. "You don't mind cereal do you?"

"I'm fine." I was fine, because I was in the clear. Nothing happened the night before. I never saw her and she never saw me. The world was good again.

Until Corey said, "He told me he saw you last night. He said you looked tired."

His mother took her keys off the counter and said, "Yeah, I really was tired. I didn't remember. Sorry." She left the kitchen and then shouted goodbye as she opened and then slammed the front door behind her.

"That's strange," Corey said going to the fridge for some orange juice. When he stepped in the spot where the orange juice had fallen the night before, he asked why the floor was so sticky.

I said, "Something must have spilled."

"And Mom didn't mop it up," he said to himself. "She must have been toasted last night or something. She never leaves a mess. Maybe she got some tail."

I almost spit the cereal out of my mouth. Did he know something? How could he talk about his mother like that? *Got some tail.* That was disgusting.

"What's the matter with you?" He asked. Corey opened the fridge but did not find any orange juice. "Damn, man. Did you drink all the juice? Greedy-ass."

"Nah." I had to cover myself but at the same time I had to protect his mother. "Actually, yeah. I drank the rest of it when I came downstairs last night."

"You said you saw her, right."

I nodded in agreement.

"How was she? Was she all clumsy and shit?"

"I told you she looked tired. That's all I can remember."

"She got me worried, man. Something happened and she's not telling me. And my mom usually tells me everything. I hope that dude didn't drop anything into her drink and take advantage of my mother. I'll kill somebody if I have to." He pulled his gun out from the back of his pants and laid it on the table. "Let someone mess with my mother and I'll blow his head off."

I swallowed hard because what he said was hitting too close to home, even if he didn't realize it.

"When are you giving that shit back to your cousin?" I asked trying to finish my cereal.

He just smiled and put it away. After I took a shower, we left for school.

The school day was dragging, so me, Corey and Nathan decided to cut out at lunch to go see a movie.

Nathan was still mumbling about the hit and how stupid those joggers were for keeping so much money on them.

"...And you're still a bitch-ass for hiding in the bushes," Nathan said to Corey. "I don't care what you say about taking a leak."

"Man, please," Corey said. "It was my idea, why would I run off?"

"I don't know man. Maybe you getting soft or something. Even this punk came out before you." Nathan was referring to me.

"Forget you, Nathan," I finally said. "We all did our part and we all ended up with a couple of bags of herb, and we all got cash for our pockets. So why are you still buggin'?"

Nathan said, "I'm just saying. That wasn't cool for ya'll to leave us out there for so long. We still boys, but you won't catch me running with ya'll like that again."

We paid for our tickets to see some Black comedy movie. I don't even remember the name, because I spent the first half of the movie thinking about me and Mrs. Jones making out. I had a hard-on the entire time.

Corey elbowed me, snatching me out of the fantasy, and pointed at two females walking down the aisle. That was the main reason why we used to come to the movies. So we could pick up girls.

"Wait for one of them to go to the bathroom," Nathan said as Corey stood up to approach the girls.

"Nah, yo," he said crossing over Nathan. "It's been a minute since I got laid and I am not taking any chances." He walked down and sat in an empty seat next to one of them.

Nathan looked over at me and shook his head. "He's gonna screw this up, watch."

I agreed with Nathan. But even if things did work out, I was not about to move in on any females that day. I had enough problems in my head. Before we knew it, Corey was back. I thought he was going to take his seat in one of the seats between me and Nathan but he didn't. He told us that the two girls were interested, so me and Nathan had to decide which one of us would go.

"Go ahead," I told Nathan. Picking up my cell phone, I said, "I'm supposed to meet up with Nina anyway. I'm picking up Lil' Darius today."

We dapped each other up and then I left the theatre. I still couldn't get Mrs. Jones off of my mind, so I needed to do something to get over that feeling. I called up Nina, but she was working at the hair salon. Nina was a year older than me and had already graduated from high school. She was in hair school and worked part-time under another beautician's license.

"Lil' Darius is at daycare," she said. "You can pick him up if you want, but you gotta make sure he gets his snack by three-thirty or else he'll have a fit."

I said, "I know my son, Nina."

"I'm just saying. I had to learn the hard way about those snacks. I'm just giving you a heads up."

I decided not to get Lil' Darius until my mother was home. Although I could easily use my father's car to pick him up, my mother is the one who knew the kinds of snacks he wanted.

There was nowhere to go if your friends weren't with you, and since I couldn't go home I felt a little stranded. I should've kept my butt in school and studied for the MCAS in the library. It was too late to go back, so I decided to walk home from Downtown Boston. It would take me about an hour or more to get there, but I was running out of options.

I only made it about a block before my telephone rang.

Emotional Rollercoaster

I was making it worse by calling him, but I needed to find my son. This was normal, wasn't it? For me to call Darius to look for Corey. I had to get this situation as close to normal as possible. When I heard his voice though, it all came back to me. The tongue, the lips, the shame. And then I wanted to see him again. But I couldn't.

"Is my son with you?" Was all I could say to his greeting.

"Um, Mrs. Jones?"

"You know it's me, Darius," I said as hard as I could. "His principal just called me and said that he cut out after lunch. And I know he wouldn't leave school without you. So can I speak to him, please?"

"H...he's not with me."

He was lying through his teeth and I wanted him to pay for that. How could he lie to the woman who had been giving him food, and a place to sleep? I was almost like his mother, and he was steady lying to me. I should curse him the hell out and...

"Mrs. Jones, about last night."

No he didn't go there. I was not about to let him take me back to that place. I was tired when that happened and he did not have to worry about anything like that happening again. It was partially his fault anyway. Darius should have pulled away.

"Darius, I have something to say to you. I need you to stop coming by my house, okay." And before he could respond, I hung up the phone on him.

No sooner than I placed the phone on the hook, than was Kael at my office door carrying another sheet of paper, and a single rose. We had to be discreet, but I was sure our smiles would give us away.

He checked to make sure that the coast was clear before he handed me the flower. It was gorgeous, and it made me realize that this is the kind of life I needed to be living. I asked him about the sheet of paper in his hand.

He said, "I couldn't remember how to find your office, so I had to ask around." As he balled up the paper, he asked me if I enjoyed myself at Cynthia's.

"I sure did. What about you?"

Kael smiled at me. "You know I did. I want to do it again tonight, but this time without Cynthia."

"I don't know if she'd allow that."

He looked at me like I was joking. "She's probably making arrangements for the two of us to eat at a restaurant right now. You know Cynthia's rooting for us."

"Don't forget I have my son. Can't you wait until Saturday? I don't want to leave him by himself, two nights in a...."

My supervisor came into my office and gave Kael the once over. Mr. Hughes asked about a student's records, took it from my file cabinet, and then walked out without saying another word.

"I guess that means I need to get out of here," Kael said putting his ink pen in his pocket.

"He's just under a lot of stress. Don't pay him any

mind."

He asked, "So about tonight?"

I thought of Darius again. There was no way I was staying in that house tonight. Although I told him not to come over, Corey would find a way to persuade Darius to be there.

"I'll pick you up at seven," I said.

"Why don't you just come by and I'll cook for you. I'm not as good as Cynthia, but I do have some skills."

So it was set. I was going on a real date with a real man. Shoot, I was old enough to actually stay the night out with him if I wanted to. As soon as work was over, I went straight home to get ready for my date with Kael. I didn't have time to get my hair professionally done or to get a manicure in one of the Korean shops. So I settled for a hot comb and a homemade manicure. I took a quick shower, spritzed myself with Bath and Body Works body splash while I tried on a million outfits. It took me an hour to find the perfect outfit for the evening. Not too flashy, not too casual. Then it was my hair. I only had about twenty minutes to get that correct, I just took the hot comb and curled the ends.

I left a note for Corey to call me as soon as he got in. He still hadn't come home from school, and there was no way I was calling Darius again. Darius had actually called me a couple of times, but I was not trying to answer his calls. Every time the phone rang it was him, except for the one time when Kael called to make sure that I was still coming.

When I first got to Kael's condo, I was mesmerized. He had built an aquarium in his living room, with all sorts of exotic fish. The furniture was Italian Leather, hard wood floors with a cherry wood coffee table and amazing African masks, sculptures and framed artwork. He gave me a tour of every room, except the bedroom.

73   Me and Mrs. Jones

Kael was respectful like that.

Throughout dinner, Kael had smooth jazz playing from his digital cable. The first course was a small Greek Salad. He wanted to make sure I had enough room for the main course. Roast duck and wild rice. This brother had thrown down and I was impressed. I had to turn down a second serving, because I didn't want to seem greedy, and besides, I didn't know if I could resist licking the plate.

We chatted for a while after dinner and then he switched the music to some 80s and 90s R&B. Our kind of music. Kael took me to the living room and, although I resisted at first, he got me dancing. Kael had the moves of an eighteen year-old, but he was still no match for me. I pulled things out of my body that I didn't know I still owned. I even pulled out some of the moves Darius taught me. I started grinding up on him like I used to do in the club back in the day.

The fireplace was simmering, the mood was right, and Kael did the all expected. He kissed me, long and hard. I pulled him in closer and laced our bodies. Although his hands gently caressed my spine, Kael continued to respect my body. I wanted him to take advantage of me, but I knew that he would not. And me, a mother of one, was not going to insist. Not this time at least.

Moments later while we were still embracing, I heard my cell phone ring. It had to be Corey. It was almost ten o'clock at night and this was his first time calling me. My first reaction was to curse him out when I answered the phone, but I could not do it in front of Kael. He wasn't ready to witness that side of me yet.

"I need to get that," I said releasing his soft hold. "It might be my son."

Kael looked disappointed, but he had to understand. He was dealing with a mother, and stuff like this was bound to happen. I reached into my purse for my phone and almost screamed. It was that damn Darius again.

I said, "What did I tell you?"

"I'm sorry Mrs. Jones, but I needed to talk to you."

"Look, Darius. I understand that you and my son are friends, but that does not give you the right to call my cell phone freel..."

"Corey was shot, Mrs. Jones."

I almost dropped my phone but I had to hold on to it. What the hell did he just say to me about my son? I was hearing things cause shit like this doesn't happen to me and my family.

"Mrs. Jones, are you there?"

"What did you say?" Tears were already pouring down my cheeks.

"He's at Boston Medical Center. I'm already here."

I just hung up the phone without a goodbye. Immediately, I ran to get my jacket and my purse. Kael was behind me, asking if everything was all right.

"No," I yelled. "Look at me. Do I look all right?"

He stepped away from me. "What happened?"

"Corey was shot! I gotta get out of here! I need to get to him."

Kael insisted that he drive me there, and I allowed him to because my head was not clear enough to be trying to drive a car. Dodging traffic, we made it to the hospital in record time. Kael let me out at the emergency entrance and said that he would meet me inside.

When I got to the reception desk, I almost had a nervous breakdown. My son's name was not in their system. I was about to start screaming, first at the receptionist, and then at Darius once I got my hands on him. If this was some kind of cruel joke then I would...

But I knew it wasn't a joke and when Darius came out to the main entrance, it was confirmed that my baby had actually been shot.

"What the hell is going on, Darius?" I asked with tears burning my eyes. "Where is my son?"

"I don't know," he said.

"What do you mean, you don't know?"

"They won't tell me anything. The last time I spoke to Nathan, he said that Corey was in surgery. But his name's not in their computers. Nathan said that they do that for his protection."

I walked away from him. At that point, Darius had become useless, and I needed to get some vital information. I headed right back to the receptionist and gave him my story. He looked me over and then glanced at Darius when he stood beside me. I guess Darius had already dealt with this young kid and couldn't get anywhere.

"You need to speak to the police department. If your son is here, then they'll have to clear you if you want to physically go and speak to him."

Physically go and speak to him? I kept myself in check and waited for a police officer to arrive. It took a few minutes before they showed up, and all the while Darius stood near by. As soon as the two officers arrived, I left Darius by himself and followed them to an administrative office, where we had to meet with the head of hospital security and with a hospital administrator.

I felt like I was going to visit an inmate the way they questioned me, checked my driver's license and made me sign forms. I was about to take off my jewelry before I remembered where I was. It didn't bother me too much, because I came to realize that whoever had done this to Corey would have little to no way of getting to him now.

Last but not least, I had to make a visitor's list for hospital security. Besides me, Darius was the only other person that I would permit to see Corey. I wasn't keen on that idea either, but Corey would have a damn fit if I didn't let Darius in to see him. But his other boys were definitely not going to be added. Hell no.

We were both escorted up to his floor. And although Corey was already out of surgery, the nurses wanted to make sure he was ready to receive visitors. I looked at Darius when we were alone, waiting for the right moment to ask.

"Now, what the hell happened to my son, Darius?"

We sat down and he started to explain about some girls they met at the movie theater. Then he said something about the girls' boyfriends jumping Corey and Nathan.

"Where were you?" I asked him.

Darius said, "I left the movie theater early and I was on my way to get Lil' Darius when you called me."

"So, first you have my son skip school and then you leave him there with some hoodlum to get shot?"

"You know Nathan," he said.

"Exactly, he's a hoodlum and I don't know why Corey hangs out with him." I was pissed. "I don't know why he continues to hang out with you either. I used to think of you as a son, Darius but now.... Well anyway, after he leaves for Atlanta I won't have to worry about him being around a bunch of street thugs who can't even graduate from high school."

I know that hit him hard. The hurt was in his face, and although I regretted saying it, I wasn't going to take it back. Darius didn't say another word to me, not until the nurse came in and asked to see both of us. The male nurse said that Corey was in ICU and could receive visitors for a few minutes.

"He's very tired though and barely conscious," the nurse said. "However, he did request to see the both of you and in this situation we'll allow it. But only for about ten minutes. Corey will need his rest."

Reluctantly, I allowed Darius to come in with me. It was Corey's request and I wasn't going to have my son getting upset for something so minor. When this was over, he would have to find new friends.

We got inside and I gave Corey a big wet kiss on the forehead. I wanted to slap the hell out of him, but he had already been through too much. The slapping would have to wait until he got home.

"Come on, Ma," Corey said trying to fight me off.

I asked, "How did you get yourself in this mess? I told you about messing with them little skeezers."

"It wasn't like that, Ma. These punks just came up and started wildin' out. I guess they were ex-boyfriends or something."

"You're going to college in August," I told him. Why couldn't he understand that? "You are going to meet some of the most beautiful and educated sisters in the world down in Atlanta. Can't you wait until then? Leave these little chicken-head females alone."

"She's right," Darius said.

I couldn't help but roll my eyes at him. He had been so quiet, I almost forgot he was there. A smile appeared on Corey's face when he saw his friend, so I moved to the side so that they could converse.

"You're lucky you left," Corey said to him. "Did you pick up Lil' Darius?"

"I was with Nina when Nathan called, so she dropped me off here," he said. "How are you doing, man?"

"Tired," Corey said. "Hey, where's that bitch-ass Nathan anyway?"

I sucked my teeth, realizing that me constantly reminding him to clean up his mouth was not working. He had too much of Stan and me in him.

Corey apologized as Darius went on.

"He was just bruised up a bit. His mom came and got him while you were in surgery. Nathan said that you were about to throw down. Had five dudes up on ya'll, huh?"

"Yeah, man, until ole' dude pulled out his piece and..."

The nurse walked back into the room and announced that our ten minutes were up. He said that he would allow for a few more seconds, but reminded us that Corey needed to get some rest.

I kissed him again and told him that he needed to call me as soon as he woke up in the morning. He said that he would and then he told Darius that he would call him too. And to make matters worse, he made a final request.

"Darius, I need to you to stay with my mother tonight." Before I could argue, Corey went on. "Mom, you're in no mood to drive and I don't want you in that house alone. I don't think that those guys will do anything but I just have a feeling that something is going to jump off tonight. I don't know what it is, but I just have a feeling."

This was just getting worse by the minute. I wanted to ask him how the guys would know where we lived, but his medication seemed to have been taking affect. Both Darius and I finally agreed and before we could say goodbye, Corey was asleep.

Jonz In My Bonz

It was a very uncomfortable walk back down that hospital hall, in the elevator and down to the hospital's main entrance. Corey's mom didn't say a single word to me, and since I was still pissed at the comment she made about me not being able to graduate from high school, I didn't have anything to say to her. Ever since she kissed me (and yes, she did kiss me despite what she may think) she had been acting like a bitch. Calling *my* cell phone and asking for *her* son, telling me not to come over her house anymore, and then hanging up in my face.

I practically grew up in her house. How could she tell me not to come over there?

That damn kiss.

I kept thinking about it though, and we did need to talk. If it took me apologizing for what *she* did, then I would. Especially after what happened to her son. I was actually going to apologize the last time I spoke to her on the phone, but she hung up on me before I had the chance to. So, until she changed that little attitude of hers, there wasn't going to be much for me to say to her.

And I hoped that she would drop me off instead of having me stay over their house. I'd cover for her, and just tell Corey that I left early.

When we got to the entrance, I remembered that I had left all of my stuff in the main waiting area. I passed a guy who was sitting next to my pile, excused myself and grabbed my jacket and my backpack. As I reached for the jacket, the guy stood up and walked over to Mrs. Jones. They hugged and then he did the unexpected. He kissed her on the cheek.

"How is he?" The guy asked.

Mrs. Jones looked at me and said, "He's fine." And then she turned back to her beau.

It seemed like she blamed me for the whole thing. It wasn't me who wanted to cut out of school early. It wasn't me who wanted to get up with some strange chicks in the movie theater. And it wasn't me who carried a knife and now a gun on me all day. Corey did this to himself, and blaming me wasn't going to make things better.

I didn't even want a ride from that woman. There were cabstands outside of the main entrance, and I could easily cough up a few dollars to get to Nina's house. After a night like this, I needed to be with my son.

Walking past Mrs. Jones and her new "friend," I excused myself and left the two of them alone.

"Where are you going?" She asked me before I could make my escape.

"I'm staying with Nina tonight," I said. "She doesn't live too far from here."

She sighed heavily but didn't say anything to me. She didn't even introduce me to the guy. His arm was tight across her shoulder but Mrs. Jones was holding up strong. No tears had shed since we left Corey in his room.

At the exit, Mrs. Jones asked the guy about her car. It was in a parking garage and he said that he would grab it and meet her outside. I was heading out to hail the taxi that had just pulled up, but Mrs. Jones called me back.

"Why are you doing this?" She asked. "Corey asked you for a favor, and that's the least that you can do. Believe me, I am no happier about this than you are, but I have to do this for my son."

Immediately I said, "I can cover for us. Tell him that I left...."

"I am not lying to Corey. I could never lie to Corey. He reads me like an open book. I have never been able to keep secrets from him."

I smiled, remembering all the times he found the Christmas presents Mrs. Jones would hide in the toughest places. She even hid a mountain bike at my house one year, and he found it there. I agreed to come over and promised to leave first thing in the morning. I promised myself that I wouldn't go into the kitchen for any late night snacks.

We dropped her friend off at home first. I found out his name was Kael. We greeted each other briefly when we pulled in front of his condo and then he and Corey's mom kissed passionately. Reminding me of when she and I kissed in the kitchen. I shook the thought from my head but it was too late, I had already gotten a stiffy.

Neither of us hesitated to get onto the porch when we got to her house. The rain had already started as Mrs. Jones fumbled with the keys. The wind blew the rain right at us and by the time she got the door open, we were both soaked. She went in first and I was right behind her.

The kitchen was warm, but I knew that if I didn't get out of those wet clothes I was going to get sick. I took off my jacket, told Mrs. Jones goodnight, and went to Corey's room. I didn't have to worry about clothes, because half of my wardrobe was in his closet, and vice versa. The only difference was that Corey was heavy into name brand. His closet was lined with Sean John, Polo, Phat Farm, and my Old Navy jeans. And the way Mrs. Jones dresses, there was no question where he got his style from. He may have gotten his attitude and his green eyes from his father, but he got his fashion sense from his mom.

Pulling off my shirt, I figured that I could use a towel to dry myself off. The towels were out in the hallway closet. So I had two choices. Go out there with my wet shirt on, which was freezing cold. Or, put on another shirt and get it all wet up. Neither seemed to make much sense, so I came up with a third option. Sneak into the hall without a shirt and pray that Corey's mom would not come out. Number three it was.

I tiptoed into the hall holding the cold, dripping wet shirt in front of my chest and snatched a towel out of the closet. Before I could turn around, I heard the door to Mrs. Jones' room opening. I turned to head back to the bedroom, and somehow lost my balance. I slipped, fell on the floor and lost my shirt.

Mrs. Jones must have heard the thump, because she was out in the hall almost instantly.

She rushed over to me and asked if I was okay. Sitting up slowly, I looked around for something to cover myself.

"Yeah, I'm cool."

She looked me over as she grabbed my shoulder with her soft fingers. With her hands sliding down my back, she was able to help boost me to my feet. There was an enticing sensation racing through me.

"Shouldn't be walking around in those wet shoes," she said and tried to walk away, but this time I wasn't going to let her.

We were going to have that conversation I'd been trying to have since the night before when we kissed. I finally admitted to myself that it meant something to me and I'm sure that it meant something to her. After all, she did initiate it.

I gently wrapped my fingers around her forearm and asked her not to go away.

I said, "We need to talk."

"Look, Darius," she started. "What happened last night was an accident. I was tipsy and... and it was wrong."

Something came over me and I couldn't hold back any longer. Despite what she was saying, I knew that there were feelings there. Although the feelings were wrong, they were there. She was my best friend's mother. She was twice my age. But still, I couldn't resist. I wouldn't resist. My lips consumed hers, tongue danced around in her mouth.

And she didn't protest. Not much at least. But soon Mrs. Faith Jones was all over me. Hands racing up and down my back. Up the back of my neck, through my braids. She pressed her wet chest against me, and my manhood stood at attention against her thigh.

"We can never tell anyone about this," she whispered. "Especially Corey."

"I know," I whispered. I couldn't believe what was happening. "He'll never find out."

We stumbled into her bedroom, where the lights were dim and 97.7 WILD FM was playing slow jams. Trey Songz was crooning over the airwaves, confirming the mood as the heat was blazing through our bodies. Mrs. Jones ran her fingers through the hairs on my chest as I released each button on her blouse and slid it over her shoulders.

Stuff like this didn't happen to me. Corey, yeah. I could imagine Corey with an older woman. He still won't come clean about his relationship with our tenth grade English teacher. There were too many late tutoring sessions and then all of a sudden she stopped working at the school. To this day, he'd deny anything ever happened. And to this day, I don't believe him.

And what was about to happen with Mrs. Jones was going to be the secret that I would take to my grave.

More kisses. More sensations. Her warm, firm breasts were pressed up against me through her lace bra. Her fingers made their way to my jeans, and she hesitated. Pulling her lips away from mine.

"If we go through with this, there is no turning back," she said. "What happens, happens. Regrets or not. I don't want you telling your little friends about this."

"This ain't my little friends' business."

And I was all set to take it a step further, until visions of Corey entered my head. How could I be doing this to my best friend? He was the one person who always had my back since the first day I met him. Now, here I was taking advantage of him, as he lay up in a hospital bed. He asked me to look out for his mother, and I was about to sleep with her. If we stopped, we would not have any skeletons. There would be no major regrets.

But I could not stop. And neither could she. We kissed again, and my pants dropped to my knees. I reached behind her and released her bra strap. Those nipples were erect and irresistible and I wanted to suck the living day out of them. I blew on them as Mrs. Jones moaned like a woman reaching her climax. Like a woman who hadn't been touched in far too long.

Peeling off her shirt, I felt Mrs. Jones' heart beating faster than before. She was still nervous, but it was something that we both wanted. Something that she needed and something that I was craving.

Heavy breathing, hearts pounding. She pulled me in closer.

"I don't have any condoms," she said as if she wanted

to do it regardless. "I can't chance anything."

I remembered the ones that I got from the school nurse when me and Corey went in for our physicals. "I have some in my wallet. They should still be good."

It took less than a millisecond to get the condom out of my wallet, but then I fumbled with the wrapper, dropped it to the floor. Hopefully Mrs. Jones wasn't losing interest because of my juvenile clumsiness. I wanted to shoot myself for acting so young at a time when I had to prove my manhood. If I didn't get my shit together, she was going to realize that it was a mistake and stop herself before anything else could happen.

The next thing I knew, Mrs. Jones was on the floor next to me.

"Lie down," she said. "Let me take care of this."

I lay flat on my back, penis standing straight up, heart beating a hole through my chest. She opened up the wrapper, slid down my boxer shorts and rolled the condom on in one motion. A professional.

Seconds later, Mrs. Jones had removed her panties and wrapped her warmth around me. The moisture, the heat, the excitement were too much for me to control. Never had a female taken me on such a ride.

I bit into my lip, trying hard to maintain the motion on that hard-ass carpeted floor. She lowered her lips to mine, moaning, smothering me. It was hurting, a good hurt. Passion had taken over and we couldn't go back. Regrets or not, we were in the moment. No turning back.

And then, before I could ask her how she was doing, I was done. Not fully limp and not fully erect, but I was done. I had reached my orgasm before she did.

We watched each other for a little while longer. No comments, no movement. Just staring into each other's eyes unsure of what we would find. Mrs. Jones stood up and straightened out her skirt, as I lay there pondering my next move.

    As she showered, I slipped back into Corey's bedroom and prayed that the event that just took place would not haunt me in my sleep. I curled up in the fetal position on the futon and thought about Mrs. Faith Jones until the shower went off. It was good. *Damn* good for me at least. Although I'm pretty confident with myself, for some reason I don't think I did her much justice. It was over, I was sure of it. Staring up at that ceiling, all I could think about was how I betrayed my best friend and wondered what he would do if he found out.

Sex-O-Matic Venus Freak

That was ridiculous and definitely the stupidest thing I ever did. Dammit! Shit! What the hell was I thinking? I can't turn back the hands of time, I can't pretend it didn't happen, and I can't go back and pull him out of me. Thirty-four years old and I practically threw myself at that little boy. Move over Stella, I could be heading to jail for getting my groove on.

"I am so sorry, Darius, for putting you through this," I whispered as the shower water ran down my body. Darius had enough on his plate, and now I add this *secret* to it. I've been putting him through all types of shit the last few nights, and here I was, adding salt to the wound.

There was no way I was going to stay the night in that house with him. It felt so good to have him inside of me that I wasn't sure if I would be able to resist tiptoeing into Corey's room to have another taste.

I must have stayed in that shower for about an hour, but the thoughts would not wash off. I was still hot and wet down there and only one thing was going to repair that. I needed to call Kael and let him take advantage of me.

Damn, I was turning into a whore right before my eyes.

When I finally got out of the shower, I rummaged through the medicine cabinet to find some Benadryl to help me sleep. It usually takes about a half hour for that to work on me. That kind of time I didn't have. I remembered the Absolut vodka in the kitchen. If I could get over there and back, without bumping into Darius I would be home free.

Drying myself off, I set the plan in motion. I threw on my robe, wrapped myself tight and paved my way to the kitchen, under the sink cabinet, way behind the extra paper towels and napkins. The first glass I saw was in the sink, and so not to waste time I rinsed it out and poured my first serving. It hit the spot almost immediately.

I was almost in my room, still sipping on my new friend, when the bathroom door opened. And it was over. Darius, although fully dressed from head to toe, was still as fine as he was when he was naked. That damn hair was still in need of a touch up and... shit, his fly was open. I tried not to stare, but the hump behind the opening was enlarging by the second.

We watched each other for a moment, both swallowing hard. My nipples were hardening, and poking through my silk robe. And he was staring.

"Mrs. Jon..." Before he could finish, his hand was already palming my breasts. Bringing me down to the floor, he slid his tongue into my mouth as I unsnapped the button on his jeans. I put my glass on the floor next to us and slipping my fingers into the elastic of his boxers, I slid them down and released his manhood, jacking him off as we lay there.

I was wetter than I'd been in the shower moments before. Sitting over me, his hand slid down past my belly button and placed itself deep inside of me. His nails were sliding up against my vaginal walls. He was overly excited and so was I.

Sweat dripped from his forehead, landing on my stomach making me want him inside me at that very moment. His fingers were appetizers, but not the entrée. I released his manhood, kissed him and then asked if he was ready. Nervously, he nodded and took away his fingers in preparation for the main course.

He snuggled inside of me effortlessly as if we were made for each other. I was grinding him and after a while I thought I was losing him.

"You okay?"

"Don't stop," he gasped. "I'm just a little nervous."

I kissed him, not because it was going to be all right, but because there was nothing else I could do or say. It was already too late. Even if we were to stop, the damage had already been done. And we weren't even using a condom. Two stupid mistakes. Still, I couldn't stop.

Half an hour later, we were still at it. I had cum about three times, and Darius was still going at it like a warrior. I straddled him, tried some of the moves I did on Stan. The stuff that used to send Stan crying to mama. But not Darius. I knew the second "cumming" took a while, but damn.

It finally happened over forty-five minutes later. This time, neither of us rushed away, and the following morning, when Corey finally called, we were lying in my bed together.

Never Let Me Down

It was selfish of me to think it, but I didn't want her to answer the phone when Corey called that morning. If she picked up that phone, then everything that we suddenly had would come to an abrupt end. *Corey's better now, we can go back to the way things were.* Not that I didn't want my friend home and all, I just didn't want to end things with Mrs. Jones.

She let him know that I had stayed the night, and even mentioned to him that I slept in his bedroom. Supposedly, I was still asleep and she didn't want to wake me.

"He was up all of last night watching television," she lied.

Mrs. Jones made a list of things to bring to the hospital: clothes, toothbrush and his newspapers. She even jotted down his telephone number so that I could call him when I "woke up." After she checked his current status: "Are they treating you okay? Have you eaten? Are you getting to the bathroom before, you know...?"

When they hung up, she told me everything he said, almost word for word.

"We have to get dressed because he wants both of us to come over to see him. I'm going to call out from work.

But if you don't think you can face him now, I can give you a ride to school or someplace until you think you're ready to visit him."

"I'll be fine. What about you?" I asked.

She said, "I'm not fine. My son was almost killed and then I go and have sex with his best friend while he's lying up in a hospital bed." Mrs. Jones apologized but kept it real. "Honestly Darius, I don't think I'm ready to deal with him being shot *and* being in your presence, after what happened."

"So this is how it's going to be from now on, huh?" I asked a little bothered. "After we kissed in the kitchen the other night, it got ugly. But for some reason, after last night I was expecting things to get better. But it's gotten worse."

Mrs. Jones said, "Don't look at it that way. Just give it a few days..."

"...Corey will be home, and all of this shit will be over." I threw the covers off of my naked body grabbed my boxer shorts off of the carpet and pulled them on. "Forget it. I'll walk to school and then stop by the hospital after I know you're gone. Maybe you can just leave me a time schedule so I'll know not to bump into you."

Mrs. Jones wrapped her fingers around my waist and gently pressed her moist lips on my back. Sliding her tongue up my spine, she slid her fingers into my shorts.

"I don't want it to end like this," she whispered into my ear. "Let's not end what we have."

I turned and kissed her. It didn't have to end. We would have to find a way to make it work.

I spoke to Corey before I left the house, and told him that I had tutoring that day and couldn't miss out. He said he understood.

"By the way, thanks for last night," Corey said.

"For what?"

"What you did for my mother."

My throat was tight and I couldn't respond even if I wanted to. I gasped for air as if I was choking.

"Are you there?" Corey asked.

"Yeah," I forced out. "I was choking."

"I told you about eating out your girl's mom," he laughed. "I'm kidding, man. But thanks for looking out for Ma Dukes. I'm sure she enjoyed your company. Even if you do snore."

"Fuck you," I said. "You know I don't snore."

"Like a damn rhinoceros," he said.

We laughed out loud while Mrs. Jones got dressed in the other room. She knocked on the closed bedroom door and told me that she was ready to go.

"Ask Corey if there is anything else he needs," she called from the hall.

"Your mother wants to know if you need anything else."

"Tell her, just the stuff I mentioned earlier. And tell her not to forget to bring the New York Times. It should have been delivered by now. The TV sucks in here, I can't even get MSNBC." I told Mrs. Jones what Corey said. "I'll need a favor from *you*, though," he said when I came back to the phone. "First I need to speak to my mother about adding Nathan and Wilson to my visitor's list. They're coming to see me after school too. I want the three of you here. I'll make sure that my mother's gone by then. Maybe I'll send her on an errand or something."

I didn't like where this was headed. With Nathan and Wilson coming, I knew Corey was out for vengeance. Not that I could blame him, but I had other stuff on my plate and it was already overflowing.

"I'll get there as fast as I can," I said hesitantly.

"Look, man. You're my boy and you know I'd do this shit for you. Don't play me now. I don't trust Nathan and Wilson the way I trust you. Especially now that Wilson's been on that fame kick ever since he became a celeb out in Quincy. And Nathan's been acting shady since we robbed that jogger. So of all people, I need you here. You hear me?"

I heard him loud and clear. *Now*, I owed him. I was *doin'* his mother, so I owed this brother the world. Whatever he was going to request I had no choice but to comply. After we ended the conversation, I met Mrs. Jones in the kitchen. I told her that I was going to visit Corey after school. She said that she would make sure that she wasn't there. Probably go and run an errand for Corey or something. She wasn't sure yet, but Mrs. Jones knew that she wasn't going to be there when I got there.

By the time we pulled up in front of the school, the homeroom bell had already rung. Without thinking, I moved in to kiss Mrs. Jones on the lips, but she stopped me before I made contact.

"Uh, uh. What do you think you're doing?"

I didn't know what had come over me, so I apologized to her. It must have been a reflex action or something. After grabbing my bag from the backseat, I removed myself from the car and shut the door.

"So, I'm going to stop by to see Corey around two-thirty," I said through the open window. I rested my hands on the sill. "And you said that you're not going to be there, right?"

She responded, "I'm going by there right now and I'll probably run to Target to buy some household items. That'll give you about two hours." She paused and looked at me with her brown eyes and perfectly chiseled nose. "I'd really feel uncomfortable if we were there together.

Not that I don't want to see you, but..."

"You don't need to explain again. I don't know if I'd be able to keep my hands off of you. You saw what almost happened a few minutes ago."

She rubbed her fingers across mine. "Do you think we made a mistake?"

I didn't know how to answer that. Of course it was wrong, but I don't think that it was a mistake. And it definitely wasn't an accident. "No, not a mistake. It's just... a little confusing right now."

"I guess it's going to be like this for a while." Then Mrs. Jones said, "You'd better hurry up inside before you're later than you already are. I'll see you tonight. I mean..."

"Don't..." I said. "Let's not say anything, okay." She nodded with a seductive smile and pulled off after I went up the stairs.

The day seemed shorter than usual and even my tutoring session flew by, which never happened. After school, Nathan was already outside waiting for me with his father's hoopty.

"I guess he can't run out on us this time," Nathan laughed when I was inside the car.

I ignored him and asked, "What the hell happened with those girls yesterday?"

"You're lucky you left," he said. "Them hoes had me driving them home to Heath Street. And you know Corey got enemies over there. But that playa would do anything for a piece of ass. I told him that we should drop them hoes off by the subway station, and he was talking all this smack about being a gentlemen, so we drive up in there, kiss the hoes goodbye and then heard a bunch of shouting."

"Corey thought it was the dude he got into that beef with at Ruggles Subway Station last month, but it wasn't. There were five big-ass dudes. They ran up on the car talking shit and pulled both them chicken-heads out the car. Next thing I know, these dudes pulling out guns. Asked us what set we were from and why we were messing with their chicks. Corey was in the back seat. He started wildin' out and pulled his piece out, told them bustas to back the fuck up. Before we could move, and before I could reach for my gun, they shot him. Corey shot back at them and almost shot one of the girls. Then they shot at me. They missed my face by a few inches. I peeled off and the mafuckers kept shooting at my car. That's why I gotta drive this hoopty around.

"I don't know what that crazy bastard was thinking, pulling that gun out. We got out of there, but Corey was losing mad blood so I took him to Boston Medical. They said he lost a lot of blood, but that he would be okay. Police showed up at the hospital and everything, procedure or something like that. I ain't no damn snitch, so I told them cops that I didn't get a good look at them mofos. But I know what they look like and pay back's a bit..."

"Thanks for calling me and letting me know what happened," I said.

"You're his boy, so I had to let you know. And since Corey was taken to the ER, you were the only one who knew how to contact his mother. By the way, how's she doing?"

It just seemed a little odd that he was grilling me about the woman I just had sex with, and he didn't even know it. This is usually something that you would brag to your boys about. They'd love to hear how I scored with an older female. I even teased myself with the idea of telling him, but leaving the second party anonymous. That wouldn't happen though, because eventually they would put two and two together. Keeping it to myself was the only option I had.

As soon as we pulled up, my cell phone rang. It was my mother.

"How is Corey?" She asked with concern. Corey was like a son to her too.

I said, "He should be fine. I'm just getting here. I was in school all day."

"I'm glad to hear that you're still concerned with your studies at a time like this. Are you coming home tonight?"

"I don't think so. Corey really wants me to stay with his mother. He doesn't want her alone in the house after what happened. He thinks that someone may try to go by his house."

"And what are you supposed to do if someone does go by there?" She asked more worried than before. "Why can't you and Faith stay here for a few days, until things cool down? I don't like the idea of my only son putting himself in harm's way. I don't care who it's for."

"It'll be fine, Ma," I reassured her. "I don't think they know where he lives."

"They might. Maybe they looked him up in the phone book and got his address."

"You're starting to sound like Corey. You know what, let me just call you later. I might be home tonight and I might not. I'll let you know."

"You make sure you call me, okay?" She said before she hung up. I agreed and told her to stop worrying.

"I'm your mother. I always worry."

We checked in at the front desk and found Nathan's name on the list. Corey must have done some major whining to get his mother to add both Nathan and Wilson's names as acceptable visitors. Nathan followed me to Corey's room and we had to wait for the nurse to give him his medication before we spoke to him. After she was gone, Corey asked me to shut the door. I did what I was told and then went to give my boy some dap. Nathan had already greeted him and was sitting next to his bed.

"You's a lousy shot," Nathan said. "I coulda took both of them fools out if I had my glock out in time."

"But you didn't," Corey smiled. "You were sitting there like a little bi-otch."

"At least I wasn't hiding, and fronting like I was taking a piss."

We all laughed, and then they started up on me.

Corey said, "What the hell are you laughing at? You were the one in those woods jerking off."

"Why were you watching?" I started.

Nathan said, "Darius was in there jerking off, thinking about your mother."

I forced a laugh and gave an uncomfortable smirk. Although I knew he was only messing around and had no idea about what happened, I felt it was time to change the subject. I asked Corey about Wilson.

"They're having a big event at school and since Wilson is like the star of the school now, he said he has to represent."

"He's bullshitting!" Nathan spat. "Wilson ain't got nothing going on at his high school. He's probably just scared."

This brother knew as well as I did, that Corey was out for vengeance. That's probably why Wilson backed out of this. I'm sure that there wasn't anything going on at East Quincy High School. I couldn't blame Wilson, though. This was already ugly, and it was about to get worse. We had to make a hit on these guys, and they were definitely going to have a counter attack.

"Forget him then," Corey said. "You two are here and that's all that matters."

"I don't know," I said hesitantly. "There're only two of us. How many guys do they have?"

"About five," Corey said.

"Nathan got a good look at them. Why can't you just tell the cops," I said. "Forget this stop snitching craze. Let the police handle it."

"Don't be a punk," Nathan said to me.

I stuck my middle finger up at him. If I'd said what was actually on my mind there would have been an unnecessary brawl in the hospital room. Nathan was a sensitive brother, and any little remark that was made would send him on a rampage.

"Naw, naw we can wait a little while. I'm still not gonna get the cops involved, shoot I have family in Heath Street and I am not trying to get them shot. Check this out." Corey looked at me and then at Nathan. "If Wilson wants to be a bitch, then let him. So let's wait until I get out of here. I'll be all right in a couple of days and then we can roll down there." Corey looked me straight in the eye. "I am not letting these chumps take me down like this. Forget that. They'll know my name before I leave this city in the fall."

Why couldn't he just leave it alone? He'd be Down South in a matter of months and all of this mess would be behind him. Those bustas would still be acting a fool over on Heath Street, while Corey was in ATL getting his education. But he always had to prove himself. It was bound to be a mistake.

After we left, I went by to see Nina at work. She was just getting off, so we decided to snatch Lil' Darius up and spend the afternoon together. We ended up at the Cambridge Side Galleria where we bought a few things for Lil' Darius and an outfit for Nina. Lil' Darius was hungry so we got a bite to eat in the food court. Nina and my son had their usual Burger King meal, and I got my favorite, chicken teriyaki from this fast food Japanese restaurant.

"I need to get a better job," I said looking through my wallet. It was almost completely empty, except for a few receipts from the purchases I just made. "My check is completely gone."

Nina didn't comment on what I said, which is unusual. Whenever I mention money, either she gets upset because she uses her check to buy everything for our son or because she makes too much to get welfare, and not enough to live comfortably. We ate in silence for a few minutes.

"You haven't talked about Corey much? How's he doing?" Nina finally asked, feeding my son a french fry.

I said, "He's fine. You know Corey, always in good spirits."

One thing I hated about Nina was the fact that she could see right through me. She knew when I was hiding something from her, and would call me on it immediately. In many ways, Nina reminded me of my mother. They got along really well, and both had their hands full with me. The worst part was when they were together and took turns ripping me a new asshole.

"He wants to retaliate, doesn't he?" She asked. "And I bet he won't tell the cops either. They are so stupid with this stop snitching shit. We got people out there getting shot every other day, but no one's opening their mouth. Soon there won't be any Blacks or Puerto Ricans left and won't nobody know what happened to us. Why? Because no one's opening their mouth to put a stop to it." Before I could say anything, she went on. "You have a son now, Darius. Corey is going to college in Atlanta. Why can't you two just move on? You know what happens when ya'll start fighting back. It never ends. You need to be the bigger man and stop this ridiculous cycle. If you don't want your son to be fatherless, you need to stop all of this before it gets any worse."

"Corey's my boy. I can't just tell him no. Don't you get it? If he doesn't man up, then people will walk all over him. In this game you can't just let stuff happen to you and not do anything about it." I wasn't sure if I was trying to convince Nina or myself.

"This ain't a game. This is real, Darius. You strike back, then those other guys will definitely retaliate. Then what? One of you will gun down one of their boys? Then which one of *you* is going to die? Tell me that."

By now, Lil' Darius was crying as if on cue. Nina didn't deserve to be a "single mom." Lil' Darius didn't deserve to be fatherless. And my parents didn't deserve to lose their son. But how in the hell was I going to break that to Corey? I owed him, even if he didn't know it. I owed this man big.

Love of My Life

The next couple of days were awkward, if I do say so myself, and I think Darius would agree. I spent every morning at the hospital with my slow-recovering son and every afternoon sneaking a quickie with his best friend in the back of my car. During the evenings me and Darius took turns visiting Corey, trying our best to set a schedule so we wouldn't bump into each other at the hospital. Then at night we got our freak on. Every night.

"I still can't believe that this is happening," Darius said after pulling out of me a little after midnight.

He couldn't believe this was happening? Shit! I'm sitting here with an eighteen year-old's stains on my new Calvin Klein satin sheets.

But damn, the boy had some stuff on him. The third time tonight, and I know that we were both ready for another round.

I looked over at his naked body, wanting to run my fingers through the strands of hair on his chest, fighting the urge to start licking him down the center of his chest and nibbling on his nipples again. His moves were delicious and kept me moist even after I was internally, physically, and mentally satisfied.

His eyes were slowly fading, and I couldn't blame him.

He worked his tail off, and had my own bones aching.

About an hour earlier, I had decided to try something a little different. Since Darius admitted to me that he was a closet romantic, I pulled out my private collection of scented candles, heated body oils, and champagne. Okay, so he wasn't twenty-one yet. I was already in a heap of shit for what I was doing, so a glass of champagne wouldn't make it any worse.

I set the candles around the room, then shut off the ceiling light to enhance the mood. I asked Darius to find a suitable CD from my collection in the living room, and told him that he he'd better not to bring back any Lil' Jon or Fifty Cent. He laughed and told me that if I didn't stop talking to him like he was a kid, he would find my old Vanilla Ice and MC Hammer CDs.

"Ice-Ice Baby..." he chanted as he strolled out of the bedroom wearing nothing but the Calvin Klein boxers I bought him when I bought the sheets. I didn't notice it before, but his boxers actually matched the sheets. Damn, I'm good.

The scent from the candles intensified my desire to have Darius back in me. I had to get a hold of myself if I was going to prolong this third and possibly last act of the night. After all, he still had to go to school in the morning. I poured the champagne into the appropriate glasses and placed the body oil on the night stand.

He strolled back in, reading over the backs of the CDs. Brother came back with some old school jams that he should have been too young to remember. Come on now, what did he know about the Staple Singers, and the Gap Band? But Darius really got me when he read off the Shirley Murdock jam that we had gotten our dance to the night of Corey's party. We were practically all over each other that night. At least now, I could admit that it wasn't either of our faults. Things happen.

I told him to play Shirley Murdock first.

He lied down on his chest, just the way I asked him to, and he got himself as relaxed as possible. The first thing I did was brush my fingertips over his ass cheeks. He almost snapped his neck, trying to give me a disapproving stare. But, I couldn't help it. When he's out of those baggy jeans he's so fond of, you can see how sexy his little ass is.

"Then take them off," I whispered into his ear.

"You take 'em off," he smiled with an attitude.

So I did... well I tried to, but the elastic got caught around his erect soldier and he had to maneuver himself before I accidently bent it the wrong way. I don't have one, but I knew that would hurt.

"Be careful," he said as he lifted his hips and slid the front of his boxers down.

I took care of the rest, got them down to his ankles, and then tossed them on the floor. That ass was shining in my face. I rubbed some oil on my hands and then gently massaged his cheeks. Darius tried to say something, but I told him to relax. He took a sip of his champagne, sighed like he was about to ejaculate, and buried his face back in the pillow.

I dragged my fingers in between his cheeks, spread them and then blew as gently as I could to accelerate the heating process. The pillow smothered Darius' growls as he began pounding his fist on the mattress. It was confirmed that Nina had never done anything like this to him. I'm sure with her it was the conventional *Who's on top? Who's going down on who?* But I'm about passion, excitement and making a brother scream. And so far, Darius had *screamed* my name every night that we'd been together.

"You ever have a *real* massage?" I asked him, spreading the heating oil over his back?

"Huh?" He was out of it.

"A real massage, boo."

"Naw," he whispered trying to keep his composure. "Nina messed my back up one day, doing something she learned in a massage class. I couldn't stand straight for a week."

"Well, you don't have to worry about me hurting you," I ran my finger along his hips. "Lift." With his ass up, I slid the heating oil up and down his over-sized penis and wiped away the excess juice from our previous encounter.

"You'd better be careful down there. You don't want to get me started too soon. You're not ready yet."

After that little comment of his, I actually wanted to put a hurting on him. I slid my hand back and told him to roll over. He was standing at attention.

"Don't move," I smiled removing my pink Victoria's Secret teddy. "And don't try anything."

I spread the oil all over, from his chest down to his toes. Once he was nice and slick, I lied down on top of him, making sure his friend was lying flat against his stomach.

"What are you doing?" he asked almost in pain. "Stop teasing me?"

"I can't handle it?" I smiled. "Maybe next time you'll keep your mouth shut and let me satisfy you in my own way. Now you have me pulling out the freak in me." I slid up and down, feeling him grow, hearing him moan, watching him bite his lip. That oil had us both heating up, and with his pubic hairs creating a light friction against my clit I was burning up on the inside as well. This little game was going to have me in flames.

I sat up on his crotch, still not allowing him to penetrate me, and finally got my tongue back around his nipples. The fruit flavor from the oil made it more scrumptious as I devoured his left nipple in my mouth.

"Forget this," he said trying to kiss me.

"I see you can't handle one of my massages." I took a sip of my champagne, avoiding his kiss. I knew that once he put his mouth on mine, all of my teasing would be over and round three would officially begin.

"This isn't a massage," he said drinking from his own glass. "You're trying to get me so worked up that I explode."

After setting our glasses down, Darius reached for the massage oil and spread it over his fingertips.

"What are you doing with that?" I asked.

He didn't respond. His hands were fully lubricated before he rubbed them over each of my nipples. I couldn't keep from moaning and I couldn't keep still. Trying to move off of him, I could feel his hands slide down past my belly button, through my hairs, into my secret place. I contracted my muscles around his warm fingers, which continued to get hotter, as he stroked them in and out.

Darius sucked on my tongue as he threatened to do things to me that have never been done before. I welcomed the challenge.

"Well, Mandingo," I said licking around his lips. "What do you have for me?"

"You're just gonna have to wait and see.'

I shuddered as his fingers found territories that haven't been visited in decades. I wrapped my fingers around his manhood, caressed the tip. Darius shrilled with pleasure as dribbles ran through my fingers. I lotioned up my tips, and placed them between my lips. Scrumptious.

He removed his fingers, licked them, dragged them across my nipples. His tongue suckled my breasts. Palming my right breast with one hand, he used his other hand to guide himself inside of me. Before I could tighten my muscles, he was already out.

"Uh, uh," he said. "No you don't."

I couldn't help but laugh. This young brother was turning the tables on me. He laid me flat on my back, spread my legs to separate sections of the dimly lit room, and penetrated me again. Two strong strokes, and he was out. I squirmed on those sheets. Grabbing his ass, I wanted to force him in me. I wanted him to gyrate those hips the way he had done earlier that evening. He thrust in one more time. Stayed a little longer, and then bailed out.

"Stop playing with me," I demanded.

"Oh, so who's the one who can't hang?"

"Okay, so this is payback? I got you."

I flipped him over, climbed on top got the bottle of oil. When my hands were nice and moist, I wrapped them around his penis and stroked him until he screamed for me to stop. By now, I knew when Darius was about to ejaculate.

His toes curled, his fists clasped my sheets, and... I let go before he was done.

"Damn!" he shouted. I started again and as soon as those toes curled I released him. "All right," he said. "The game is over. You win."

We tongued each other down, him tasting what was left of his orgasm in my mouth, me tasting my sweet juices on his tongue. I straddled him with ease, warmth wrapped around his penis, and tightened my grip. Back arched, I moved my body like I was Dale Evans riding in an old Western, trying to tame the bull. Throbbing, sweating, feeling his penis explode inside of me.

Squeals escaped his mouth, his hands released the sheets and toes relaxed behind me. Climbing off of him, I watched his stuff ripple onto the bed.

"Oh, you are so lucky I got the shot the other day," I

said. "Why didn't you pull out?"

"I was lost in the moment. You see what you did to me?" Darius was sitting up staring down at his puddle. "Did you... um....?"

"Yeah," I said rubbing his damp and enticing upper body. "Twice."

"It was like three times." This time he drank from my champagne glass.

"What are you talking about, three times?"

He shared the glass and then placed it back.

"I know you when you do. You make these expressions, and you tighten up your—"

"Okay, I get it."

After he made that comment *I still can't believe that this is happening*, I laid my head on his chest, I closed my eyes and held on to that moment for as long as I could. There was no telling how much longer we would actually have whatever it was that we had. It felt good to have a man understand me the way he did, down to knowing my orgasms. Shit, knowing how to give me an orgasm. And although Stan was a good lover at times, I never climaxed more than twice while I was with him. When Stan was done, he was done. Sometimes he kissed me, sometimes he turned over and went to sleep.

Darius always kissed me, before and after.

"Well it's happening, boo. And I can't say that I regret any of it. If there were a way that this was acceptable, I'd be ready to take it to the next step. But it's not acceptable and probably never will be."

"Never, huh?"

"Can you imagine what Corey would do? Your parents? Friends, family? Oh, I hate to even ponder the thought. This will never amount to more than what it is."

"It's true, I guess. But why can't we just say fuck it, fuck them? This is our life, we're both consenting adults."

I wanted to tell him to clean up his mouth, but shit. He was sort of right. *Fuck them.* But Corey was my priority. And *he* was a part of *them.*

"I couldn't do that to Corey. And he would definitely not approve."

"What about that family in Alabama. Fourteen-year-old O'Rourke boy who married that forty-one-year-old woman. He was like best friends with her son."

"Were they white?" I asked matter-of-factly.

"Yes."

"Well, I rest my case. Corey is not some impressionable fourteen-year-old. He is practically a grown man. Seventeen, about to go to college. He'll hate the both of us."

"If you ask me, Corey has a lot of growing up to do."

"Hey, that's still my son you're talking about. And your best friend."

He paused, before he said something that he would possibly regret later. And I was glad he did, because if he said something else against my son, I know I would have said something that I would regret.

"Let's not talk about this anymore. We're cool right now and that's all that matters. Corey is getting better and will be out of the hospital soon. Let's just enjoy what we have and let the cards fall where they may."

Darius summed it up nicely. His arms wrapped around me, squeezed me tight, filling me with tranquility. He held me close until the moment I drifted off.

closer

My baby needed to come home. I sat next to his hospital bed, holding his hand as he fell asleep. Visiting hours were coming to an end and I was ready to go and hit the sack myself. It was hard to let go though, and watching him lying there, made me think about what would happen if he hadn't made it. Atlanta couldn't have come along a minute too soon. Boston was just too crazy and I hoped that I could get him out of town before anything else happened to him. And if I knew Corey, he was planning to retaliate. That boy definitely had his father's attitude. Don't take no mess from no one, and always strike back. This time I hoped he would let it slide.

But I doubted it.

When Corey was five years old, some little boy in his class took his ice cream sandwich during snack time. So my son took someone else's ice cream and smashed it in the bully's face. Then he paid the other kid fifty cents and told him to buy another one.

In the sixth grade, Corey had a crush on this girl named Jennifer. He asked her to a semi-formal dance, but she said that she didn't' want to go with him. She ended up going with another kid from their class. A few days later Corey took the bee-bee gun that his father bought him, and tried to shoot the girl. He ended up shooting the gym teacher, and got himself expelled from the METCO busing program. That's how he ended up in the public school system and that's when he met Darius.

Since then Corey had calmed down a lot. Well, as far as I knew. The older my son got, the less I heard about his extracurriculars. I didn't even know if he was dating anyone. Come to think of it, I could have been a grandmother and wouldn't have known it. Corey stopped telling me stuff when he and Darius became seniors. I was hoping that Darius had been keeping him out of trouble.

The nurse came in and told me that visiting hours were over and that if I wanted to stay, she could bring me a cot to sleep on. She recommended that I go home and get a good night's sleep because it looked as if the doctor was going to be releasing Corey in a day or two. I thanked her, kissed my son on the forehead and went home.

When I pulled in front of the house, my cell phone started ringing. To my surprise, it was Kael. I hesitated answering the telephone, but decided that it wasn't fair to him if I ignored his call.

"Hello," I said as I unlocked the door to my house.

"Hey," he said. "How's it going? I've been calling you all day but I kept getting your machine."

"I know. I was in the hospital with Corey so I turned my phone off." I was beginning to wonder if Darius had called me as well. I was still not sure if he was coming by that night.

"I was thinking about coming by," Kael said. "I know it's late, but I'm pretty sure you haven't eaten properly. And I think I made too much food so I'll bring it over."

I tried to interrupt, "Um, Kael..."

Me and Mrs. Jones

"And I won't take no for an answer. I'm already in my car, engine started.... I just pulled out of my parking spot... and now I'm on the main street."

I was sitting on my couch holding in my laughter. He was so bizarre, but it was cute. Honestly, I didn't mind seeing him and I was starving. I just didn't know what was happening with Darius. There was no way I was going to have two men in my house. I'd have to call Darius and ask him not to come.

"Okay, okay," I said as Kael continued to give me locations and landmarks. "I get that you're on your way. I'll see you in a bit. I just need to freshen up." I hung up the phone and then checked my voicemail for messages. I had three. Two were from Kael asking me to call him back. The last one was from Darius telling me that he had his son and was going to sleep at home.

With Kael headed to my house, it was good that Darius was staying home tonight. Not surprisingly, I would have rather had Darius stay with me that night. But I guess this was working out for the best. Corey would be home in a couple of days and whatever Darius and I started would have to end anyway.

I decided to call him and tell him that I received his message, and to have a good night. But instinctively, I decided to call his house just to make sure that he was there. It wouldn't matter if his mother answered the phone. I hadn't spoken to Olesia in a couple of weeks so if she did pick up than I would just have to spark up a conversation. We used to be closer back when our boys first started hanging out. We were always complete opposites, but we tried to stay in touch for the sake of our sons. That way they couldn't get away with much.

Benjamin, Darius's dad answered the phone. He recognized my voice immediately and asked how Corey was doing. I told him that he pulled through nicely and that he was in good spirits.

"I'm surprised you answered, aren't you still doing those three to elevens?" I asked him.

"Yeah, but I took a few vacation days so I can do some work around the house."

"Well, I was calling to thank Darius for going to visit Corey today. It meant a lot to him."

"Those guys are like brothers. There was no way Darius wouldn't have gone to visit Corey. Anyhow, I haven't seen Darius all day. He's staying the night with Nina, but he should be home in the morning. He usually brings Lil' Darius over on Saturdays."

"Oh, are they still together?" I asked innocently.

"Who knows with these teenagers? I just hope he doesn't try to bring home any more babies."

We both forced a dry laugh. I told Benjamin to relay the message to Darius and to also tell him that Corey could be coming home in a day or two. We said our goodbyes and I went to get myself all spruced up for my "date." If after the last few nights, Darius could have his own fun, then so could I.

I'm Sprung

It wouldn't even work when Nina rubbed her hands across my lap. I just wasn't feeling her and I wanted to get out of there. But after what she said to me about being around for our son and the whole family-thing, she was somehow able to talk me into staying the night.

I left a message for Mrs. Jones, telling her that I had my son and that I was going to be sleeping at home. It wasn't a total lie. I did have Lil' Darius, and Nina's house was like a second home to me.

But truth be told, I was a little scared about being with Mrs. Jones that night. I wanted to be away from her and from Corey just so I could get my head straight. The hit on those Heath Street dudes was running through my head and I had to find a way to change Corey's mind. It was going to be hard especially with Nathan encouraging him to carry it out. And what if that put a rift in our friendship? What was going to happen to me and Mrs. Jones?

Nina undressed in front of me as usual and asked if I had anything to wear to bed.

"Just what I'm wearing now," I told her.

She was down to her bra and panties. The sight that usually got me hot and erect was turning me off more and more by the second. I wanted her to put some clothes back on.

"You all right?" Nina asked me. "You still thinking about our earlier conversation?"

"I'm just thinking that.... I don't know. I need to go home."

Actually, I needed to go to Corey's home. I imagined myself up under Mrs. Jones' soft breasts with her smooth skin gliding up against mine. Damn, I needed to get out of there. I did promise Mrs. Jones and Corey that I wouldn't leave her at the house by herself. What if someone did stop by there and I wasn't there to protect her?

"What are you talking about? You need to stay right here with your son. He hardly sees you as it is."

"And whose fault is that?" I spat. "I used to see him almost everyday before you started sending him off to the babysitters. And if you let me take him during the week like I wanted to then I would see Lil' Darius more often." I reached to the floor, pulled on my sneakers and tied the laces. Nina sucked her teeth and started cursing in Spanish. Those were the only words I knew, and although she is Puerto Rican, sometimes I wondered if those are the only words that she knew. "Cut it out," I said. "What if your mother comes in here again? I don't feel that comfortable."

She said, "Forget you, Maricón!"

I put my jacket on and headed to the door. I half expected her to say something crazy, maybe something about Lil' Darius not being my son. Even though little man looks just like me – same eyes, same nose, same complexion – she tried to pull that 'I'm not the father' B.S. when she got upset with me. To my surprise she didn't try it this time. She let me walk out the door without saying a word, except...

"Don't forget to say goodbye to your son."

When I got to his bedroom he was snoring like his dad, with his juice cup lying next to him in bed. Yeah, the little player looked just like me. He was definitely going to be a heartbreaker when he got older. Unlike when I was growing up, Lil' Darius was going to be taught about relationships and the games that women play. There wouldn't be any accidental pregnancies for him. Lil' Darius was going to know how to protect himself in bed and on the streets. I was going to be real with him. I kissed him on the forehead and promised him that I would never let anything happen to him. He could believe that.

Before I left, I said goodbye to Nina's mother. The old bat never had much to say to me, and after the ordeal in Nina's bedroom our dialogue was cut even shorter.

My phone rang when I got outside. It was Corey, so I immediately picked it up.

"Hey man, wasup?" I said.

He was extremely excited for some reason. "Where are you now?"

"I just left Nina's house. I'm about to head over to your crib now. Why, what's going on?"

He started ranting. "Nathan just saw one of the guys down near the Forest Hills subway station. Nathan was leaving his chick's apartment and spotted the dude hollering at a shorty."

"What did Nathan do?" I asked anxiously. I was hoping that Nathan didn't need me for anything. I didn't have a car, and I wasn't trying to catch a city bus to meet Nathan. It was bad enough that I had to catch one to see Mrs. Jones.

"His stupid ass ran up on dude and pulled out his piece. That man was out, left his shorty there and everything. I'm just telling you this in case they try to retaliate or something. I need you to stay at my spot until I get out of here. I don't trust them mofos. I don't know what they know about me. So I really need you on this one, man. Like I said, you're the only one I trust."

There wasn't a problem staying at his house tonight. But there was no telling how long my mother would allow me to keep doing this. She was nervous and had the right to be. I was starting to get a little scared myself, especially after this news.

"I thought you told him to wait for us," I added in.

"I did," he said. "You know he don't listen. He's hardheaded like that. After we take care of this, I'm cutting both him and Wilson off."

"Did Wilson ever call you back?"

"Naw," Corey said sounding a little disappointed. "I left him three messages today and he never called me back. He's been our boy... for how long now, Darius?"

"Since we were in the eighth grade and he was in the seventh," I said walking to the bus stop. "We met him the year after me and you started hanging."

"Can you believe that? And you see how he's playing us? I have the mind to call his girl and tell her how many times he's come to Roxbury to mess with his old girlfriends."

"She probably already knows. Virgins have that kind of insight. Shoot, sometimes, I wish I was still a virgin." I thought about how easy my life would have been if I never messed with Nina. I wouldn't want to give back my son though. We've been on and off since high school and there have been a lot of girls during our many breaks. And now there's Mrs. Faith Jones.

"Shut the hell up." Corey was sounding a lot better than before. "You haven't been a virgin since you let Rebecca give you a blow job in eighth grade."

"Damn, you remember that?" I almost forgot about

that myself.

"I was envious as hell. I honestly think I started jerking off the same day you told me about that. I didn't get a BJ until..."

"Until Shonda in ninth-grade," I cracked up. "That skeezer."

"She was nice, though. You have to admit."

We joked around a bit until my bus arrived. I climbed on the bus and paid my fare. I told Corey that I had to call my parents to tell them where I'd be and then told him that I would call him when I got to his house.

I couldn't wait to get myself into her sheets again. Doing it on the carpet had caused a burn on my back and I wasn't trying to leave there with injuries this time. During the bus ride, I thought of the numerous positions that me and Mrs. Jones could try. Although Nina was a freak, there were a number of things that she wouldn't do. But Mrs. Jones was a freak's freak. If she were doing me, then I'm sure she would be willing to do a lot of things. My favorite position was the one with Sharon Stone in Sliver. Actually all the positions in the movie were my favorites, especially when William Baldwin hit it from behind.

Speaking of sexual positions, I even thought about buying some Jell-O pudding or an ice cream cone to practice going down on her. My older half-brother used to have me watch pornos so I could learn moves. I should have borrowed one of those before tonight.

Now, I am no amateur when it comes to eating a girl out, but Mrs. Jones was used to older, experienced men getting busy on her. The girls I've been with were just happy to have my tongue down there. I was trying to take this to another level with Mrs. Jones, though. Whirlwind tongue, teeth suckling the clit. Man, I was trying to leave my mark up in there.

Hopping off the bus down the street from the house, I almost fell into a skipping mode. I had to catch myself before I embarrassed myself. I spent a few seconds doing some tongue exercises, arm stretching and heavy breathing. This night was going to be a long one and I needed the energy to keep myself going. Before I knocked on the door, I thought about going into the bushes on the side of the house to jack off. There was no way I was going to "cum" up short tonight and if I had done it inside the house, she would probably find it disgusting.

I peeked inside the window before moving to the side of the house. The coast was clear. Her car was parked in the driveway so she must have been in her bedroom watching television or something. I stood in the bushes and kept my eyes on the living room window just in case she walked in the room and saw me standing outside. Even though the house next door was completely dark, I kept watch on those windows too.

After undoing my pants and zipping them down, I pulled my man out through the flap in my boxers. He was already at attention and ready for some action. In a minute boy, in a minute. I needed to get myself into a comfortable position.

Spreading my legs just enough, I made myself comfortable and I was jacking off. Slowly at first, caressing my own skin as I thought of Mrs. Jones in my mouth. My eyes were closed tightly, tongue cycling like a motorboat. Oh, shit. I sped up as I felt the pressure rising down in my groin.

The next thing I knew, there was a roar of laughter coming from nearby. The first thought of course, was that I'd been caught and probably by Mrs. Jones. My eyes popped open and I looked around. Lucky for me, no one was there. Then where'd that laughing come from?

That's when it hit me. I looked into Mrs. Jones' window and she was sitting on the couch cracking up at something on the plasma television. After a sigh of relief, I felt for my jones again. It was still ready for some action. Now that I knew where she was in the house, I could finish up quickly and then get inside for some one-on-one action.

It didn't take much to get me back into my previous state and just as I was about to duck down and go to work, somebody else walked into the living room. A tall decent looking brother came in carrying sodas. He sat down on the couch, and I got a good look at his face. It was that dude from the hospital. What the hell was his name? Keenan or some shit. Naw, it was Kael.

Come to think of it, there was a strange car parked in front of the house but I figured it belonged to one of the neighbors. I couldn't believe she let that man in her house after the last few nights. Was she fucking him too? That's all I needed to know, and if she was it would be all over after that. I gave up a night with Nina and here was this woman screwing some other dude.

This was not happening.

I rushed to the front door ready to throw down with this man. It wasn't about Mrs. Jones anymore. Forget her. So what if some dude from Heath Street rolled up over here, I didn't care anymore. And who the hell was Corey anyway, trying to set me up and get shot over his mother. My mother was right, I didn't need to put myself in harm's way. Instead of staying over at the Jones', my plan was to punch this old cat in the mouth and then walk home. On second thought, I'm sure my invitation to stay at Nina's was still available. I needed to get my shit off before I got a case of blue balls. And I was already feeling it coming.

My jones was still hanging out. I tucked it away and

redid my pants. And then I took a deep breath and rang the doorbell.

Didn't Cha Know

This was unbelievable. In the back of my mind, I knew who was at the door and I almost didn't answer it. In his voice message, Darius said that he wasn't coming so when Kael said that he would stop by, I didn't put up much of a fight. I decided that it was going to be an innocent evening. There would be eating and some conversation, but definitely no kissing. I wasn't a trick and since I already gave a piece of myself to Darius, I couldn't play myself with Kael although there was almost a moment when I gave in to his advances.

"I'm not ready for that right now," I told him when he tried to kiss me after dinner. He was helping me rinse the dishes and put them into the dishwasher. While he was removing a dish from my hands, Kael held onto me longer than usual. Then with ease, he brought my soap-covered hand close to his lips and tried to kiss me. I snatched my hand from his grip and wiped the suds off with a dishtowel.

"Is it Corey?" He asked trying to keep his dignity. I don't think a woman has ever turned down this man before. Shit, Kael was fine and he had style. That night he was wearing Diesel everything. Khakis, a blue and white striped dress shirt and probably matching boxer shorts.

If he was wearing boxer shorts at all.

"Yeah," I lied. "Until he is home safe and sound, I don't think I can get involved with anyone. Corey is my priority. My needs come second. So I can't find pleasure until my son is okay. It's not you, so please don't take this personally." Well most of it was true, but I could have used a little comfort right around then. But the comfort I was hoping for was in another man. A younger man who had satisfied me more than any man had done in years.

"I understand and don't worry, I'm not offended."

Earlier that afternoon, the Good Times season three DVD collection came in from Columbia House. From our previous conversations, I knew that Kael was a big time J-J fan. I, on the other hand, was a James Evans fan. When he left the show after season three, their ratings dropped so much that the show eventually left the air. Thelma was my girl too. I grew up wishing that I looked half as good as her. I was even going to name my first daughter after her – but that never happened. Instead, I got blessed with Corey.

We decided to watch as many episodes as we could stay up watching and then made plans to view the rest at a later date. After dinner, Kael was in the kitchen fixing us some sodas, so I went to put on the first DVD. I couldn't wait for Kael. The season premier came on and I was already laughing out loud. Mean-ass James and that stupid J-J were always going at it.

By the time Kael came to the living room, I was almost in tears. He was complaining that it wasn't fair that I was watching the episode while he was making us drinks.

"It shouldn't have taken you so long," I said accidently rubbing his knee.

We made eye contact and before he could make another advance, I decided to restart the episode from the beginning. And that's when the doorbell rang.

Like I already said, I didn't want to answer it, but I was sure Kael would have started asking questions if I didn't. I told him to wait in the living room and to start watching the episode without me.

"Normally I wouldn't, but this is payback," he smiled. "I'll just watch up to where you left off."

At the door, I glanced through the peephole. Just as I had expected, it was Darius. I threw open the door, and had to stop him from barging in.

"Where the hell is he?" He asked.

"Excuse me," I said placing my hand on his chest. "Who do you think you're talking to? And why are you here? Shouldn't you be at home with Nina?"

"That's none of your..."

"Just like this is none of your business." I stepped out onto the porch with him. Surveying the area, I said, "Look. Don't make a scene."

"Fuck a scene," he said in a whisper, which helped calm me down. "I can't believe you have some nigga in there after... after... us."

"Well, I can't believe you were over at Nina's house probably getting your stuff off... after us."

"I didn't do anything with Nina. I was with my son and spent the entire time thinking about you, while you're over here getting your groove on with Keenan."

"His name is Kael and we were just watching some TV."

"After you boned him? You weren't even in the living room with him that long."

I was offended and shocked all at the same time. Instead of slapping him and telling him to get the hell away from my house, I said, "What were you doing, stalking us? You're starting to make me nervous, Darius."

He turned to walk away from me and before I called

him to come back, Kael was behind me.

"I'm just checking to make sure everything is all right out here. J-J is in there acting a fool, you gotta come see this." Kael snickered as Darius walked back towards us. "Hey, aren't you Corey's friend? Darius right? It's good to see you, again."

Darius looked like he was ready to pounce on him so I intervened.

"Darius is still upset about Corey. Maybe you should go inside and finish watching the episode. It's getting late and we won't have enough time to get through even three episodes before you leave. I'll be there in a few."

"Oh, you're trying to get rid of me, huh?" He smiled. "I thought you wanted me to stay here all night."

Darius was fuming, and I swear that I saw smoke coming out of his ears.

"Don't play like that," I said seriously. "Darius is about to go, and after a few episodes you're going to be leaving as well. I'm going to be in my house alone tonight. And it's going to be that way until Corey comes home from the hospital."

Kael took the hint and went back inside. I could hear the audience laughing as I came back to Darius.

"Look," I said. "This is getting to be more awkward than I would have wanted it. Now I'm going to have to explain to this man that you are just looking out for me, because you're like a son. I should have remembered how jealous you got when that girl broke up with you in the seventh grade. Then when Rebecca left you for the ninth-grader when you both were still in the eighth grade. And you and Nina are always going at it." That's when it hit me. I had been a part of this kid's life for years. So what if he was eighteen, I was still a pedophile. Darius was just a baby! My stomach was boiling over with acid.

"You need to leave," I told him as I tried to shut the

door on him.

Darius wedged his foot in between the door and the frame. He moved his face closer, and then brought his lips to mine. His tongue entered my mouth and I did not resist. I would have probably taken my clothes off right then and there if it hadn't been for Kael calling my name.

"I'm at the end of the first episode."

I pulled myself away from Darius and shut him out. Resting against the door, I had to gather my composure before I went back into the living room with Kael. If I didn't get myself under control I would have ended up asking Kael to leave, and then brought Darius upstairs to my room and performed all sorts of sexual acts on him. He wouldn't know what hit him.

Before sitting on the couch next to Kael, I had to catch my breath and pretend that everything was normal. Although my heartbeat was accelerated, and my stuff was moist, I had to pretend that I was in the same state that I was in before Darius rang that doorbell.

"Is everything all right?" Kael asked. "He seemed a little pissed."

I said, "Darius is going to be all right. I'm like a mother to him and he has just been looking out for me since Corey's accident."

He simply nodded and I was hoping he believed me. We watched a total of two and a half episodes before we both decided that it was getting late. Kael didn't even bother shaking my hand when he left. All I got was a wave and a "see you later," which I knew would never actually happen.

So I was spending the night alone, just as I said I would. The first thing I did was call Corey to tell him goodnight, and then pulled out my little blue friend. Shit, I could have had the real thing that night.

She Don't Have to Know

Last night I was so upset with Mrs. Jones that I boned the hell out of Nina. I was on some sneaky stuff when I got back to her apartment, and climbed in through her bedroom window. There wouldn't have been a problem if I came through the front, but my head was all messed up. I was horny, I was getting blue balls, and I was pissed.

I called Nina from my cell phone when I was outside of her window. She asked me what was wrong with me and why I wasn't going through the front door.

"I don't want your mother to know that I'm here," I said. "Just open the window and I'll climb in. I'm right outside."

"What happened with you going home, Maricón?" She said into the phone as she appeared at the window.

Instead of answering her question, I just closed my phone and grabbed onto the ledge. She was still acting like a bitch and didn't help me climb in at all. All she did was move out of the way and let me fall inside onto the floor.

Nina shushed me and said that her mother was still awake.

"It's after midnight, what is she still doing up?" I asked taking off my shoes.

Me and Mrs. Jones

"She's watching her novellas on the TiVo." Nina was still wearing her bra and panty set, and although it wasn't doing for me what it used to, it was more appealing than earlier. Shoot, a naked picture of Martha Stewart would have put me in the mood.

As soon as Nina sat next to me, I started kissing her. She tried to resist, but I wouldn't let her. This was what she had expected earlier, and this is what I was hoping for, only from someone else. I snapped loose her bra and she finally gave in. She moved back a little and lifted my shirt over my head. I undid my jeans, where my manhood was once again, ready for action. I pulled down my pants and my boxers and kicked them away from me.

Almost instantly, I was inside Nina. First, I went down on her and satisfied her like she had never been satisfied before. Forget the Jell-O, I came up with my own whirlwind. Mrs. Jones didn't know what she was missing. We went at it all over the floor, then on the bed. I tried out some new moves where I had her up against the wall, and got her from behind. Move over William Baldwin.

Nina tried to pleasure me, but I didn't want it. I wanted to do what I had to do to get all of my frustration out. I plunged myself back into her, she pleaded for me to slow down because she was having her third orgasm and was becoming tired. There was no way I was pulling out.

Grabbing the bedrail, Nina squinted and forced a tear out of her eyes. But I didn't care, she was going to have to take all that I had until there was nothing left to give. I licked the salty tear from her eye.

An hour later, and I was finally done, and I was exhausted. I dropped my head on the pillow and felt like putting my thumb in my mouth. Nina rolled over and climbed out of bed. I didn't even see where she had gone, but I heard the door open and close.

The next thing I knew, I was in Mrs. Jones' arms suckling her breasts as she nursed me to sleep.

Then the door opened and Nina was back, waking me up. She asked, "Who is she?"

"What?" I didn't know why I was surprised that she could read me like that.

"I know there's someone else," Nina said. "I'm not upset or anything. Even though we've been over for a while, it's still good to have someone familiar every once in a while. It's almost like a safety net."

"There is no one," I lied. "I'm just so concerned with passing this stupid MCAS test in a few weeks and now with Corey being in the hospital, it's all so much."

She took a pre-rolled joint out of her nightstand and sparked it up. After a few tokes, she passed it to me.

"Whoever she is, you must be really angry at her. So much that you took it out on me. I'm not your whore, Darius but I realize that we all need a good piece of ass now and then. Next time, tell me so I can be prepared. Or else there won't be a next time."

I could care less what she was saying. We both wanted something and we both got it. I should have been the one upset, because I got mine from the wrong person.

I Wish I Wasn't

Not that I was expecting anything different, but I was still hoping for a late night phone call. For a second, I even thought of calling him. At three o'clock in the morning I was still awake. My blue friend couldn't do me like he used to. Poor thing was no competition for a big, black, juicy live one. I even added some new Duracell's just to see what happened. It kept going, but I wasn't cuming.

For a while, I lied there, flat on my back wondering what was going to become of me. When it comes right down to it, the whole thing was my fault. Meeting a man like Kael was a godsend. I had been looking for a man with dreams and aspirations ever since Stanley. A quality brother, who was making things happen for himself. And when I finally met him, I screwed it up for a little boy who can't even keep himself in check.

That relationship was never going to amount to anything, so I couldn't understand why I was feeling this dude the way I was. The heart sucks!

After only an hour of sleep, Corey called and woke me up. It was just about seven in the morning. My boss had let me have a couple of days off so that I could take care of my son. I hopped out of bed and cleared my throat.

"Hey, boo-boo," I said.

"I told you don't call me that," was his usual response. "They're discharging me this morning. They said that you should come and pick me up because I'm too weak to take public transportation."

"Of course I'll be there," I said excitedly. Did he think that I wouldn't come and pick up my only son? What kind of drugs did they have him on?

"I should be ready around eight. The doctors are filling out the discharge papers now."

There was only an hour left before Corey was going to be released, so I had to hurry and get myself together. Before I left, I took a five-minute shower, threw on some jeans, a fitted t-shirt and some white Reebok Classics. To top it off, I had on a white baseball cap to match my sneakers. Even in those rags I still knew I was looking good.

I hopped right into my ride and sped off to the hospital. At the entrance, I decided to call Darius to give him the good news. It wouldn't hurt to hear his voice either.

The telephone rang about four times, and then it went straight to voice mail. I cancelled the call and then hit redial but there was still no answer. Instead of leaving a message I turned off the phone and tucked it away into my jeans.

The time was now a quarter to eight and my baby was about to be released from the hospital.

Corey was sitting on the hospital bed, dressed in the new Roca Wear jean set I had bought him the day before. Even though we were not sure when he would actually be discharged, I had to make sure he had something new to wear home. I instructed the nurse to throw away the bloodied clothes he had worn into the hospital. We didn't need to be further reminded of the shooting.

I hugged him gently so that I wouldn't irritate his wounds. My baby had stitches in his stomach and in his arm. It would be a few days before he had to come back and have them removed.

"How are you feeling?" I asked as I helped him put on his jacket.

"As well as I can be," he said. "I just want to go home and have some of your homemade brownies."

"Why didn't you tell me? I could have baked some last night."

"I didn't know I was getting out of here today."

"I would have brought them to you regardless," I said as if he didn't know. We sat back down and waited for the doctors to bring the discharge papers for me to sign.

"No offense," he started. "But I couldn't eat your brownies here. It just wouldn't be right. Besides, it was giving me something to look forward to."

"Brownies?" I asked slapping him lightly on the head. "You were looking forward to the brownies instead of your mother?"

"But Ma, those brownies are off the hook. Even Darius says so."

I did not respond. I just kept holding a smile on my face. Together we sat and waited for the doctor so that we could go home.

Itzsoweezee

My boy was on his way home and I was too embarrassed to go and see him. Now ain't that messed up? My ace dawg, money-man fifty-grand was out of the hospital and I would not go and visit him on his sick bed. I used MCAS as an excuse again, and although he promised that he would tutor me, I turned him down and went on to school instead.

All day, I thought about Corey and about rolling out to the projects on Heath Street to get at these dudes who got my boy laid up in a hospital bed. Then I thought about me and Mrs. Jones rolling around fully naked on her queen-size bed.

"What is the measure of angle B?" Mrs. Robinson asked from the whiteboard. There was no response from the group. "Let's see. Darius, choose the correct answer in the book."

I looked down at my practice booklet and tried to figure out where we were. What did that stupid triangle have to do with real life anyway? Three angles, I didn't give a damn. Which is the measure of each angle? Ask the idiot who created the triangle.

"Need some help, Darius?" She asked. "I can walk you through it, although I've already walked you all through half the problems on this page. I will not be there when you are all doing this retake."

I did need help and it wasn't just on the paper, I needed answers for the situation with me, Mrs. Jones and Corey. If Corey found out, what would be the consequences? How would my relationship with Mrs. Jones affect my friendship with Corey? How would it affect their relationship?

I guess if Corey was the largest angle, say angle A of an isosceles triangle then both me and Mrs. Jones would have equal size angles. Regardless of what happened to either Mrs. Faith Jones or myself, the biggest impact would always be on Corey. And whatever happened to Mrs. Jones, would happen to me. So the only *thing* I need to be concerned with is Corey. I finally worked through the problem and gave Mrs. Robinson an answer. It was wrong, but I still had an answer for my real issues. I had to make sure that Corey didn't find out, and I would have to put an end to what was left of my relationship with his mother.

It wasn't too hard of a conclusion to come to since I hadn't spoken to Mrs. Jones since that night Kael was at her house. I even avoided most of her calls. She may think that I'm immature, but so what, I just wasn't ready to speak to her yet. I mean, she did have some dude at her house after everything we'd done. And I have to admit, I was still feeling a little guilty about sexing Nina.

After school, I called Corey while I was with Lil' Darius and told him that I would come by after Nina picked him up. Then I let my son speak to his godfather.

"Make sure you holler at your boy," he said sounding half asleep.

"What do they have you on?" I asked.

"Some pain killers. I can't remember the name but its some kind of narcotic."

We were both silent for a moment, and then I heard Mrs. Jones in the background. She was mumbling something about him needing rest.

"Mom Dukes wants to come and change my bandages before I go to sleep." He coughed a little. "Can you believe she made some chicken soup earlier, but didn't make me brownies?" Before I had the chance to say anything, Corey called his mother. "Darius wants to know why you didn't make me any brownies."

There was silence on his end until he came back.

"She said that I need to get off the phone. Mom's been acting kind of funny since I got back. She must be really worried about me. How were things when I was away?"

"Away my ass. You sound like you were on vacation." I chuckled.

"Just give me the four-one-one. Was she scared?"

Lil' Darius started to cry. "I need to get lil' man his snack before he has a fit. I'll call you later and tell you what you want to know."

Corey was gone before I could say goodbye. He must have really been tired. If I did decide to stop by later, he probably wouldn't be conscious enough to recognize me. By the time Nina came to pick up Lil' Darius it was after ten at night and I was sure that Corey was still asleep. So instead of calling him, I called Mrs. Jones' cell phone.

"What are you doing calling me? I haven't heard from you in a while," she whispered.

"Sorry, damn. I guess I just missed you."

She sighed, and told me that she missed me too. This was going to be harder than we had expected. I apologized for the way I acted the other night, and told her that I needed to get over what I was going through. Mrs. Jones said she understood, so I told her of my epiphany in Geometry class. Not that I had expected an invitation to come over, but I was expecting her to say something besides, "okay."

"That's all you have to say?" I asked.

"I'm kind of glad this is happening," she said. "We were getting in way too deep. And now with Corey home, it's probably best that we just end it, now. I mean, it was fun right."

I agreed. It had been fun.

She responded quickly. "Corey is the most important person in my life. So anything that I can do to keep my son protected and out of physical or emotional harm, I will do."

There was a brief pause.

"I spoke to someone at Morehouse today. They have a pre-freshman program that begins in June. I already signed him up."

"Does Corey know about this? He was looking forward to hanging out with the fellas this summer."

Mrs. Jones cleared her throat. "His safety is much more important than hanging out with *the fellas*. I know Corey, and he has a vengeful side to him. You may not want to tell me, Darius, but I know he must be planning some sort of retaliation. And if you're the kind of friend that I think you are, you'll talk him out of it."

Corey was my best friend, and despite what Nina said, I would never snitch on him. Especially to his own mother. I still owed Corey, so I had to make sure I didn't betray him this time either.

"He hasn't said anything to me about going back to those projects," I lied.

Mrs. Jones was no fool, and by her not responding, I knew she was aware that I was lying. By the time she spoke, I was expecting her to explode on me.

"Okay," she said again. And that was it. Mrs. Jones asked if I could come over and see Corey. She felt that it would keep things normal and Corey wouldn't start asking questions. "It'll be better for everyone."

I decided to do just as she asked. My father dropped me off after he got home from work. In the car, my father started up with a discussion of my own safety.

"Your mother doesn't mind you spending time with your sick friend," he said when we parked in front of Corey's house.

"He's not sick, Pops. Corey was shot."

My father acted like he didn't hear me. "We're concerned about the gang that did it to him. What if they come by here and you end up getting shot over nothing? Do you know what that would do to us?"

"Nothing's going to happen to us, Pops. Stop worrying so much. You sound like Mom."

"I sound like a parent who loves his child. You remember when your brother got stabbed by those guys. You know how crazy that had me."

"I know, but dad, Deon was a trouble maker. He kinda asked for it. Even his mother said so."

Dad couldn't respond, because he knew it was the truth. My half-brother and I had two completely different upbringings. Deon's mother could be a little on the neurotic side, but she was easy going. On the days when she wasn't cursing him out for the smallest things, Deon could get away with murder and his mother would not say a word. Our dad treated us both the same, but I guess since I had Dad to myself most of the time, I ended up developing a stronger conscience. And Deon ended up doing whatever he could to get attention.

Half the time, my parents wouldn't let me out of the house. And most of the time, Deon's mother was kicking him out.

Dad rubbed my head like he used to do when I was younger, and then sent me inside. I told him that I would call them in the morning.

"Give Faith and Corey my regards, and tell them to call if they need anything."

"Mom already spoke to Mrs. Jones the other day and she told her the same thing."

"And we mean it." Pops looked me in the eye.

"I know," I said. "I'll see you tomorrow."

Inside, Mrs. Jones was in the kitchen filling a bowl with almond praline ice cream. Earlier, she told me that the backdoor was going to be left open in case they were asleep when I arrived.

"You locked it back like I told you to, right?" She asked placing the container back in the freezer.

"Yeah, I did."

This was a sight of beauty that I was not prepared for. Her jeans defined her perfection, and her fitted t-shirt teased her curves. Her soft hair was pulled back into a ponytail, giving her the look of an early twenty-something year old. My manhood jolted forward, and it took her less than a second to recognize it.

"You'd better put that away," she smiled.

"I can't help it."

"Can't help what?" A slightly familiar voice called from the distance. It was a little groggier than I could remember, but it was close enough.

"Corey," I called.

Mrs. Jones asked, "What are you doing out of bed? I told you I was going to bring this ice cream to you."

"I'm bored, and when I heard this punk-ass boy right here I wanted to scare him."

"I didn't get scared until I saw your face," I chuckled. "But it's been like that for years. You'd think I'd be used to it by now."

Corey tried to throw a fake punch at me, but then he placed his hand over the spot where he'd been shot. When his face knotted up, I was immediately at his side, helping him back to his room and into the bed. Mrs. Jones brought in his bowl of ice cream and asked if I wanted anything. I was all set, so she closed the bedroom door as she left.

"So, man," he said. "It took you long enough to come by and check me. What's going on? How's the tutoring going?"

"It's cool. I should do all right on the retake."

"Damn, the test is in a few weeks, right? Time flies, man. Can you believe that I'll be leaving in a few months for college? I think I leave near the end of August, but I plan to make a couple of trips so I can get acquainted with the area. You should come with me so we can check out the honeys."

"I don't know about that..."

"Check it, we can even get an apartment together because compared to Boston, the rent is really cheap. I'll have my boy with me and we'll be banging hoes all across ATL. I hear that there are like ten women to every one man down there. So, it's like together, we have twenty and we can trade them back and forth."

Not to upset him, I said, "We can talk about it." I suddenly remembered that his mother didn't tell him about the program in June. Corey was going away for most of the summer and he didn't even realize it yet.

"Okay, it's like that, huh?" He asked scooping ice cream into his mouth. "Well then, let's tend to business. Nathan called me, and after I illed on him again about stepping to that dude, we came up with a plan for those Heath Street mofos."

"Why don't we just leave it alone, Corey?" This suggestion was not only because his mother asked me to talk to him, but I was genuinely concerned for my boy. "Listen, if you kill this shit with Nathan, I'll go to Atlanta with you. I just don't want to see you get messed up because of some project chicks."

"It's not about the chicks," he said. "Look what they did to me, Darius. I almost died, and you're telling me to let them dudes slide? You're on some old punk shit right now."

"Look, Corey. I never told you this, but you've been my ace since day one when you helped me beat them brothers down in middle school. I've been looking out for you just like you've been looking out for me. I got mad love for you, man and I don't want to see anything happen to you. You got a good life ahead of you. If this happened to me, yeah I'd be ready to retaliate, but because I know you're going to college soon, I wouldn't ask you to get involved. I wouldn't want you to jeopardize your future."

"So you're telling me that you don't want to help me?" He spat.

"Naw, Corey that's not what I'm saying. I don't want you to do anything at all. Maybe report it to the police or something."

After contemplating for a few seconds, Corey looked at me. "I can't let this slide. So what, if I'm going away, I'll be back every Thanksgiving, every Christmas and every summer. You're asking me to leave here a snitch and to come back as a snitch."

"Forget this snitch shit. If you do retaliate, you may not be going anywhere. You'll end up in jail or dead." I hated to be so blunt with him, but it was necessary.

"Fuck you, you punk ass," he said turning away from me. "I've never heard you talk like such a bitch before. I want you to get the hell out of my house."

I didn't have a chance to make a comeback before Corey added, "Even if you didn't want me to get involved, I'd still back you, just like I did back in the seventh grade. You wouldn't have to ask me."

Corey had never spoken to me like that before, and I can't honestly say that I could blame him. This dude was angry and embarrassed. If I had been there when this mess popped off, then we would have been able to talk each other out of going back. But instead Nathan was there, and he was still pumping Corey's head with ideas.

"I'm not leaving." I was sure about that.

"Ma!" He called at the top of his lungs.

Moments later, Mrs. Jones was at the door about to hyperventilate.

"What's the matter?" She asked catching her breath.

He said, holding up his bowl, "I just wanted some more ice cream. And can you walk Darius out? I think he needs to leave."

After she picked up the bowl, I followed Mrs. Jones out of his bedroom into the kitchen.

"I can't talk him out of it," I whined.

"He's trying to go back to Heath Street, isn't he?"

"It's that damn Nathan. He's on some stuff and he's keeping Corey all hyped up and shit... excuse me. But Nathan is the only one he's listening to."

"There's nothing left that I can say to him," Mrs. Jones said. "All I can do is stick around here and try to keep his contact with Nathan as limited as possible. Corey is a sneaky kid. I can't monitor him twenty-four hours a day."

Her face lowered as her hand reached across to wipe a tear from her eye. I slid my hand across her shoulder to provide her with a little comfort.

"Some people just don't understand. A parent can try to keep their children out of trouble, but there's only so much we can do. Believe me, if I could lock Corey up inside of his room until it is time to leave for Atlanta, I'd do it in a heartbeat. If I could keep him on a sick bed until then, I'd do it. But he needs to go to school, he has to live his life. I can't hide him from the world."

"My mother tries that with me." I sat down beside her. "She was a nervous wreck while I was staying over here those last few nights. She even invited the both of us to stay at my house until this was over. But the way Corey's talking, it'll never be over. It's going to keep going back and forth until one side ends it. That's just the way it is."

Mrs. Jones wrapped her arms around me and I rested my head on her shoulder. It didn't cross my mind until much later that Corey was in the next room. We released each other and I told her I was leaving.

"Don't leave," she insisted. "I don't care what Corey says. You're his only real friend. Forget Nathan, you have always been by his side so don't let this divide you. Corey will come to his senses and he'll need you to be there when he does."

That night, I slept on the couch with my best friend in one room and my lover in the next. Half the night I spent worrying about what was going to happen to Corey, and the other half I spent playing with myself, thinking of Mrs. Jones. By the time the light shined through the blinds, I had made three attempts to go into Corey's room and four attempts to sneak into Mrs. Jones'.

Let it Go

It was Saturday and although I wanted to go to this little restaurant on Blue Hill Avenue to have breakfast with Cynthia and Kael, I decided to postpone the invitation and prepare something for Corey and Darius. Darius tried to excuse himself most of the morning, but I insisted that he stay. Despite what was happening between us, Darius was Corey's only true friend. Corey knew that, but when he was upset he would forget about those most important to him. The two of them had gone through something like this before. Just like brothers, they were always fighting.

The house had never been as quiet as it was that morning. Corey was still not speaking to Darius, and he was upset with me for allowing Darius to stay. Believe me, if it hadn't been for him being stuck in bed, he would have left before the sun came up. In fact, I felt bad for the both of them, but in time Corey would come around.

Darius sauntered into the kitchen and took a seat at the island. A light sigh was released as he rested his head on the counter.

"Still nothing?" I asked flipping over the pancake in the frying pan.

"Nope, and this is getting ridiculous. I even asked him

if he wanted me to rent some of our favorite movies. Remember how much we used to watch 'Juice'?"

"Oh, I couldn't stand Tupac in that movie," I said. "His acting skills were so good that I actually hated the character he portrayed. What was his name again?" I asked.

Darius smiled. "How could you forget Bishop?"

"The only one I can remember is Q. That fine-ass Omar Epps." I took the pancake out of the skillet and piled it on top of the plate with the others.

"Oh, so he's fine now?" Darius said as he crossed his arms over his chest. He had to know I was kidding, and I decided to play along.

"Oh yeah. Omar has always been my heart. You know my favorite movie is 'The Wood.' I got a good enough glimpse of his..."

"Got it," he laughed. "I really don't need the visual."

After taking the egg carton from the fridge, I asked Darius if he had ever tasted my Black-Mexican omelet. He hadn't, and he said that he was not sure if he wanted to try it. Darius had never been much of an adventurer. Corey, on the other hand, would have tried anything once. That characteristic had its moments. It could be cool, but it could cause a lot of trouble too. I can't count how many times I had to go to the nurse's office at Corey's schools to pick him up because he tried something crazy.

A couple of years before, Corey tried to climb the side of his school after watching Spider-man. He climbed the tree next to the school and got halfway to the roof, but the tree was only so high. He thought that he could use the bricks, like he did on the rock climbing wall at Boston Bowl. He ended up crashing back into the tree, and eventually made his way to the ground. He was laid up for about a week after that.

There was this other time when I bought Corey a MINI bike, just like the one that Darius had. Darius' mother told me where I could find one at a decent price. Corey was ecstatic of course, and had already learned how to ride from using Darius' MINI. But the day he got his, they were ready to race. Hadn't even test-drove it yet, and this kid was ready to show off. So, they raced up and down Darius' dead end street.

Before you know it, they were off the street, over by Washington Park trying to race motorcycles. They both knew better, but Corey had to do his thing. It was no surprise that Darius was the one who tried to talk him out of it. Especially when one of the older bike riders offered to let Corey ride his motorcycle instead. He said that it would even-out the odds. Corey had just learned how to ride that MINI and now some teenage thug was convincing my baby to ride a Honda CBR.

This boy was on the bike, revving up the engine, when Darius finally told him to get off. It seemed as if that was all it took to get Corey off that bike and he admitted to me later that he was actually afraid to ride, and he was hoping Darius would have found a way to get him off. To this day, I don't think Darius knew how much Corey appreciated what he'd done.

"So," Darius said stepping behind me. "What goes in a Black Mexican omelet?"

Standing that close to me with my son still in the house was not a smart move. I was ready to mount this kid right there on the kitchen floor, in front of the fridge where this secret rendezvous started. He knew as well as I did that it was not safe to rub himself against me.

Stepping away from the island I went to the cabinet and took out Lawry's seasoning salt, black pepper, and hot sauce.

"The hot sauce is what makes it *Black*," I smiled. "It

takes the place of the salsa."

"And the Lawry's," he said. "Is there anything Black people don't put Lawry's in?"

"Come to think of it, probably not. That seasoning salt does wonders on fried chicken, home fries, french fries, vegetables. Damn, you *can* use it on anything."

"That's how my mother used to get me to eat string beans."

I grabbed the onions, garlic and tomato sauce from the fridge and sat everything on the island. Darius was back in his seat, after catching my hint, and immediately took an onion.

"Do you want me to start chopping these?"

"I'd appreciate it." I handed him the knife and watched as he cut each piece to an almost perfect size. When I let Corey cut up my vegetables, I would always have to fix them before I put it in my mix, so this came as a surprise. "How's Olesia? She called yesterday, but I was busy fixing Corey's lunch."

"She's cool. Mom is just ready for me to graduate. She wants me to go to Northeastern University, but I want to go to... never mind."

I watched as he carefully sliced the onion down the center, and then trimmed it into smaller portions. Before sliding it to me, this young professional peeled each layer away and piled it into a bowl.

"Come on. Tell me where do you want to go?" I said, admiring the work he had done on the garlic.

"I want to go to Johnson and Wales for culinary arts, but my parents don't think it's a sensible decision. My mother told me that although all men should learn how to cook, I shouldn't make a career out of it."

He passed down professionally-chopped garlic cloves and watched as I went to work on the egg batter.

I asked, "What does Benjamin have to say?"

"My father never picked up a frying pan in his life so he doesn't see a need for him to spend money for me to go to cooking school. I figure I'll just work and maybe go to school for something I really want, later."

"I love Olesia, but that doesn't make any sense to me."

"Tell *her* that." He walked towards me and stood over my shoulder as I poured the batter into the frying pan.

"I mean, if you like to cook and you want to become a chef then you should go to school for it. I have a friend who didn't follow her dreams. She wants to open up her own restaurant, but for some reason she won't make it happen."

"I don't know." He paused. "Like I said, maybe I'll just work and make enough money to pay my own way to Johnson and Wales. That way if it doesn't work out, my parents can't say I told you so."

Darius removed the spatula from the counter top and reached over to fold the omelet in half.

"I don't think Olesia or Benjamin would make you work to pay your tuition. You know them better than that. And I'm sure they wouldn't say I told you so... they may think it but they wouldn't say it. If you show them that this is what you really want to do, there is no way they won't support you."

I reached the hot sauce and passed it to him. Our fingers traded the bottle and the spatula, as Darius quickly went to pour the sauce into the skillet.

"Is this right?" He asked shaking out drops of the Red Hot.

I gently took it from him and twisted the rubber cap off. "You gotta get the flavor in there." I poured a generous amount on top and then placed the bottle on the counter. "So, what are you going to do about your parents?"

"I don't know. Johnson and Wales is just an idea

that's been running through my head. I haven't even applied yet and I'm sure the deadline has passed. Plus, Corey wants me to move to Atlanta with him."

"Oh goodness," I said. "You know there's no rush. Not that I don't want you to explore your options and I know you want to be with your boy Corey. But sometimes it's best that you discover yourself first, before venturing out. And if you do decide to move with Corey, I'm sure Atlanta has some nice restaurants where you can find a job. Maybe you can become the next G. Garvin."

He smiled as he put the omelet on a plate. "Isn't it true though, that sometimes you have to leave your nest to find who you are?"

"It's true, and a lot of people have no idea what they are chasing. Corey's leaving the nest because he has an idea where he's going. Although his agenda may change as soon as he lands in Atlanta, at least he has direction. I'm not knocking you at all, Darius. I'm just afraid that if you go just to be going, you'll end up helping Corey find himself, and you'll get lost in the midst. You have to make sure you can achieve something wherever you go."

"I never thought of it that way," he said.

"And if you go to Johnson and Wales, you may actually fulfill a dream that you weren't even sure was there."

"Honestly, right now my only concern is getting out of high school. I'm not thinking about the prom, and could really care less about the graduation ceremony. I just don't want to be twenty-three or twenty-four years old still fighting to get my diploma. The time is now."

We poured the remaining garlic and onion into the batter and I added the seasonings. Darius watched everything that I did. Although I was fighting it, the thought of him leaving was hitting me almost as hard as when Corey decided to go the Morehouse. However, if

Darius did move away, it would give me the opportunity to get closer to Kael. This thing with me and Darius was temporary at best. It was definitely a pleasure, but there was no way it was going to last. How could it? What would people say? 'Hey look, it's Darius and Mrs. Jones.'

I can't Let Go

A few days later, I was in my room reflecting on how unproductive the week had been. I hadn't studied for MCAS and I didn't do any homework. I tried calling Corey a few times, but he wouldn't speak to me. And with Mrs. Jones trying to uphold her end of the bargain, she kept our conversations as short as possible. It was getting to be too much, and even my parents were starting to worry about me.

During dinner one evening, my mother asked me about Corey's recovery.

"He's doing fine." I took a sip of my soda.

"You haven't been spending a lot of time over there since he's been home," she said. "Is everything okay between the two of you?"

"You know how it is," I started. "I've been studying and stuff. He's been trying to get better. So we decided to spend some time apart. Just until after MCAS."

I didn't give her the opportunity to ask another question. I told her about a concert I wanted to go to. Although I knew it would send her into convulsions, I also knew that it would lead us into another discussion.

"You're not going to a concert on a school night, are you crazy!" She yelled standing up from the table. "Didn't you just say that you have to study?"

I said, "Ahh, come on. A friend of mine has one extra ticket and he invited me. Plus, I've been studying all week, I could use a break."

In all honesty, there was no concert. Well there was a concert, but I wasn't going. I wanted to spend a few hours away from all the craziness, all the aggravation. It would be a few hours of me time, at a hotel, in a Jacuzzi, alone. All I had to do was to get my mother to say yes to the concert and to the car.

"No, no," was the extent of her vocabulary for a while.

"I could really use this," I said.

"A concert?"

"I know I'm going to pass MCAS this time. There's no doubt in my mind. So this is like an early award for passing."

"Isn't it a little too early? You haven't even taken it yet, let alone pass it." She collected the empty dishes and put them in the sink.

There was one last strategy that would work. Threatening to pair my parents against each other. It was an old, but modified trick that always seemed to work for me. Both parents think they have the power, and would hate to have their ruling overturned by the other.

"What if I ask dad?"

"What is that supposed to do? If I say no and he says yes, then I'm the bad guy. You know what, if you're going to go I might as well be the one that gives you the okay. I'm not about to get into an argument with your dad about this."

I hugged her, kissed her on the cheek, and then ran to the stairwell. Before I bolted up to my room, I asked her about using the car. I told her that I felt safer if I drove, and that I didn't know if my *buddy* was going to be drinking or not. After a brief hesitation, I got the keys and my night was about to begin.

    I sat at the bar ordering virgin pina coladas and sodas for about an hour. There was a band playing in the next room for someone's fiftieth birthday bash. The reception hall was so packed that I almost invited myself in. But I wasn't there for that, I was there for a few hours of peace and relaxation. After a few more drinks, I was going to sneak into the swimming area and chill out in the Jacuzzi.

    As soon as I ordered a strawberry daiquiri, without the alcohol, my cell phone went off. I was pissed that I hadn't turned it off. After all, I was supposed to be at a concert. I checked the number. Mrs. Jones.

    "Is everything all right?" I asked stumbling with the phone.

    "Yeah, um, are you all right?"

    "Oh, yeah," I said. "I'm sorry. It's just that I haven't—"

    "I know. Well, Corey's got his cousins over here and their playing Play Station. Kicked me out of the room and everything. It reminded me of the times when you two used to sit around here playing, all night long."

    I could feel her trying to force a smile.

    "Am I the real reason why you stopped coming by?"

    I said, "Definitely not. Corey doesn't want me around."

    "I know what we agreed, but I'm having a hard time with this. It's like every time the phone rings I'm hoping it's you. When someone comes to the door, I want it to be you. Even if it's just as friends, it would feel good to be able to see you."

    Damn, that was deep. I sipped on my drink, cooled down my intestines and then told her where I was.

    "Do you have a room yet?"

"No. I wasn't planning on staying the night. I was just going to hang out in the Jacuzzi before I headed back home.

"Are you at the Howard Johnson's in Dedham?" She asked as if she hadn't heard a word I said.

"Yes, but I—"

"I'll see you in an hour. I'll call you from the main lobby," Mrs. Jones said, and then hung up the phone.

About an hour later, her name showed up on my caller-ID. I answered it immediately and she told me that she was getting a room and would call me back with the room number. Ten minutes later, she called again.

"Meet me up stairs. Room five-eleven."

I waited a few minutes before heading out of the bar and to the elevators. I wanted to make sure that no one suspected that we were together. I don't even think that anyone looked my way.

I knocked on the door and waited for her to let me in. During the few seconds that I waited, I thought about marching back down the hall to the elevators, out the main entrance and back to my house. But there wasn't enough time or enough willpower to do it. When she opened the door and flashed that mesmerizing smile, I was done. I floated into the room, checked the layout and suddenly found myself sitting on the flowered comforter.

"You're making yourself a little too comfortable a little too soon, don't you think," she said sitting at the desk across from me. "I thought we were just going to be friends."

I walked over to her and offered my hand. "Okay friend," I said as she slapped my hand away. "What do you want to do first? Did you bring the oil?"

"Seriously, Darius. If we are going to be friends, then we have to stop doing what we've been doing."

I plopped back on the bed, knowing she was right.

But still, it just didn't feel that good.

"I know. Because of Corey, right?" I said. "Nothing's been right since he came home. I hate saying that, but it's true. Me and him. You and me. If I knew that he was going to stop talking to me anyway, I might as well have kept seeing you. Do you know how hard it was for me to be sleeping on that couch the other night after being in your bed for over a week?"

"I almost slipped out there and brought you back to bed with me. How do you think that made me feel? I'm sleeping with my son's best friend and I can't let go of him. I'm in a damn hotel with him for goodness sake. Look at me, thirty-four sneaking around with a teenager. I thought those days were over. The next man I thought I would have in my bed would be the man that I was going to marry."

"Who, like that Kurt guy?" I said. "That's the kind of man you wanted to be with?"

"I guess you can say that." At least she was honest. "Kael, is the kind of guy I was supposed to be with. The kind of guy that I needed to be with. And I'm here with you."

"Thanks, I feel a whole lot better," I said. "Really, I'm glad you decided to meet me here." I stood up and was about to make my exit when she grabbed my arm.

"Can't you see, Darius?" she said. "I'm here with you and I shouldn't be. You should be with a nice young girl who you can grow old with. Not some old maid that's robbing the cradle."

"You're not an old maid. Shoot, you're nowhere near old. And you are sexy as all hell. Do you know how many guys wanted to get with you while we were growing up? Corey illed on our gym teacher one day when you came up to the school. He was checking you out, and Corey put him in his place, telling him to respect his mother before he beat his ass," I said. "Mr. Jones was an idiot for messing up with you, and I know Kael loves you. I just wish I could have been your whole fantasy. But I guess Aaliyah was wrong. Age ain't just a number."

We stared at each other in silence. We didn't need any oil or champagne. All we needed was each other. Mrs. Jones stood up and placed her lips on mine as I reached behind me and turned off the light switch.

Then I undid her jeans, slid them down and kissed her belly button.

Ex-Factor

A few days later, Kael called. Corey still wasn't speaking to Darius and I had only spoken to him once, since our night at the hotel. So I guess we were finally moving on.

I have to admit it was good to hear Kael's voice again. Although I had been invited to breakfast earlier that morning, it was Cynthia who had done the inviting. I hadn't actually spoken to Kael in a couple of days.

"I just want to apologize for anything that I may have done to upset you," were the first words that came out of his mouth.

"What are you talking about?"

"Well, you haven't been calling me lately and I really do miss you. So if it's something that I did to cause this rift between us, I am sorry."

"You didn't do anything," I said abruptly. "Corey's home and I've been spending every waking hour at his bedside."

"Wow," he said. "Congratulations. How come you didn't tell me?"

"The way Cynthia runs her mouth, I figured she would have told you. I haven't been to work since he got shot and now that he's home I need to take care of him. That's why I couldn't go to breakfast with the two of you the other day."

"Breakfast?" He asked surprised. "What are you talking about?"

"Cynthia invited me to breakfast with the two of you. She didn't tell you?"

"I know she didn't want to eat at that restaurant on Blue Hill. She knows that I hate that place. I wouldn't be caught dead in that joint."

"Have you ever actually eaten in there? The food's not that bad. The service is even good, for an African-American owned restaurant."

"No. It's owned by The Nation of Islam, and let's just say they're not high on my favorite-people's list. And that's all I have to say about that."

"Okay, Forest Gump. But now I'm wondering what Cynthia was up to. She invited me to eat breakfast with the two of you, at a restaurant that you hate. And you were never even informed."

"Oh, Damn. Don't tell me she's up to her old tricks again."

I was well aware of most of Cynthia's games. But being that Kael was her cousin, I was willing to bet everything I own that he had a lot more stories up his sleeve.

"What kind of tricks?"

"I told her that I hadn't spoken to you in a few days even though I'd been calling you at least three times a day. Cynthia must be trying to tell you about how I'm such a great catch and that you shouldn't lose out. Blah, blah, blah. Stuff like that."

"Oh please. Knowing Cynthia, she wouldn't waste her time with some BS like that. She was probably going to tell me how much you were admiring me. How you became a stalker and that I should be careful, with my fine-ass, in case you try to sneak in my backdoor wearing your birthday suit."

The brother was speechless. "Is that an invitation?"

I needed to somehow take that back.

"Um, I was joking. You're not outside of my house are you?"

"I can be there in less than twenty minutes."

"Please, Kael. For the next few days it's going to be all about Corey."

"Believe me, I understand that. My mother is the same way with me. I had a bad case of the flu a few years back, and my mother would not leave my side. Even though I appreciated it and I love her for all the times she's been there for me, but I did need some breathing room. She wouldn't let me do anything, except watch TV and eat whatever she cooked for me."

"Your mother loves you and you should not b—"

Kael cut in, "The point is, Faith. You don't want to smother your son. And you do need to get out that house and take care of yourself. Let me take you for a quick ride, or maybe a walk through Franklin Park."

"I don't know, Kael. It sounds nice and all, but I don't want to leave Corey for too long. What if he needs help going to the bathroom? What if I need to change his bandages again? What if he gets hungry?"

Clearing his throat, Kael continued. "It'll take me twenty minutes to get there. You can cook him something to eat, check the bandages, make sure he uses the bathroom before we leave, and make sure he has a phone next to him. Franklin Park is only a few minutes away from your house. So if *anything* happens, he can call your cell phone and we'll be back to the house in no time."

I was taken aback by his concern. "With *you* driving, I can believe that."

"I would never do anything to hurt your family. You

may not realize this, but Faith, I care about you a lot. I haven't felt this way in a long time."

"That line is so tired," I said trying to keep myself from being pulled in.

"It is tired, but I'm hoping that my gestures can show you that I really mean it. I'm not about the game. I'm tired of playing with chicks that aren't taking life seriously. Part of my attraction to you *is* the way you take care of Corey and your concern for his friend Darius. You have so much love in your heart and I just hope that one day you'll let me in."

My heart dropped. This man was heating me up internally, I felt like I was going to burn the hell up. I reached over and turned my fan on high and stuttered into the phone.

"W-we can walk around the park for twenty minutes only. Okay. But then I have to get back."

"See in you a few."

And before I could say anything else, Kael was off the phone and I was looking for something to wear. This was the challenging part. Since I was *kind of* with somebody else, I couldn't go out with another man looking my fly-old self. And I couldn't go out there looking rough either. Some of my colleagues walked the trail at Franklin Park and if they saw me all scruffy, I would be the talk of the campus. Especially if Rita spotted me, she would be the one to start it off. Monday morning the gossip would be all about me out there looking busted and walking with the Down Low guy.

I searched for my pink and white Enyce jogging suit and my white on white Nikes. The suit was new. I had recently bought it on sale at Macy's and the tag was still on it. The sneakers had only been worn twice. It bugs me when females buy white sneakers and they wear them until they're gray. Not me. I wear my white sneaks a few times, and when they get marked up I toss them and buy another pair. The Nikes were only a month old. My Classics were only like four months old and were only worn five times.

The floor of my walk-in closet was filled with shoes and sneakers. I started tossing my Bandinis, Manolo Blahniks, and Steve Maddens onto the bedroom floor, hoping that my Nikes were not scuffed up. If they were, Kael was going to have to take me to Lady Footlocker before we got our walk on. I was not trying to let Rita see me with even a hair out of place.

Eventually, I found one of the shoes and it was in good condition. There was just one more to go. I saw the bottom of it and was about to snatch it up, when the house phone rang. I jumped for it, just in case Corey was asleep, and received the shock of my life.

"You are receiving a call from a correctional facility. The inmates name is Stanley Jones. To accept the call press one, to refuse the call press two?" Damn Stan again. This was not the time for his bullshit. I considered pressing 'two' before the recording even offered the choice. This wouldn't have been the first time that I refused a call from Stan, and it certainly wouldn't be the last. If I didn't accept the call though, he would call again later, probably while I was gone and would have disturbed my son. At least if I was there, I could monitor the call and make sure that Corey wasn't aggravated by him.

Immediately after pressing 'one' and hearing the collect call charges, Stan's voice came on. "Wasup, boo. You know I'm still missing you like crazy."

"What the hell do you want now, Stan? I'm on my way out."

"You're on your way to come and see me, I hope."

"I can't talk now, and Corey is asleep. So is there

anything I can do for you before I hang up?"

There was a heavy sigh of aggravation from the both of us. "Corey was supposed to come and see me. What happened?"

"He's not feeling well right now."

"What's he got?"

"A jackass for a father."

Stan started laughing like he always did when I put him out there like that. Honestly, I don't know why he continued to call and talk to me like I was going to give him another chance. Since the day when he held that gun to my head, it's been over. He's lucky I didn't take it from him and shoot him in the ass or go Lorena Bobbitt on his ass and cut his shit off. Just wait and see what happens if he ever gets out and tries to come visit me.

"I miss my son and my wife."

"You should have received the divorce papers by now. My lawyers are waiting for you to sign them."

"I ripped them shits up. We are not getting divorced. I promised myself that no matter what happened in my life, I would never get a divorce."

"It doesn't matter what you promised yourself. You're in prison for trying to kill your wife. You tried to kill your son's mother. You don't have rights," I shouted into the phone. I had to get myself under control before I woke Corey up. "I was trying to be rational and make this a mutual agreement but I can see that it is not gonna happen. I'll just do what I have to do and lose this sorry-ass last name."

"Baby..."

"Don't fucking baby me, you bastard. You held a glock to my head."

Every time this topic came up, my eyes got watery. The flashbacks hit me like stones, and I thank God every night that I'm still alive.

"I was on that stuff, Faith. You know this. I've been clean since I been in here."

"You're always clean when you're in there. I hope you never come out so you can die in there –clean."

I hung up the phone, waited a few seconds and then took the receiver off the hook. He would call back but neither my son nor I would be speaking to him. And so, without a phone it meant that I wouldn't be going walking with Kael.

I was still brooding when the doorbell rang. I opened the door and Kael pulled me in for a strong hug. I invited him in. He was not very receptive when I explained to him why I couldn't go.

"When are you going to get from under your ex's power? You already have a son that you are living for. Do you honestly need another man controlling your every move?"

Although Kael was right, I was not in the mood to deal with the issue right then. Until Corey was an adult, which I wasn't about to let happen any time soon, I needed to allow some sort of communication between him and his *father*. Despite what happened between the two of us, Stan was a half-decent father. And I would continue to allow him access to his son... at my discretion.

"This is another part of my life that I need you to stay out of," I said to Kael.

"I'm not trying to get in the middle of anything. I just want to make sure you're taking care of yourself. Just like I said on the phone."

"I appreciate that, but right now I need to be by myself. I don't know why I even promised that I would go."

Lines formed in Kael's forehead and he looked like he was about to explode. If he was, the brother needed to leave because I was not about to get into another... anything... like that again.

"Maybe you're right," he simply stated. "And maybe I should stop trying."

Without a goodbye, Kael walked out the front door.

Corey and I sat in the living room watching television for a few hours that night. He said that he was well enough to stay up, and he was also complaining that if he stayed in bed all day he was going to get bedsores. Of course I argued, but I eventually I gave in.

His not talking to Darius was disturbing to me, but I hesitated talking to him about it. I didn't want him getting upset with me again, so I decided to just sit quietly and not discuss it. And that's when the jerk called. An hour after I put the phone back on the hook because Corey wanted to call his grandmother.

Until then Stan had slipped my mind, so when the phone rang I told Corey to answer it.

Corey wasn't excited when he heard the voice, he actually sounded a little annoyed. I almost thought it was Darius, and I tensed up a bit.

"Who's that?" I asked.

"Dad." He turned back to the phone and told the bastard that I was just asking who was on the phone. After a brief pause, Corey asked me, "You didn't tell me he called earlier."

"Sorry, I forgot." I turned back to the movie and listened to the conversation as best as I could. I couldn't make out what Stan was saying through the phone, but I could only guess based on Corey's responses.

"No, I'm not seeing anyone... yes I'm going to Morehouse... they gave me enough money... I don't know when I'm coming to visit, I'm busy at school... okay bye."

After Corey hung up the phone I asked him if he was going to be all right. He rolled his eyes at me and then stood up to walk away from me. "Why do you two keep doing this to each other? Doing this to me? Now I can't even think straight. This nigga wants me t—"

"Corey!"

"Sorry, Mom, but he wants me to come and visit him. I can't go visit him after what he did to you. Why do you keep giving him the number to the house? You changed it like six times and you keep giving it to him."

I wasn't expecting that. All of these years, I thought I was doing him justice by allowing him to have a male figure in his life. Lord knows there is a shortage around here. Now it seemed as if I was only doing him harm. The confusion in his eyes was enough to burn a hole in my chest. Stan had already been away for two years and it seemed like Corey had been suffering with it ever since.

"I thought you wanted to have a relationship with him. A lot of your friends have fathers in their lives. Besides, Stan has always treated you like the prince that you are."

"Yeah, but look at what he's done to you. Look at what it's done to us. What kind of father would treat his family like this? So what if he bought me a bike when I was seven. He was too strung out to teach me how to ride it properly. I ended up learning the right way on my own. Forget him. It's always been just you for me and me for you, Ma. I don't need his image to make me feel better about myself. I have all I need right here."

We were not one of those huggy-feely families, but after his little *Cosby Show* speech, I felt like grabbing my son and smacking a wet one on his cheek. That was not about to happen, so I just smiled at him, he smiled back.

"I'll call the phone company in the morning."

He said, "While you're at work?"

"I have a few more days off." The family disability option works wonders.

"Look at me, I'm fine." There was no way I could deny that he had gotten a lot better over the last couple of days, but I still wasn't convinced.

"Corey, I don't know about that."

"Look, woman. I am a man and I want to be treated like a man. I said I want you to go to work and you are going."

I gave him the only look that would stop this boy in his tracks. The *look of death*, as he used to call it. It meant that if he wouldn't do what I told him after giving him *the look*, then he might not make it to the next day. *The look* worked.

"What?" He said squirming in his place. "I was kidding."

The look turned into a genuine smile. "I know you were joking, but I don't think you should be by yourself."

"I told you that I'm all right. I was more worried about you being home alone then about me."

After the Kael fiasco, going back to work would be a relief. I needed to get out of the house and back into the real world. Certain things needed to be fixed, and the only way to do that was to stop sitting in the house and being idle. However, facing Cynthia was going to be a chore in itself.

"You know what? I'm going to go to work and leave you at home by yourself. But I want you to talk to Darius about getting some make-up assignments. You're already behind and you need to play catch up before it's too late."

"I am not speaking to that sell-out."

"I still don't understand what's happening with you two. And if you don't want to talk about it, I'll understa—"

"I don't want to talk about it!" After his little

outburst, he limped back into his room and shut the door.

Dreamin'

The moment I walked into his studio apartment, my half-brother Deon knew something was up. He tossed me a bottle of Budweiser and followed me to the sitting area. The bottle opener was already on the coffee table, so after I sat down on the queen-size futon I picked it up and popped my beer open.

"So what's up, little brother?" He swigged a large amount of his beer. "You got another chick pregnant?"

I took a quick sip and then placed my beer down on the table. "Naw, no more babies for me."

"Like you got control over that. You still messing with your baby mamma, Nina? She sure did have a fatty on her, Darius."

"I stopped messing with her a while ago, where have you been?"

"You don't come by to see me like you used to. Like you too good for your big brother."

"I've been busy with school. I'm trying to graduate, so excuse me if I don't make time to come over and smoke with you as much as I used to."

"Fuck you," Deon said searching his pockets. "I don't even have any more weed."

We both cracked up, clinked bottles and then he

turned the CD-player on. I couldn't make out the music that was playing. It was some underground mix CD that he bought on one of his trips to NYC.

"Seriously though. How are things? You sounded a little anxious over the phone."

I told him all about Corey and how he got shot because of a girl. Then I explained the whole hospital visit and that Corey wanted me to help him retaliate against the dudes.

"What did you tell him?"

"I told him to leave it alone. Corey has a scholarship to Morehouse. Why would he want to mess up his chances because of some punks in the Heath Street Projects? He should just leave it alone, move to Atlanta and not look back."

"I grew up around Heath Street, the dudes there aren't that bad. It's like every other community – just a few knuckleheads that cause the drama. But Darius, you know as well as I do that Corey is not the type to let this kind of thing slide. This is your boy, you should realize that."

"I do know it, but I was hoping that going to college would make a difference. Wouldn't you want to leave this life behind you if you had the chance?"

"I'm cool where I am. If I had the opportunity to move away, then I wouldn't mind taking advantage of it, but my life is still here. I would like to be able to come back whenever I want to without having any shit over my head."

Lighting a Black and Mild, Deon took a few puffs and passed it to me. What Deon said was making a lot of sense to me. So what if Corey was going away for the school year, he would still be back during the breaks, and next summer. He couldn't hide from these people. No matter what happened, it would still be hanging over his head.

"Okay," I said excited about a thought I had. "Say he does retaliate and then he leaves. Won't those same dudes be looking for him no matter when he comes back?"

"It's definitely a no win situation. But it's a decision Corey has to make. And as his boy, you gotta support him."

"I don't want to get shot over no—"

Deon cleared his throat and said, "I didn't say get involved. I said show support. Shit, if something happens to you then it means I gotta get involved. You think I want to get shot over some craziness like this? I mean... you don't owe him your life do you?"

While finishing up my beer, I considered telling Deon about me and Mrs. Jones. This was eating away at me, but there was no one that I could talk to about it. Deep inside, I knew that our rendezvous would never be much more than just that. A rendezvous. I wanted to get married someday and I couldn't imagine walking down the aisle with Corey's mom in my arms. Our dilemma must have crossed her mind. What was she actually expecting from this?

"Um, Deon," I started.

He swallowed the last drop of beer, and placed the empty bottle on the table.

Before I could get my thoughts into focus, his cell phone rang. Deon told me to wait and then answered the call. His voice turned to a whisper and eventually he stood up and went into the kitchen area. Moments later, he returned with a confused expression on his face.

"You want to take a ride?"

We pulled in front of the Unity Caribbean Club and

parked. Deon didn't tell me what was going on. He hadn't spoken much at all since we got into his black Ford Explorer. When he asked me to come with him, I simply agreed and followed him down to the car.

A short line was formed outside of the club, but Deon had so much clout that we just walked straight over to the bouncers. They dapped Deon up, gave me the once over and then allowed both of us to go inside without a pat down, or paying an admissions fee.

Buju Banton was blaring through the speakers as we made our way to the bar. The ladies on the dance floor were wearing practically nothing at all, making me feel like I was at the West Indian Festival, where the women wear little less than what *should* be considered legal. If my memory served me correct, I could have sworn that I saw a female covering her *stuff* with a handful of feathers. Oh yeah, she did have two more to cover her nipples.

At least in the club they were actually wearing minis. But they were so mini that I got a few glimpses of the thong-thong-thong-thongs. Not that I'm complaining, but... Never mind, I'll just say that I'm not complaining.

While we were sitting there, Deon offered to buy me a drink. I reminded him that I was only eighteen, but he shushed me and told me to tell the bartender what I wanted. Rum and Coke. The same drink that I usually have when I'm out. I just never had the opportunity to have it made professionally. The bartender was back in a few minutes with my drink and with Deon's Budweiser. The same drink that he has everywhere he goes.

"So what are we doing here?" I finally asked him.

He guzzled down half of his drink and put it back down on the bar.

"Frandy called me and told me that that hoe-ass Teresa was supposed to be down here with some other dude."

"I thought you two broke up." I took a swig of my drink and almost choked on it. That drink was stronger than I was used to. Deon laughed and patted me on the back.

"You gotta watch that Caribbean rum, my brother. That shit is strong." We watched as the bartender tried to hide his own laughter.

"So what's up with you and Teresa?" I asked.

"We're actually not speaking right now, but I just want to catch her in the act. You know what I'm saying. If she's down here with some other buster, I want to see her and I want her to know that I see her."

"With all of the chicks that you're always bragging about, why do you care if she's with somebody else?"

He finished off his beer. "Let me tell you what this bitch did. I was getting my freak on at the crib, right? This is after I broke up with Teresa. I was waxing that, Darius. We were like an hour into it. I'd bust a nut already, but I was hitting her back up and then before I could bust another one, Teresa's gonna walk up in there and start bugging."

"What do you mean she walked in there? This sounds like some crazy dream."

"I was thinking the same thing when I first heard her voice. I thought I was imagining it, but then I remembered that she had a key."

I needed another rum and Coke by then. Deon was telling me every brother's worst nightmare.

All I could say was, "Ah, damn."

"I told her to get the hell out, but by then she was ready to fight this hoe that I was with. Talking about, we were still together. Man, me and Teresa had been split up for like two days and she was still bugging like that."

Deon had this rebound thing down packed. Give him an hour after he's broken up with someone and he was ready for a new piece of tail. His motto went something like this, "If the first chick messes up... try, try again." And I kind of admired him for that. If I were more like him, I wouldn't be dealing with the issues I was having with Mrs. Jones. I could have just moved on.

"Two whole days," I said jokingly. "That's like a record for you. Isn't it?"

"I had already bagged that chick the same day that I broke up with Teresa. I actually hit it in the bathroom over there." He pointed towards the rear of the club. "I met her here and we literally hit it off that night."

Laughing off my buzz, I looked around the club, hoping to see something that I liked. If Deon could hook up with somebody, then I knew I could meet someone. I was young and more attractive then he was. Deon would never admit it, because he thinks that he is the next Will Smith. He has those standout ears, and a pretty decent build. However, I have the baby-come take advantage of me-face. My braids were done-up last night by Nina, so I knew they were tight. I was a little cut, not as much as Deon, but my wide-eyes made up for that. At least my stomach wasn't protruding my t-shirt like some of the other fellas in the club.

My eyes caught the attention of this young looking sister. Light-skinned, shoulder-length curly hair. My dream lady. I had actually caught her looking my way a few times while I was swigging down my drink. She was in the middle of the dance floor, with two other females. Although they weren't fully dressed, they still weren't putting themselves on display.

"Yo, that's her right there," Deon blurted out.

Since I never met Teresa, I crossed my fingers, praying that he wasn't talking about the girl in the center. Deon had been messing around with her for about six months, but he was sort of private with his women. I've only met about two of his girlfriends. One was his date to the prom, and the other was the girl he got pregnant in college. Dad offered to pay for the abortion, so I went with them to talk to her parents.

"The one on the wall standing next to that dude." He told me to wait at the bar for him because he wanted to go and talk to her.

"I'm going to dance," I said. "I'll meet *you* back at the bar."

He followed my gaze over to the girl in the center and then turned back to wink at me. It was a wink that meant that if things went well, I'd just meet him back at the apartment. And if things went really well, I'd call him in the morning.

My jam, 'Dreamin' by the City Slickers came on just as I approached her. I never could dance to hip-hop, but that night I was going to fake the funk. As her friends separated from us, I fell right into the motion. I didn't get up on her immediately. I've already told you, females don't like it when guys just come up and start grinding on them, so I left a little space.

We faced each other, both smiling. When the next song came on, she told me that she hated it, and I agreed with her.

"I don't know why they keep switching the music up like this," she said as she wiped some sweat from her forehead with a handkerchief. "They should just *play* some more reggae or some soca."

"If I wanted to hear a bunch of hip-hop I would have gone to The Officer's Club." Not that I went to clubs much at all, but I had to have some sort of contribution to the conversation.

She smiled. "Where are you from?"

"I'm from here. Been here all of my life. What about you?"

Me and Mrs. Jones

Looking around for her friends, she waved towards the bar. "Atlanta." This was the first time I noticed her accent. "I'm here with my friends, they're all from Boston. We go to Spelman together."

So, she was a college girl. These are the types of women that Corey was talking about hooking up with. I may have to take him up on his offer and move to Atlanta.

"So you were born and raised in ATL?"

"Right outside, in Marietta." She fanned herself with her hankie and her eyes began to glisten as she looked to the side of me. Either she was bored or there was someone more important coming around.

"You're a lifesaver," she said as a hand reached from behind me holding a glass.

It was one of her friends.

My dance partner drank half the glass and sighed with relief.

She said, "That joint hit the spot."

"You all right, Mya?" Her friend asked giving me the once over.

Mya took another sip. "I'm cool. Me and... I'm sorry I didn't get your name."

"Darius."

"Me and Darius were just talking about how the music sucks. I thought you said they played a lot of Caribbean music."

"They do," the other girl said. "But they also play whatever hip-hop jams are hot at the time."

The next track that came on was some old school Sean Paul. When we both started to bust some of the moves from his videos, like the *ponytail* and *the signal the plane*, it seemed like we were aging ourselves. By the time the song went off, I started looking around for Deon. I tried to steal a glimpse in the direction where he had gone, but I didn't see him. Then I looked at the bar. Still no sign of him.

"You looking for your friend?" Mya asked me.

"My brother, yeah. Why, did you see him?"

"He went outside with a girl a few minutes ago."

I told her I'd be right back, and I headed outside. If he was about to cause a scene, if he hadn't already done so, I needed to be there. I was sure that the bouncers would have his back if anything went down, but like he said I needed to show support.

Outside, the cool air hit me hard. I hadn't realized how sweaty I had been. Looking around, I didn't see my brother, and after a while, I noticed that his SUV was gone too. I looked at the bouncers, and they eventually recognized me.

"You Deon's brother?" One of the muscle heads asked. "He said to call him if you needed a ride home."

"Did he leave by himself?"

"Naw, he had Teresa with him. I called him and told him how that trick was down here with some other man. I didn't expect him to come pick her up and take her back home."

I went back inside and searched my pockets for my phone. I checked all of my pants pockets. Then I remembered leaving it on the dashboard in his SUV. Now, I was stuck at the club without a ride and without enough money for a cab. Even if I did find a way to call him, he wouldn't pick up. Deon was known for not answering his telephone if he was with a honey. And if he were with Teresa, I wouldn't hear from him for another couple of days.

Near the coat rack, Mya was waiting for her friends. She noticed that I was still there and came to ask if I needed a ride to my house.

Embarrassed, I accepted.

It was a quiet ride to my house, and I was sure that Mya would not bother giving this sorry brother the time of day... or night.

Before I got out of her car, she slid me her cell phone number.

"I'll be here for a few more days so we should hook up."

And then they were gone. I opened the front door and soon realized that I hadn't thought about Mrs. Jones in the last few hours. Maybe I could get over her if I actually made an effort to. I forced myself to believe that until I got up to my room and masturbated to the image of Faith Jones in my head.

The next couple of days were ridiculous. I hadn't spoken to Corey all weekend, but Mrs. Jones had managed to call me a couple of times. We spoke briefly each time. The first time she called was to ask me about getting Corey some make-up work from his teachers. Corey was supposed to call me himself, but we both knew that he was too stubborn to do that. The agreement was for me to pick up the assignments and then drop them off at her job. I recommended that I leave them in the office mailroom so that I wouldn't have to bump into her and she agreed.

The first few days were fine. By the end of last week and even earlier this week, she was *accidently* bumping into me while I was sliding the papers into her box. Her excuse was that she just happened to be collecting her mail at the same time.

I'm sure she wasn't stalking me, but it was obvious that she was meeting me at the box on purpose. There was something more that she wanted from me and she was not ready to ask me.

However, last night when she called me, I was with Mya. It was the third time we'd been out since I met her, and things were going strong. Mya was a sweetheart, and since it was her last night in town I was planning on doing something special.

Earlier that morning, I made reservations at the same hotel where me and Mrs. Jones spent our final night together. It wasn't that expensive, and although it felt wrong, it was the only place I could afford. A brother's pockets were kind of tight. I booked the room, made a slow-jam mix CD, and then during lunch I went out and bought some heart-shaped chocolates and flowers. I checked-in by myself and left my supplies in the room. I still had to grab some massage oil, bubble bath and condoms.

Mya never agreed to have sex with me, but after what I had planned for her, she couldn't turn me down. And if she didn't want to sleep with me, so be it. I would still call her in Atlanta and maybe even arrange to visit her. Sex wasn't the priority, but it was an option and I wanted to be prepared and protected just in case.

Our first stop that night was at Legal's Seafood in Copley Square. I left my mother's car with the valet and we took a walk through the mall. It had been years since Nina and I actually went anywhere in public together, and just thinking of Mrs. Jones reminded me that we could never take a walk in public. This thing with Mya was just right. She was down-to-earth, intelligent and self-confident.

We stopped at a few of the stores, and I ended up having to dip into my savings account so I could buy her some earrings and her favorite perfume from The Limited. Then, before we left the mall she bought me a bottle of Kenneth Cole's *Black* cologne from Neiman Marcus.

There was not a single moment of silence, and the conversations were not just a bunch of chitchat. Mya was a freshman at Spelman. She said that a lot of her high school friends were there with her so she never felt out of place. She did miss her mother, even though she was only a few minutes away. Mya wanted to be a pharmacist, she planned to get married by the age of twenty-seven and have kids by the age of twenty-nine.

"Does your fiancé agree with the plan?" I asked.

Sucking her teeth, she said, "I am not settling down with anyone this soon. At this age, a man would only slow me down. I'm just chillin' and having a great time doing it."

I heard the sistah loud and clear. Mya was keeping it real and not ashamed to show it. To my surprise, she was not turned away by the fact that I had a son. She even asked me to email her a picture of Lil' Darius since I didn't have one in my wallet. I was not too keen on sending my son's picture over the world wide web, because you never know what perv out there may accidently get his hands on it. I promised to show her a picture before she left for Atlanta.

We were already at the hotel by the time Mrs. Jones called. Mya was in the bathroom changing into her bathing suit so we could go swimming in the indoor pool. When the phone rang, I almost didn't answer it, but she was calling from the home phone and I thought it was Corey.

"Is Corey with you?" Is the first thing she asked before she even said hello.

"You know he's not with me, Mrs. Jones. Why would Corey be with me? I haven't spoken to him in over a week." I hadn't spoken to him since the night I stayed over there. And even then, he didn't speak to me.

"I know and I'm sorry, but he left. He said something

about going to visit Wilson in Quincy. But I don't trust him right now. Have you spoken to Wilson or Nathan?"

"I spoke to Wilson yesterday, but he didn't say anything about Corey going to Quincy, unless they just decided this today. I honestly don't know."

"I need you to find out for me. I'm worried and I don't know what else to do."

At that very moment, Mya came out of the bathroom, wearing a two-piece bathing suit. Her dimples were deep and her light cheeks had become a deep shade of burgundy. She had curves that only God himself could have blessed her with. No amount of Jenny Craig could build thighs and an ass like that. A plastic surgeon could not have shaped the breasts of this goddess. Not even Michael Jackson's. Mya was putting Beyonce's jelly to shame.

I almost dropped the phone when she asked me about her outfit.

"So what do you think?"

"Uhhh."

"Darius, are you okay?" asked Mrs. Jones.

"Oh, yeah, yeah," I said. "I'll call Wilson and call you back."

I closed the phone and walked over to my queen for the night. "Are you sure you don't want to just stay in here?"

"After all the cash you paid for this hotel. We need to get your money's worth. I want to hit the pool, the hot tub and the sauna. Shoot, we should hit the gym too."

I hated myself for this. "Actually, I need to make a few calls and then I'll meet you at the pool. I don't want to chance this phone not working down there."

Mya's dimples faded as she wrapped herself in a complimentary towel. She kissed me on the cheek and told me not to be too long. Nothing was going to keep me from her for too long.

Wilson knew nothing about Corey coming to Quincy. For some reason, Corey never called him about going to Heath Street either. This was going to be one of those nights. Wilson promised to meet me in Boston as long as I was the one to call Nathan. Both of us damned Corey for not getting himself a new cell phone. I guess he had gotten comfortable using mine.

Dialing Nathan's number was painstaking. I didn't want to speak to Nathan and I'm sure that if he saw my number on his caller-ID he wouldn't pick up. So instead, I used the room phone.

"Who the hell is this?" was the first thing that came out of his mouth.

"Let me speak to Corey."

There was a little chuckle, and then he asked Corey if he wanted to "speak to this bitch-ass, Darius."

A sneeze, a grunt, and another laugh. "What the hell do you want, now?"

"Where are you going?"

"You didn't want to be down with us. You wanted to be a bitch, so you don't need to know where I'm going."

"I'm serious, Corey," I said. "Are you going to Heath Street with just Nathan? You know he's crazy, man. Don't get your shit messed up because of him. Why didn't you call Wilson?"

"You called Wilson?" He asked. "What are you going to do next, call my mother or the police? Why don't you call my father while you're at it, you snitch! You want his telephone number in prison?"

"Look, just pull over somewhere and wait for me. I'm coming with Wilson. You're my boy, so if you're that serious about doing this, I want to be there. So just tell me where you are."

Not surprisingly, Mya was not at all happy about my

early departure. I told her the entire story when she got out of the pool. She said that she understood, but she was adamant about me not going.

"If he wants to be stupid and throw his life away, then let him," she said. "Why should you throw yours away right behind him?"

I said, "He's my best friend and he would do the same thing if the tables were turned."

"The tables wouldn't be turned. You wouldn't put yourself in that kind of predicament. You'd take that scholarship and walk to Morehouse with your head held high. I wish you were the one with the scholarship to one of the most prestigious Black colleges in this country. Yeah, Corey is your *boy*. He *is not* you."

Everything and everyone was basically reiterating what I already knew. But Corey was my boy and if they were in the same boat, they would all do the same thing. Talk is cheap, because their actions would prove otherwise.

I asked Mya to stay at the hotel because I was coming back and I wanted to spend the night with her. She didn't decline. Actually, she said that she had a surprise waiting for me in her duffle bag, and she would give it to me when I got back safely. Then she made me promise that I would try to talk some sense into Corey before either of us did anything stupid.

Instead of calling Mrs. Jones, I called Wilson back and told him to meet me at the hotel. And afterwards he would drop me back off at the hotel so I could spend one final night with Mya.

To Zion

The moonlight glare smacked right up against my windshield. With the water already soaking my eyes, the brightness was making it almost impossible to drive. I tried calling Darius again, but he stopped answering his phone. Either he and Corey were up to something, or he was just as clueless as I was. But if he was in the dark, we should have been together to find my son.

I made one last attempt to call him. This time from a payphone outside of a Mobil gas station. If for some reason he was avoiding my calls, the unknown number would get him to answer the phone. The phone rang a number of times, and there was still no answer. I hung up before the machine picked up again.

Thinking back to our last conversation, I wondered why he answered the phone at all, unless he was expecting it to be Corey. After all, I did call from the house phone that first time. And who was that woman in the background? It didn't sound like his mother, and there was no Spanish accent, so it couldn't have been Nina. Maybe he had found somebody else. If that's the case, then more power to him. I guess I'd eventually be happy for him.

I drove through Roxbury and then Dorchester. I even

passed Heath Street expecting to see Nathan's car out there. After waiting a few minutes, I decided that for my own safety I would report my speculations to the police. If something did happen, and if Corey was at fault, a record like this would destroy his Morehouse enrollment. Even if they allowed him to enter the school, there was no doubt in my mind that they would recant his scholarship. But if I didn't tell the police, Corey could end up dead.

Maybe he was really going to Quincy to see Wilson. Darius was my only link, and with him not calling me back, I was going insane. He was probably sexing that little hoochie-mama while I was on the road pulling my hair out.

I drove back through Dorchester, hoping that I would see someone familiar on the streets who would have an idea where Corey was. Getting desperate, I called my house thinking that Corey was back at home. When the machine picked up, I demanded that if he were home then he needed to pick up the phone immediately. I waited the entire thirty-seconds, until the machine disconnected the call.

Next stop was Darius' house. It didn't matter to me that it was after ten at night. They could have all gone back to Darius' house to talk about old times and wish Corey a safe trip to Atlanta. That would have been ideal, but truthfully it was a simple fantasy. They were not at his house and Darius' parents probably wouldn't have any idea where he was. Still, I decided to stop in and say hello.

Both cars were gone and all the lights were off in the house, which meant that Benjamin was still at work, Darius was not home, and Olesia was in bed. There was no need to burden her with my issues.

 I sat in front of the house for about five minutes, hoping that Darius would pull up. Even if he were with someone else, at least he would allow me the opportunity to talk to him about Corey. He owed me that much. There was no denying the fact that I messed this whole thing up. And I honestly believed that he and Corey wouldn't have the issues that they were dealing with. The guilt is written all over Darius' face.

 By ten thirty, I was back on the road heading towards my apartment. I pulled onto my dark street, passed the memorial for the little girl who got shot on the corner the previous year, and pulled into my driveway. The house seemed darker than I remembered leaving it, not a single light indoors. Not even the sound of Corey's radio blasting through the night.

 A sigh and a yawn later, I turned off the ignition and sat there.

 Prayers came naturally in times like these. It seems that once people are in crisis, we turn to the only ear that will listen with the hope that He hasn't forgot about us. These prayers always start with an apology about the gap in time between prayers. Then we talk about how great His power is, and finally we get down the point. We need His help and we need His guidance. We end with a thank-you and an Amen.

 That's when the phone rang. I fought to get it out of my purse and didn't even bother checking the caller-ID. There was only one person I was expecting to hear from.

 "Hello," I said filled with excitement and fear.

 "Hi, Faith," he said from his end. "Is everything all right?"

 Kael. Once again to the rescue. This was a night when I needed as much company as I could get. If that phone rang again, I would need someone with me to get whatever news there was to get. And if Corey came home without a scratch on him, I needed someone there to keep me from bashing his head in.

"I don't know about this," he said. "After what happened the last time. I don't know if I want to be put in that situation again. I was calling to check up on you and Corey, that's it."

"What if I come over there? I'm serious, Kael. I think I need to get away from this for a little while."

The tears were streaming down my cheeks, like Niagara Falls. Maybe Kael could hear it in my voice and if so, who cares. Everything that was happening to me and my family was weighing on me more than I could have expected. In all honesty, I don't even know if I could drive to his house in my condition.

"Yeah, come on over, Faith," he said. "I'll wait for you downstairs."

Kael was outside just like he said he would be. A stone-cold gentleman to the core. I parked my car in the visitor's parking space and walked over to him. Even in the dark, I could make out his wonderful physique and bright smile. The first thing I did was hug him, and inhaled the sweet aroma of his African Musk oil. We laced our fingers and headed up to his condo.

Once we got to his living room, the first thing I did was remove my shoes and plop down on the couch.

"I was surprised you wanted to come over. Dealing with you is very confusing." Kael was smiling as he fixed us a couple of drinks. From where I was sitting, it looked as if he was mixing Absolut vodka, Parrots Bay and cranberry juice.

"What's this," I asked as he placed the glass in my hand.

He said, "My own twist of a Cape Codder. I put Absolut in everything."

Toasting our glasses, we both took a couple of swigs and I was fascinated with the taste. It was better than I had expected it to be. I should have known though, especially after the night he threw down on that roast duck.

We cuddled on the couch, listening to a mix Neo-Soul CD that Kael had recently made. It had the new Jill Scott single, Erykah Badu's On & On, a lot of D'Angelo and of course John Legend and Maxwell. All of my favorites. It wasn't making sense to me why I hadn't chosen him.

It felt wrong for me to be sitting there in comfort while my little boy was somewhere out in the streets. Kael kicked off his sandals and rubbed his soft feet against mine.

"You seem so tense," he said. He brought my hand to his lips and kissed each and every one of my fingers. Tingles ran across my arm, down my spine, into my stomach and through my baby girl. This time instead of walking away, I just leaned back and trusted his direction.

"There is just so much going on right now, that I can't keep my life in order. You were so right."

"It's not about being right. It's about taking care of yourself. Corey may be your priority, but if Faith isn't taken care of, then she can't take care of Corey."

Kael hit it right on the money. All along, he'd been trying to tell me that but I was too stubborn to listen. I was so wrapped up in myself and Darius, that I allowed this stuff to build up inside. Now it was tearing me apart.

By the time my drink was done, Kael was already up making me another one.

"You're not trying to get me tipsy, are you?" I asked playfully.

He laughed. "No, Cynthia already told me that you have a very high tolerance. I'm the one that has to be careful of you trying to take advantage of me. My tolerance is very low. I think I'll be drunk after this next one."

"The way you're walking, it seems like you're already drunk."

This laugh felt really good and I was happy that I decided to come. My phone was still attached to my hip, so the slightest vibration would send me into convulsions, but I had no other choice. Good news or bad news, I needed to be notified.

Kael almost tripped as he made his way back to the couch. Luckily he caught his balance, because I was not trying to catch his big ass.

"Oh yeah, I meant to tell you, my niece is in town," he said handing me my second drink.

I told him to be careful not to spill any of it on me.

"What niece are you talking about?" I asked.

"The one from Spelman. She's in town with some friends. She's been staying here from time to time."

"Oh, yeah the girl Cynthia was talking about." I remembered that Kael was trying to hook my Corey up with that little hoochie.

"Don't listen to Cynthia. My niece is a good girl despite what her mother has done in the past. And in case you were still wondering, she is not my daughter. We had the blood test done years ago and Cynthia is well aware of it. Besides, Mya looks nothing like me."

"Then she must be pretty," I smiled. Kael smiled back. "Mya is a nice name. How long is she here for?"

"She's leaving tomorrow morning. Supposedly, she and her girlfriends are hanging out at some hotel tonight before they go. I didn't like the idea, but they came up to Boston together so I figured they're trustworthy. I wish you and Corey would have had the opportunity to meet her. She is such a sweet girl."

"Maybe next time around. I'm actually thinking of having Corey go down to Atlanta for the summer program at Morehouse. It wouldn't be a bad idea for him to have a friendly contact. And don't worry, I won't tell Cynthia about it."

"What are you going to do with yourself after he's gone?"

"What do you mean?"

"I mean just that. You spend every waking moment worried about him, catering to him, and doing for him. What's going to happen when the empty nest syndrome hits?"

"Believe me, I've been thinking about that for a while. But right now I'm not thinking about what I will do after he goes away to college. I'm thinking about what I will do if my son gets killed. I can deal with missing him during the school year, as long as I have the vacations to look forward to. But I can't deal with not having anything to look forward to. I'm not like those mothers who think that they'll see their child in heaven. No. I'm going to do whatever it takes to make sure I see my child on Thanksgiving, Christmas and spring break."

"You know, during spring break students usually go to Cancun, right?" His light smile brightened the dim room.

"Shoot, I may be there right next to him. They have some fine-ass college boys hanging out in Cancun. Have you seen those six-packs?"

Kael lifted his shirt so that I could see the slices and dices across his abdomen. His stuff was cut up like that model Bradly Tomberlin. Detailed lines, like a professional stitched them. I couldn't keep my fingers from gliding across them.

"Those college boys ain't got nothing on me."

"All I see is one big pack," I said trying to hide my

infatuation. The next couple of minutes flew by and it was about time to change the CD. "Do you have Anthony Hamilton's first CD?" I asked him.

"Nah, I let my cousin borrow it, and you know what that means."

"You're not getting it back."

"You got that right. It's been years since I loaned it to her and do you think she's even mentioned it?"

I looked through his CD collection, but couldn't find anything that I wanted to listen to. Not that his taste in music was bad, it was just that his collection was similar to mine and I was in the mood for something different.

"Wait, I have something you'll like." He turned on his Apple Powerbook and turned up the speakers. "I downloaded a few mix joints. Lauryn Hill, the Roots. It's not hardcore, but it's not all slow either. I think I even have a few Anthony Hamilton remixes on there."

Before he could get the music on, my cell-phone buzzed. I almost jumped into his arms when that vibration hit me the way it did. After I calmed down, I was reminded of my unused blue friend, I promised myself that after I cursed out Corey and Darius I would use it to put me to sleep.

The telephone number didn't register, so I had become a little nervous.

"Hello?" I said into the phone.

"Mom, I'm staying out in Quincy with Wilson."

"Stop lying to me, Corey. Where the hell are you?"

"I just told you. I'm at Wilson's house now."

"Where have you been all day? I've been calling around looking for you. I drove all over Boston looking for you. Are you okay?"

"Yeah, I'm fine. Darius is actually with us too. I met up with him and Wilson."

"Ask Darius why he never called me back to tell me

that he found you."

Corey asked the question in the background, and then came back to the phone. "He said that he left his phone somewhere. You know how he's always putting it down and leaving it."

"Yeah, I know. He's almost as bad as you, but at least he keeps finding his." Corey told Darius what I said and they both laughed.

"Okay, Mom. I'm going to get off the phone now. I'm exhausted and I want to get some sleep."

"Have a good night, and call me in the morning, okay?"

"Sure thing. Goodnight."

As he was hanging up the phone, I thought about Darius and the MCAS retest. He only had a couple of days left and he needed to spend every waking hour studying for it. I had a good mind to call him right back and tell him to let Darius go home and study. Making him stay out like that was very selfish of Corey. And it was very stupid of Darius to tag along. Well, since I wasn't his mother, I couldn't tell Darius to go home. His next move was up to him. And my next move was up to me.

Climb

I got back to the hotel a few hours later, and of course Mya was gone. Although she'd promised to wait for me, I found a note that said she had something she needed to do and to call her in the morning. She was hoping to see me before she left for Atlanta the next day, but I'm sure she knew as well as I did that that was not going to happen. Flopping down on the bed, I accepted the fact that I had just wasted a full night.

When Wilson and I got to where we were supposed to meet with Corey and Nathan, no one was there. We waited a few minutes, trying to convince each other that Corey would not stand us up and then discussed how much we've all changed over the years. When we met Wilson in middle school he was a nerd. Big glasses, beat-up shoes and bootleg designer t-shirts. I was quiet, used to walk on my tiptoes and always had my guard up. Wilson would say that I looked nervous all the time and that was why the other kids used to pick on me. Corey was always the cool one. He had the best gear, the smoothest haircuts and was the first one of us to have his ear pierced.

By high school, we had all changed. Wilson was wearing contacts and had joined the school football, basketball, and track teams. He was a year behind us, and somehow over the summer after he graduated, Wilson had discovered that he had a knack for sports. Corey already knew that he had a way with women before I met him. Girls loved his green eyes. Rumor had it, he slept with almost every girl in our eighth grade class. Although I was the first one to get a BJ, the rumors still circulated around about Corey. Off the record, Corey was a virgin until ninth grade. But even in the eighth grade, he never denied the allegations. It just made it easier for him to get dates with girls who were eager to give it up. In high school, a lot more girls were willing to go all the way. In eighth grade, most of them were usually teases.

I was shy until ninth grade, and I didn't really come out of my shell until the following year. Because of my personality, I wasn't the type of guy to stand out. I didn't play sports like Wilson. I wasn't as popular as Corey, and my grades were fairly decent. Not that I didn't have girlfriends, but the girls I went out with just wanted to hold hands and talk on the phone. My first real kiss wasn't even until I got to the tenth grade. And that was with this girl named Alkia. I couldn't believe that she actually laughed at me after our first kiss. Lucky for me, she didn't spread the news around school that I was a bad kisser.

Alkia taught me a lot. She got me practicing kissing using my fist, Karma Sutra, and the basics of satisfying a woman. After a few weeks together, Alkia popped my cherry and I have not been the same since. I had found my niche. I was good at sex. Books, pornos and magazines. If school would teach stuff like how to work a woman, rather than just why you should wear a condom, I would ace all of my classes. Maybe they should add some questions on the MCAS retest about sexually pleasing a woman. Fondling her clitoris and caressing her breasts. I could even teach them about self-pleasure.

But just like Alkia kept the kissing extravaganza from the school, she also kept my newly developed talent from the other girls. I had to show and prove. By junior year, Corey, Wilson and I had made our marks on the world and even though Wilson had transferred to Quincy, he was still a legend at our school. Half of our class would go and see him play during football season. We ran so deep that we had those white kids scared as hell.

On my way back to the hotel, Mrs. Jones called me again. I stopped answering the phone after Wilson saw the number show up on the caller-ID. Thinking that it was Corey calling from home, he told me to answer it.

"Naw, it's his mother," I said. "She's been calling me all night about him. And I don't want to talk to her until after I find him."

I guess there was something awkward about the way I responded, because he asked me, "You feeling Mrs. Jones?"

"What?" I couldn't understand what brought that on.

"You got that look that you always make when Nina calls you. You front like you don't want to talk to her, although you know you really want to. Tell me, Darius. Mrs. Jones *is* fly for an older woman."

"Forget you, Wilson."

Outside of the hotel, Wilson was still at it. Talking about how he used to have wet dreams about this woman. I couldn't take it and told him he needed to get serious about his girl in Quincy.

"Don't bring Damita into this," he said copping an attitude. "I don't want to call up Corey and tell him about you and his mother."

I opened my side door and headed out. "Look, I'll talk to you tomorrow all right. If Corey calls you let me know."

"Why, so you can call Faith back?"

I slammed the door and went back to my room. How in the hell did he figure that out from just one look? Was I that obvious? Shit, if this got back to Corey I was a dead man. He was already pissed at me, and then to find something like this out would push him to grab a gun or something.

A moment or two passed before I picked up the phone to dial Wilson. Halfway through, I placed the receiver down. It would seem like I was whining if I called him, and it would prove my guilt if I asked him not to say anything to Corey.

"Wilson, please don't tell Corey what you said," I whined. "He'll get mad at me."

"I already told him," Wilson would respond. "You know I have a big mouth. I can't keep shit like that to myself."

"But it's not true, Wilson."

"If it's not true, why are you calling me, and whining like a little bitch?"

Yeah, there was no way I was calling Wilson. I would just have to let the cards land where they may. The next few days went by in a flash, and I still hadn't spoken to Corey or Mrs. Jones, and I never got the opportunity to say goodbye to Mya. It wasn't until the night before the MCAS retest that she called me.

I was in my room doing some last minute studying when my cell phone rang. It was way after midnight, and from the tips from my prep course I should have been in La-La Land by then. But I was up, eating a Snicker's bar and blasting 97.7 FM WILD through my headphones. The only way I knew she was calling was because the light was glowing from my phone.

"Hey, I didn't think I'd hear from you again." I was excited. "What's up?"

She was just as excited as I was. "I thought I was going to hear from you the morning before I left. I've been waiting for you to call."

"I didn't think you wanted to speak to me after what happened."

"Honestly, I didn't want you to call, but I knew that if you did then I would have accepted it. I've been kind of worried too. I was praying that you would answer and that you didn't get hurt."

I said, "Thank you for that. And I miss talking to you."

"Same here."

We spoke for about an hour, until it was time for her to go to bed. I should have done the same, but I had a little more studying to do. I promised myself that I would study for only half an hour more, and then hit the sack. The promise was somewhat kept, I only studied for fifteen minutes and I fell asleep at my desk.

My telephone woke me up, and this time it was a definite unexpected call. When the number showed up, I couldn't identify it. It was a good thing I couldn't because from the indi-glo clock next to my computer, I could see that it was five-thirty in the morning. This call had better be important.

Clearing my throat, I greeted the caller.

Whispering, the caller said, "Darius, it's me Corey."

"What? Where are you? What are you doing?"

"Chill man," he said. "I need you to come and get me. I'm down at the area B-3 police station."

"You've been arrested? For what?" I was already up and still dressed from the day before. I rubbed on some Degree deodorant and found my shoes.

"Me, Nathan and Ricardo got pulled over last night for speeding and we got arrested for possession."

I almost felt like undressing and going to bed. This dude was messing his life up, and amongst the four of us, he was supposed to be the smart one. Commonsense and book smarts are two totally different things.

"How much is bail?"

"Like fifty bucks. I'll give it right back to you."

It only took me a few minutes to get there. I borrowed my mother's car and left her a note that I would be back by seven. She needed to leave the house by eight-thirty but if I were late, she would easily hop on the bus and then curse me out after work.

His bright cheesy smile almost blinded me, and his breath smelled of stale shit. He gave me a half-hug, dapped me up like old times and then marched out to the car behind me. The release process took longer than I expected. The bails bondsman didn't get to the station until after seven, so I sat out in the waiting area with Ricardo's girl-toy. Apparently, since Nathan was an adult now and since he had a record, they were going to continue holding him.

"I really appreciate this," he said buckling up. "Do you think this will go on my record?"

"What the hell is up with you, Corey?" I spat. "Of course this is going on your record. You may have to kiss that scholarship goodbye. You may be at your mother's school after all, this September."

"Why are you always so cynical?"

I grunted, and told him to forget about it. I even told him to forget about the fifty dollars.

The ride home was almost silent, until we got to his crib.

"Do you need me to come in and cover for you?" I asked as I put the car in park.

"Naw, I'll just tell her that I stayed the night with you or something." He shut his door and then walked around to the driver's window. "One more thing. Could you not come by as often as you used to. Especially if I'm not here."

"What are you talking about?"

"Nothing really. I mean, I really appreciate that you were taking care of my mother when I was in the hospital, but people are starting to talk shit."

"Wilson?"

"I know he's full of it, but I just don't like my mother's name being put out there like that. If it's just you and me, then it's cool. But when they start pulling in names and shit, I'm not feeling that at all."

Here it comes. "Corey, there's nothing going on between me and your mother." The big fat lie.

"I know this. Of all of my boys, you're the one I trust the most. I'm still not cool with how you've been acting, but I trust you more than anyone else. You're my brother, and nothing's ever going to change that." He laughed a little. "Can you believe Wilson said that? And now he has Nathan and Ricardo talking that shit. My mother is like your mother. That's just nasty."

I chuckled along with him. All the while, the inside of my stomach was being attacked by killer butterflies.

We dapped each other up and I went home to vomit. It was at that very moment that I decided to put a final end to me and Mrs. Jones.

Of course I was late for school, but because I was taking MCAS the school let me slide. They were just happy that I showed up at all. The testing room was filled with tenth and eleventh graders. There were only two other seniors taking the retest. I was the last one in our crew to have to pass the exam. I still wonder how in the hell Nathan passed. Although it was on his second try, it still amazed me that he passed before me, even if it was by one point.

Me and Mrs. Jones

I wore a dark t-shirt, in case I needed to wipe the sweat from my brow, I wouldn't stain up a good white one. Halfway through, the bottom of my shirt was already soaked. Even though I could hear the motor running, I couldn't feel a bit of the AC they claimed was blowing. And by the time I broke my third pencil of the morning, my neck was aching.

The cone shown below has a radius of 9 feet and a height of 15 feet. What is the volume of the cone? Carol removed one marble without looking, and she recorded the result. She placed the marble back in the box and repeated the procedure one more time. What is the probability that Carol removed a green marble followed by a yellow marble?

I remembered the steps but I couldn't get the order. And it was like that for the entire three hours that I was taking that damn test. I could only hope that I scored high enough to get by. Proficient of not, as long as I passed the damn thing the score itself was the least of my concerns. Right after I turned in my booklet and answer sheet, I bolted out the main entrance and headed to my mother's car. She called me twice that morning and told me that I could use the car for the day, as long as I picked her up at the subway station by six o'clock. There was still about four hours before I had to get my butt over there, so I drove to my brother's crib to have a drink.

Deon was sitting on his couch smoking a blunt when I walked in. Already zoned out, with his head slouched to the side, I would have sworn he had overdosed if I hadn't found him in that position before. The first time I saw him like that, I was about to slap him across the face to get him up. But his reflexes were too quick for me, and he snatched me up before I made contact.

"Damn, I almost forgot you had a key." He hadn't even moved.

"What were you gonna do if I was a robber? Offer me

a smoke cause you sure as hell weren't gonna get up and fight me."

His hand slid between the cushions and pulled out a glock nine. He wasn't fool enough to aim it directly at me, so he pointed it at the door that I had just come through.

"If someone was stupid enough to try to run up on me, then he wouldn't be running back out of here."

"I didn't know you had a gun." I let out a small sigh of relief when he lowered that piece of metal. "Let me take a look."

"Get away from me with that nonsense." He placed it back between the cushions before I could say *Amen*. "You'd hurt yourself without even knowing it."

"What are you talking about? I'm not dumb enough to shoot myself, but if I did I'm sure I would feel it. Don't you think it would hurt?"

"It's not about shooting yourself, idiot. You should never put your hands on nobody's gun. If something goes down and that fool uses it after you've touched it, then your prints are on there too."

I smirked.

"No, I'm serious," he said. "Especially that stuff you've been telling me about with Corey and your other boys. If they have a gun and you touch one of them, who do you think they're going to go after if that gun is used in a murder?"

"The person who killed the victim?"

"Don't be a wise-ass. They're going to go after whoever's prints are on that gun. Even if you were just profiling with it, your prints are on it."

I took the joint from between his fingers.

"You hear me?" He asked.

"Yeah, yeah. I won't touch anyone's gun."

"And don't go out and get one of your own. If you

need a gun, I'll come and use mine." All was quiet as I finished off his joint. "You selfish bastard," he laughed preparing to roll another one. "How was the test today?"

"I took both parts today, but I don't really want to talk about it until the results come in. I think I passed, and that's all I'm gonna say."

"Good, because that's all I want to hear. Actually, tell me about that honey you were all up on the other night in that club. The last time I saw you I forgot to ask you about her. So did you hit that?"

I'd only seen Deon twice since that night at the club. The first time, was the next day when I went to pick up my cell phone. The next time was about a week later, when he came by the house to borrow some money from our father. Lil' Darius was there and he was crying for his afternoon snack, which I forgot to take from Nina, so Deon and I didn't have much time to catch up on things. He had some explaining to do to me, too. I wanted to know what was up with Teresa.

"Naw, I didn't get the chance to get with her. Mya goes to Spelman and she was only here for a few days."

"A few days! That's enough time to sleep with her a *few* times. Man, you slipping. You should have let me get at that."

"You were all up Teresa's ass that night. Left me at the club and everything."

"I told you I was sorry about that. Things happen. You know I really love that girl."

"You thinking about marriage?"

"Sometimes, I do. We've been off and on for about... how long has it been?"

"About six months, now."

"And sad to say, but that's the longest relationship I've ever had in the twenty-four years that I've been on this earth. That night after the club, Teresa and I had a nice long talk. The guy she came to the club with was her cousin who just moved into town. He even came out to dinner with us one night. Terrell is a nice guy. I'm supposed to take him out to play pool tomorrow night. You should come with us."

Tomorrow was not good. Not because I had already made plans, but because I *didn't* have anything planned. After school, I was going to do a lot of nothing. I wasn't going to have my son, I wasn't going to study for any stupid-biased test, and I wasn't going to think about any females. Maybe I'd rent some movies or burn some CDs. No matter what I decided to do, I wasn't going to let anyone disturb me. I was known for losing my cell phone, so tomorrow was going to be one of those *lost cell phone* days.

"I'm busy tomorrow," I said with a straight face. Unlike Nina, Deon could care less if I wasn't telling the truth.

"Alright then, another day. So, back to this girl Mya."

"Yeah. She's real cool people. I was feeling her. Smart as hell, sweet. I wish I had spent more time with her. Not just because I wanted to sex her, but because she was legit and I'm not used to that. I'm used to chicken-heads like Nina and Alkia. You remember Alkia don't you?"

"Hell yeah. She had you crying like a baby when she broke up with you."

"I was not crying. There was something in my eye."

"For a week. Damn, if that was the case, you should have gotten that checked in the ER." He lightly punched me in the arm.

To pay him back, I took his new joint and exhaled the smoke in his face. The next thing I knew, my brother had snatched me off the couch and had me on the floor. We were rolling around throwing soft blows at each other like old times. He stood over me and busted out with some Hulk Hogan moves. Talking about his biceps.

"Whacha gonna do when these 24-inch pythons come crashing down on you?"

I cracked up and told him that his pythons looked more like a three-inch garden snake. Deon hopped on top of his coffee table and tried to pull a diving elbow drop. Although I knew he wouldn't actually make contact, I rolled out of the way and Deon landed, pretending to be hurt. To finish him off, I busted a leg drop onto his chest, and then laid him down for the count. One-two-three. Ding-ding-ding. The match was over and I had won again.

This was something that I needed, and it was moments like this when I was happiest to have a blood-brother. Someone who wouldn't turn his back on me just because I didn't agree with his decisions. Not to say that we've never argued, because that's just what brothers do. It's different though. I may see Deon much less than I see Corey, but we always know that we can count on each other. What happened between me and Corey, and then him not being where me and Wilson were supposed to meet him, got me really thinking. Maybe Corey and I were growing apart. The last thing he said to me was to stay away from his house. He claimed it was because of what Wilson said about me and his mom. Maybe it had more to do with me and him.

I let the thought escape my mind as an unfamiliar scent entered my nose.

"Oh, shit!" Deon shouted looking over at the couch.

He must have dropped the joint on the cushion, because there was smoke coming from the exact spot where he was sitting. The first thing he did was grab his gun before it got too hot. He yelled for me to snap out of my trance and to get some water.

"You don't have a fire extinguisher?"

"This is no time for a lecture, *dad*." He placed the gun in his inseam and tried to pat the fire out with the decorative pillows that my mother had gotten him. If they got damaged, she'd understand. And then she would ask him why he didn't have a fire extinguisher.

I poured a pitcher of water on the small blaze. Intense black smoke rose through my nostrils, and I almost choked. Deon was already on the other side of the room letting up the windows.

"It smells like you burned up your dinner," I laughed.

"Smells like I burned up the entire house. I just hope the landlord doesn't hear about this. He's already informed me that I am not his favorite tenant and that if I screw up one more time, I'm outta here."

"You can always come home with me. We still have that little guest room."

"Guest room my ass. That's your old room. You took mine when I moved in with my mother. Don't forget that. If I do decide to move back there, then you'll be going back into that little ass guest room."

"Have you seen these 45-inch pythons?" I laughed. "You think you can handle these bad boys?"

Deon dived for me and we rolled around on the floor for another half hour. I would love for my brother to come home, and I would gladly give up my bedroom to have him there. He knew that, but I don't think he'd ever come home. He and our dad repaired their relationship the day Deon moved in with his mother and I don't think either of them would want to jeopardize that. Besides, if I didn't pass that MCAS retake, I was going to need a place to stay.

Love Rain

This was just what I needed. It had been weeks since Kael and I officially started dating. And at my age dating doesn't mean sex, it means going out and spending a lot of quality time together. Oh, yeah and a lot of kissing, which Kael was really good at.

Today, this brother hooked me up and took me to an all day spa at a big resort in New Hampshire. The suite Kael rented for the weekend was decked out with a fireplace, two pedicure chairs and a steam room. We started off with a romantic couples massage in the privacy of the living room. Anita was my therapist. She was a sistah-girl from New Mexico, and had been living in New Hampshire for two years. She was only twenty-five years old and already had three children. Anita had only been a massage therapist for two months. It may have seemed odd for me to become that acquainted with my therapist, but I like to know a little bit about a person before they start rubbing my body.

Kael agreed to let Lano massage him. Lano was this bronze colored, Australian guy with a deep seductive accent. Although he was attractive, it looked like he'd overdone it in the weight room. It was a little weird for me to watch at first, because I'd never seen a guy feeling up another guy like that. Years ago, Stan took me to this cheesy little Asian massage parlor in Rhode Island. It actually turned out to be a whorehouse in disguise. Besides watching a woman practically jerk-off my husband under the sheet, the only other thing I didn't allow to slip my memory was when Stan almost went off on the manager when they tried to give him a male therapist. He screamed out that he didn't want no faggots rubbing up on him like that. So watching Lano rub up Kael made me feel a little queasy.

Eventually, I came around. I had to tell myself over and over that Kael was just very secure in his manhood and it didn't matter who gave him a massage. The only person going to bed with him that night was me.

Yes, I made up my mind to sleep with Kael.

"You alright over there?" Kael was staring at my wide grin.

"Mmm Hmm." I continued smiling, and he immediately returned the gesture.

It had been about a month since I met Darius in that hotel room. It had been longer since Darius last stopped by the house. I have to admit I was missing him, but this was good for the both of us. He could go back to his baby mamma or whoever, and I could move on to a grown man. Yeah, this was going to work out fine.

After our pedicures and manicures, Kael took me out to a restaurant halfway across town. He wouldn't tell me where we were going, but I knew that it was someplace special and I knew that I was going to be very, very pleased. And I definitely was. When we pulled in front of that five star restaurant my mouth almost dropped.

We walked along the garden, where we could hear the live reggae band doing a rendition of Bob Marley and the Wailers' 'Easy Skanking'. I was already feeling high, way before the maitre d greeted us at the entrance and led us to our reserved seats. My toes were tingling when we sat down in a corner seat with a clear view of the kitchen as they prepared food for the other patrons. My primary goal was to watch them after I ordered to make sure no one spit in my food.

"So what do you think?" Kael placed his napkin across his lap.

"This is magnificent. I never expected anything like it." I picked up the tulip, which decorated the center of our table. "Are we still in New Hampshire? You took a lot of side streets and back roads. At first, I thought you were taking me somewhere to whack me off."

"I don't want to say," he chuckled. "If you ever want to come back here, you're going to have to come with me."

"I can't think of anyone else I'd rather come here with."

The maitre d showed us the wine list and then the menus. Not far behind, was the waitress delivering a fresh serving of Texas toast and sparkling water. We were introduced to the house specials and then it was left to us to make our selections.

"Give us a few more minutes," Kael said as the two left us alone.

"It's so expensive here," I said checking out the thirty-dollar hamburger. They'd better be slaughtering the cow to-order," I smiled at myself. I was acting like I'd never been out on a real date before. In reality I hadn't. This guy was really special and I didn't want to lose him for the world. I think I was falling in love with him.

"Order what ever you want. I've been putting in overtime just so I could bring you here."

That really made me feel bad. He'd been working double shifts for two weeks now, just so he could blow it all in one night. There was no way I was taking advantage of him like this. I wasn't some cheap hoochie mama looking for a Daddy Warbucks. I had my own money and I was prepared to go fifty-fifty this weekend.

"Kidding," he said. "Damn, it looked like you were about to blow up. Put your purse away and enjoy yourself. I got it, believe me. And I didn't work all those shifts just so that I could bring you here. That was for something else, which I'll tell you about later tonight. But for now, just enjoy the evening. We've got a long night ahead of us."

Oh my God! He was going to propose to me. I couldn't marry Kael, could I? Damn, it's all so sudden. Wait a minute. I was still a married woman. That stupid-ass Stan was trying to contest the divorce. He was really pissing me off. The whole divorce thing was going to take a little longer than I had expected, so even if I wanted to marry Kael I couldn't. But did I want to marry him?

Dinner was excellent. I have to admit, the chef still had nothing on what Kael could put together, but the over-all experience was magnificent. We walked hand-in-hand along the boardwalk not too far from the resort.

"I love watching the stars." I thought back to when my parents used to take me to Nantasket Beach when I was a kid. My world was so innocent then. I never envisioned that one day I would be the *single* mother of a teenage boy, sleeping with his best friend and on the verge of a divorce from a man who had tried to kill me.

The stars reminded me of the times when my dad used to throw me up on his shoulders so that I could try to touch one of them. My mom was always so worried that I would fall if I reached too high. But I never fell. Even if I did, Dad would have caught me.

"They are beautiful, aren't they." He led me to a bench where we could sit and watch the ocean.

"Thank you for bringing me here. I haven't been to a

beach since Corey was a little boy. And even then, it was different. I was the parent, making sure that my son didn't get hurt. But now, I'm here with you, stress-free." I reached up to grab a star and then placed it into my pocket.

"What was that about?"

"It's a game me and my dad used to play. I'd reach for the stars, and then I'd grab one and keep it safe in my pocket. He said that if I reached for the stars, then I could have anything I wanted. When I was a kid, I wanted the stars so I kept them in my pocket."

We both laughed out loud, and then he did something I don't think I'll ever forget. Kael reached up to the stars, grabbed one and handed it to me.

"Could you hold this for me, too? Tonight I'm hoping we both get what we want."

When I stepped into the steam room, I was surprised to see Kael wearing absolutely nothing. I still had on my bathing suit from the pool, because he told me not to change, but when I saw his trunks lying outside the door I knew what he was up to.

"If I'd known this was a skin-only party, I would have come prepared." I immediately removed my two-piece and dropped it onto the bench beside me. Neither of us knew where to start, and I wasn't too sure if I wanted to make the first move. Kael placed my hand in his and then brought it to his lips. The touch was so tender, that even in this heat, I was getting shivers.

We explored each other's bodies as if we were exploring new, sacred territory – afraid to break any part of the order. I looked down at his bulging friend, expecting nothing less than what I saw. He was an all around big guy and I was satisfied with the addition to our relationship.

Moments later, we were making out in the bedroom, dripping sweat all over the floor. I wanted him more than anything. This was the move I needed to make, to take our relationship to the next level. After all, if I was going to marry this man, I had to at least know what I was getting myself into, right? But for some reason I couldn't.

"Stop," I said. "I can't. Not yet."

"Wha-wha- are you okay?" He was filled with concern. And I genuinely felt bad for what I had done.

Tears were streaming down my face. Kael reached for a few sheets of tissue and gently wiped my face.

"I'm so sorry," he said kissing my moist cheeks. "I didn't mean to rush you."

"No, don't say sorry. I'm the fool that keeps messing everything up. You are the perfect man. Sometimes I think that you are too good to be true, but I keep screwing with your head. You deserve better than this. You deserve better than me."

"I want you," he said. "And that's all. I don't care if we never sleep together." He paused momentarily, probably contemplating what he had just said. "I want to be with you, Faith Jones and I want to make you happy no matter what it takes."

"That's just it, you are every woman's dream come true and I want to be with you too, but this may be a little fast. We've only been dating a month, and..."

"Faith, don't explain anything to me. This can wait as long as you want, okay."

All I could do was smile. It was okay, I guess. But what if I was never ready to have sex with him? Although he said he was cool with it, that little pause of his had me thinking. Was he getting his shit from someone else? Naw, Kael wouldn't do that. This man was too perfect. Maybe that was what kept scaring me.

Kael held me all night long. We both slept in our birthday suits, and we woke up at the crack of dawn. I told him that he should get some more sleep, while I went to shower and check out the breakfast menu that was sitting at the writing desk.

I tossed all of the dried out Kleenex tissue into the wastebasket before taking a shower. If he knew the real reason why I hadn't slept with him, he would have needed a few pieces of tissue himself. As soon as Kael and I hit the bed last night, I was slapped with visions of me and Darius' last night romping. I remembered it all too well, and it wouldn't have been fair to Kael if I had gone through the motions with him, while another man was on my mind.

The shower merged with my tears, making it difficult for me to get out. Kael was not going to be able to see me like this. I was going to stay in there until I washed all of my sorrow away.

"Are you trying to drown yourself in there?" His sweet masculine voice called.

"I'll be out in a minute," I called back.

"What if I come in?"

He was still trying, but it was too soon. "I'll be out in a minute."

Then it hit me. Kael never got around to talking to me last night. I guess I really screwed that up. He was definitely not going to propose to me now. Instead of turning the shower off, I had to let the water wash away the new tears that had emerged.

I Try

Who the hell did Corey think he was, calling me in the middle of the night to tell me that he needed me to pick him up from some girl's house? I hadn't spoken to him in about a week, and all of a sudden he wants to call Mr. Dependable for another ride. Just because his ass got caught up in some chick's closet at two o'clock in the morning, now he wants to give ole' Darius a call. Well forget him. I told him to call Nathan or Ricardo. Since those were the guys that he got locked up with a couple weeks ago, they should be the ones that helped him get out of his latest predicament. Then I hung up the phone.

After all that'd happened, Corey was still being admitted to Morehouse in the fall. And I guess Mrs. Jones also eventually informed him that he was going to be attending the summer academy at Morehouse. Corey wasn't happy about it, and when he found out that I already knew and had agreed with it, he got pissed at me again. By then, I'd gotten used to him not talking to me, so this current hissy-fit didn't faze me. Sooner or later he would call because he needed something, and as always he did.

It was hard rolling over and going back to bed. To be honest, I did feel guilty about disconnecting that call, but what was I supposed to do? Sneak my mother's car again? Get *my* ass in trouble so that I could save his ass? Not this time, and probably never again. And forget moving to Atlanta with him. If we got into it while sharing an apartment, I don't know how it would feel walking around the crib with him avoiding me twenty-four hours a day.

After tossing and turning for another two hours, I threw on an early Eddie Murphy film, which put me to sleep almost immediately. The next thing I knew, my mother was shouting for me to get my lazy butt up. I yawned after my brief sleep and forced myself out of bed. Before heading to the shower, I checked for missed calls on my caller-ID. Corey had called three more times from that chick's house. Lucky for me I turned the ringer off after the first time he called me. If I had received the calls, I'm sure I would have ended up giving in to his whining.

The school day dragged by, and I was happy as hell that it was Friday. The weekend was here and I was ready to shoot some pool with Deon and his new best bud, Terrell. For some reason ever since he and Teresa got back together, he'd been hanging out with her cousin Terrell almost everyday. I didn't trust him, but I didn't know him that well either. That's why I decided to spend some time with the two of them. Cousin or not, I think Terrell was up to something and it was time to find out what it was.

There was nothing out of the norm about this pool hall. Smothered in smoke, sticky floor and cash sitting on the edges of most tables. Deon racked up our table in the back of the hall, and told me to wait the first game out. Odd. Despite who was with us, Deon would always play me first saying that he wanted to show off his little brother's skills since he taught me everything I knew about shooting pool.

"Seriously?" I asked him.

"Just this time okay," he said. "I want you to see how good this brother can play. I taught him everything he knows about shooting pool."

That sounded vaguely familiar.

"Damn, Deon. I guess it's cool." I wasn't about to start complaining.

"You can go first if you want," Terrell said. "I don't want to steal your brother from you."

"Steal my brother?" I laughed. "You can have him if you want him."

Deon chuckled as he sideswiped me with the pool stick. "Just sit this one out. You got winners."

I watched them play four straight games, and they were tied up. In the first game it was so close that Terrell wanted an immediate rematch. I took a swig of Deon's beer and said that they could go ahead.

After winning the second game, they had to break the tie. Third game, Terrell beat Deon by a landslide, and of course I was to blame.

He said, "You drank all my beer, man. You know how thirsty I get when I'm playing."

So they played again. The score was now two-two, and my pool stick was already back on the rack. This was not how I had expected to spend my Friday night, especially if I was spending it with my brother. Ever since we were kids, I had always been the center of his universe. Deon always put me first, and it wasn't just in pool. Now Terrell was invading my space, and I was going to have to put an end to it.

"Deon, I want to stop by Ricardo's on the way to your crib tonight."

Deon glanced at Terrell and then at me. "You were going to stay over tonight?"

"I *was*." I'm sure he could hear how disappointed I

became.

"Terrell and I were about to drive down to Rhode Island to check out this new strip joint. You have to be twenty-one and..."

"Like that ever stopped us before."

"This time I don't have any connects. How about we pick up Corey and the two of you can stay at my crib tonight? I have enough videos and alcohol to keep you two occupied for a while. Shoot, I even have some porn if you want to feel the vibe we're gonna be feeling in Rhode Island."

Terrell laughed as they slapped palms "It won't nearly be the same. These dancers get up close and personal where we're going. I wish I could get you in Darius, but they're extremely strict and the bouncers don't make friends that easily."

I didn't want that character doing me any favors, and I was not about to have Deon pick up Corey. The best thing for me to do would be to go home, sleep in my own bed, and in the morning figure out my future plans.

And that's exactly what I did. I slept until noon that Saturday, came down for breakfast, and then thought about what I would be doing in the fall. I drew a blank almost immediately. With things the way they were with Corey, there was no way I was moving to ATL. However, I really wanted to get down there to see Mya. If I didn't pass my retest, then I wouldn't be able to get into any college except one of the two-year community colleges. Going to school where Mrs. Jones worked was out of the question. What the hell did the future have in store for me? That one stupid exam was holding me back from everything I wanted to do. It just didn't make sense.

"Are you gonna stay up there all day?" My mother called from the bottom of the staircase. "It's a beautiful day out there and it would be nice to take my grandson out to the park."

"Why don't you go get him, then?" I spat. I was instantly ashamed of my tone.

There was a pause. I knew she wanted to rip into me, but she didn't.

"I think I will..." she said. "...and fix your little attitude before I come back with him, because the three of us are going to that park together. So go and get ready."

"I don't feel like going to no park. I just want to stay here and sleep."

I could hear her footsteps gradually making their way up the stairs. My door slid open and Mom found me lying on my bed in my pajama bottoms.

"Mom," I called, throwing a blanket over myself. I don't know why I did that, this is the woman who used to breast feed me.

"Boy please, I've seen you butt naked all your life. Don't forget, I used to breast feed you."

"I know, I know." I mashed my head into my pillow hoping she would get the hint to leave me alone.

Snatching the pillow off my head, she tossed it to the edge of the bed.

"You've been moping around for weeks now. What is wrong with my boy?"

"Nothing, I just want to sleep."

"Is it about graduation and all the pressure we've been putting on you? You know your father and I only want the best for you, that's why we stay on top of you all the time. We only want the best. You deserve the best because you're a good kid."

"Nothing's wrong with me. I just want to be left alone."

She said, "Then is it Corey?"

"Why would you say that?" I asked.

"He hasn't been around lately. Me and your father

were just talking about it the other day. It seems like you've been spending a lot more time with Deon than you usually do. That's not a bad thing. It's good to see that you two are bonding. However, Corey is your best friend and if something is going on, one of you needs to be man enough to step forward and apologize. Isn't he leaving for Morehouse right after graduation?"

"How'd you know that?"

"Faith called and told me. She's really proud of him, but she's sad that he's leaving."

"When did she call?" I asked hoping that I wasn't giving myself away.

"I actually just got off the phone with her. She calls from time to time to chat. Faith is such a nice young lady. You know she's dating someone. Some guy named Kevin, or Kerry..."

"I think his name is Kael, Mom."

"Yeah, Kael. Me and your father invited them over for dinner next weekend. Maybe you should bring Nina and the baby."

There was no way in hell I was going to be at the dinner with Mrs. Faith Jones and Kerry, or whatever his name was. And I was not about to bring Nina around my family so that she could get the impression that I had any interest in her. If Mya were in town, I would have brought her instead just so that I could show-up Mrs. Jones and her new beau.

"You know I'm not with Nina anymore."

"I know but, it would be nice for us to sit down like a family and—"

"She's not my family and neither is Corey," I said as calm as possible. "Anyway, I'm spending next weekend with Deon."

Mom didn't get upset and she didn't demand that I show up. She just released a simple sigh and said, "That's fine, but as I was saying before. Either you or Corey needs to stand up and be a man. Someone has to settle whatever tiff you are having before this boy leaves. And I don't care what you say, they have been family since he beat up those two boys for you."

"He didn't beat anyone up for me, he just—"

She cut in, "Like I said. Corey and Faith have been family for a long time and that's not going to end over some stupid misunderstanding." I was about to speak but she gave me that look every mother gives her child. The one that makes you shiver until you are old and gray. I think Corey calls it *the look of death*. "I am about to go and get my grandson, and I expect you to be dressed and ready to go to the playground when I get back."

With that she was gone, and I got my butt up and went to take a shower. I wasn't dumb enough to not be ready when she got back.

Days had gone by, and I still hadn't spoken to Corey. He must have been even more pissed, I'm sure. Even Wilson called and asked what was going on between me and Corey.

"I just got off the phone with Corey, and as soon as I mentioned your name, he started wildin' out," Wilson said as we sat on my back porch.

"He's probably mad because I didn't pick him up the other night from some trick's house," I said taking a puff of my Black and Mild.

It was late in the afternoon and my mother was out clothes shopping with my father. She was trying to find something to wear for the dinner with Mrs. Jones and Kael that Friday. I still hadn't spoken to Deon about me staying the weekend with him. Now that he was hanging with Terrell, it's like I had to check in days in advance before I went by.

"It wasn't like this growing up, was it?" Wilson said, more as a statement than a question.

"Remember we used to fight over simple things, like who had the best sneakers..."

"Which Corey always won," Wilson laughed.

"...And who had the best girlfriends...."

"Which Corey also used to win."

"Damn, what did the two of us have?" I asked taking another drag.

"Well, you always had the best looking mother," he said. "And me, I think I was the best runner."

I passed him the Black and Mild, but he refused. "That's why you're so good at sports now." Instead of taking another hit, I dropped it on the porch and crushed it with my shoe. "I never told you how much we admired you when you were a freshman. We were a little envious, but we had to give you your props. We were both sophomores, and here comes our freshman friend. Went from JV to Varsity in a few weeks, right?"

"Felt more like a few days. Man, I know you guys look out for me. We've always had each other's back and that won't stop that easily. A lot of kids from the high school still come over to East Quincy to watch me play, but it means more to me that you guys are there. That's why you and Corey need to settle this mess ya'll are going through. Ever since my parents separated and I moved to Quincy with my father, I've been afraid of losing my people. Now with you and Corey falling apart, it's messing up my head.

"I depend on what we have here to keep me going. It's going to be hard enough when he leaves, but knowing that our friendship is still going strong, it's all good. I figure, when the two of you move down there, I'll grab my scholarship and come down myself. It'll be the three musketeers again, running through them girls in Atlanta."

"I don't know about that," I said. "I may not be going to Atlanta. If this retest doesn't happen, then I don't know what I'll do. But no matter what, I won't be attending classes where Mrs. Jones works." Speaking of Mrs. Jones, I had a few questions for Mr. Wilson about his comments to Corey. "Before I forget, I need to ask you something."

"What's up man, I'm an open book."

I spat, "What's this I hear about you telling Corey that me and his moms is... I can't even explain it."

"What?" He was clearly taken aback. "What the hell did he say to you?"

I explained the conversation that I had with Corey in detail, and Wilson burst out laughing. "I can't believe he said that. Man, you know how we do the dozens. I said something about me and you running a train on Mrs. Jones, and he started bugging, asking me why I added your name to the pile."

"Corey didn't tell me all of this."

"Of course not. Corey's my ace, but he's always the victim. So, when I told him that you must have been hitting that every night while he was in the hospital..."

"You said that?"

"Don't sound so stunned. I've said worse in the past. But, Darius, you know it was all in good fun, but Corey started taking it to the next level, saying that none of us are allowed near his house if he ain't home. You know the real reason why he's mad about the move to ATL? It's because he thinks we're scheming on her or something. Now Mrs. Jones is nice, but like I said, it's your moms that ya'll should be worried about. That woman has an ass on her that makes me want to do things to my..."

I punched his arm hard enough for him to know that

the joke needed to end before it turned serious. Lucky for him he caught himself just in time, because he was starting to piss me off. Now, I could understand why Corey was so pissed that I already knew that he was being shipped out, and to make the situation worse, I wasn't going with him.

Later that night, I called Corey. We spoke briefly, making plans to meet up and discuss everything that had been happening. Something in me wanted to confess my relationship with his mother. Although I'm sure he would have eventually forgiven me, I didn't know how he would react to Mrs. Jones.

Climbing into the passenger seat, I made myself comfortable as I took his joint from the ashtray. Corey was driving his mom's car for the first time in a while. The last time I knew of him driving the car was when the two of us were racing Nathan on his bike. Of course, he sped past us, and we ended up getting pulled over by the cops and received a one hundred dollar ticket. It was just lucky that we had finished smoking a half an hour before, and we didn't have a stash in the car. Since that was his third offense, Mrs. Jones stopped allowing Corey to drive her car.

"It's been months," I laughed exhaling smoke. "I guess you're on parole or something."

"Since I'm leaving, Mom eased up a little. I've been driving for about two weeks now."

"Damn, it's been that long and you never even came to pick me up." I was joking, but from the way Corey gripped the steering wheel, I could tell he didn't see it that way.

"Well, it's not like you came to pick me up when I was in a jam. I still can't believe you did that to me,

Darius. I stayed there until like eight in the morning. The honey had to play sick so she could stay home from school. Her mom was trying to stay with her, but she talked her out of it. Of all my boys, I never ever thought you would have done something like that."

"Man, it was three in the morning. I had Lil' Darius with me," I lied trying to save face.

"You've been shady for the last few months, Darius."

"Corey, you sound like you're trying to forget that I bailed your ass out of jail not long ago. You remember that?"

"Yeah, but then you started lecturing me like you wanted to be my Daddy. You ain't my Daddy. Sometimes you act like you ain't my boy either."

"Look, if it's like that, than maybe you should just drop me back off at home. I thought we could hang out like old times, shoot the breeze and get pass this before you leave. But you acting like a straight up punk right now, Corey."

"Get the hell out of my car, bitch," Corey snapped.

"What? You better turn this car around and drop me off at my crib. You tryna leave me down here in the middle of Franklin Field Projects to get shot up. You know I still got enemies down here."

He stopped the car right in front of that dude Marcel's building. We hadn't seen Marcel since we finished junior high school. After Corey took my back in that fight after school, I later found out that Marcel had been waiting for the day to get back at me. We almost went at it during graduation from the eighth grade when he had his brothers with him. Of course, Deon was ready to throw down and luckily it was squashed before any of our parents found out.

"I saw Marcel at the club the other night," Corey smiled. "He got big as hell and he said he's been looking for you."

"Oh, yeah?" I said holding in my anger. This was not happening. Corey was not about to set me up over some BS. Brothers don't do that to each other no matter how ugly their relationship gets.

Looking up at the metal door, Corey started blowing the horn.

"What the hell are you doing, Corey?" I wasn't afraid or anything. I was just very confused as to what was about to happen.

When he blew his horn again, with this silly smile on his face, he told me to calm down. The metal door slowly opened, and as far away as we were from the entrance we could still hear the squeaking metal. I balled up my fist, ready for some action. There was no way I was going to run from this character and make myself out to be a punk. Whatever happened, I was going to take care of Corey next.

The door got stuck, there was some pounding, and then the door pressed forward. Corey reached over and patted my shoulder, as if to tell me that it was all good. He had this smirk on his face, one that I had never seen before.

The door finally opened, and out came two feet raised above the cement, next came two huge wheels and the body of a handicapped young man, about our age, rolling himself forward. This guy was wearing a black suit and bow tie. I cut my eyes at a hysterical Corey Jones, who was now squeezing my shoulder.

"I thought you were about to piss your pants," he said in tears.

Marcel had been shot two years before, in a drive by shooting near Heath Street. It was by the same guys who shot Corey. After his time in the hospital, Marcel took to reading the Qua'ran and the Final Call, eventually becoming a Muslim. He and Corey met up at the club a few nights ago, and discussed Corey's situation. Although Corey had no interest in converting to Islam, he decided to leave the whole Heath Street thing alone. That's why he decided to pick me up and talk about things. But with Corey, everything had to be difficult.

We all had a good laugh at my expense, and then discussed how our lives would soon be changing. Corey was moving to Atlanta, Marcel was accepted to NYU and was taking off in early August to get situated. I still wasn't sure what I was going to be doing, so I told them that I planned to work for a year and then head back to school. We promised to get together before Corey left, and I recommended Friday- the day of the triple-date at my house. Since I still hadn't been able to get in contact with Deon, this was a good enough excuse as any. There was no way I would be sitting across from Mrs. Jones and Kael that weekend.

What's Come Over Me

This boy was in my house again, and I had a guest in my living room. At least with Corey there, neither of them would have started up. Not like the last time. I have to admit, it was kind of nice to see Corey and Darius hanging together again. Corey had been moping around the house for over a month, ever since I told him that I signed him up for the summer program at Morehouse. He kept complaining that he wasn't a punk and he didn't want to be sent away. He thought that it would make everyone think he was a punk. I told him that this excursion would be good for the both of us. He would get away from the nonsense, and I could practice not having him around.

"You just want that nigga to stay up in here," he spat after I told him. Of course he was referring to Kael.

"Not that I need to explain myself," I started. "But you know that Kael has nothing to do with this. I don't want you to go anywhere, and I would have been a whole lot happier if you would have just gone to school here. It was your choice to go away, and I had to accept that."

"And it has nothing to do with me being shot?" It sounded like he was trying to convince himself.

"To be honest, that was just the icing on the cake.

When you got shot I thought I was going to lose you forever. And as soon as I got you back, I signed those papers and said *yeah*, my son is getting away from this place so that he can start over. It seemed like the best thing for both of us." At that point, I knew that if I reminded him that Darius also agreed with me then that would have opened up a whole can of worms. So, I left his name out of it that time.

"Long time no see, Darius," I said when he came into the kitchen wearing a new Prada outfit with some Nike Air Force Ones, and sorry to say, he was looking good as hell. He smiled at me, said that he'd been busy with school, and then slipped into Corey's room.

I sat down on the couch next to Kael, and told him that Corey had come in with Darius.

"Are we still going over to his parent's house this Friday?" He asked.

"Well, that's up to you. I already confirmed, so I'm not trying to back out. If you, on the other hand, have something planned..."

"You've been acting kind of funny since you mentioned this dinner thing to me. You haven't sounded too enthusiastic since the invitation. If you don't want to go, why did you agree to the dinner?"

"What are you talking about? I do want to go. Olesia and Benjamin are some of my closest friends, of course I want to spend the evening with them."

"Then it must be me," he said as he sniffed his armpits. "Do I stink or something?"

I hit him over the head with a pillow from the couch. This man was so amusing sometimes, that he made it difficult not to enjoy his company. Surprisingly, after the little rendezvous in New Hampshire, he and I had still been going strong. He never showed any anger or frustration towards me because I didn't sleep with him that night. However, the one thing that did begin to bother me was that he never told me whatever it was he was going to tell me. Everyday I replay the comment in my head, *I didn't work all those shifts just so that I could bring you here. That was for something else, which I'll tell you about later tonight.*

It had been about a month, and he still didn't talk about it. Was he going to propose? I was actually ready to say yes, until Darius walked back into my kitchen, right by the refrigerator where all of this started. It had been about two months since Darius and I had been together and I thought about him often. I even lowered myself to calling his house just to say hello. The first time I did it, his mother answered so I ended up having a nice long conversation. That's how this whole triple date thing came about. Supposedly, it was going to be Darius' parents, Darius and Nina, and me and Kael. I was not trying to go sit across from Darius and that young girl of his. The problem was that Kael was looking forward to the evening and I couldn't disappoint him.

I grabbed my purse from the couch and told him that I was ready to go to the mall whenever he was. I still hadn't bought anything to wear, and Kael promised me that we could go shopping for something. We headed out to the South Shore Plaza where my first stop was Arden B. I picked up this baby-doll tube top with halter beads, a pair of flare stretch jeans and I bought some pumps from Nine West.

It only took us three hours to find something I was somewhat satisfied with. Not that I wasn't happy with my purchase, but as always, Kael was huffing and puffing about finding something for himself at Macy's. He wanted to go without me, but I needed him right next to me to tell me how I looked in each outfit. I mean, he had to be happy about my purchase since he was going to be walking in with me.

But honestly, I wanted to help him pick out something myself. Yeah, the brother could dress, but I didn't want him to over do it and end up spending five hundred dollars on a suit he was only going to wear once. Olesia told me that it was casual, because Benjamin was not in the mood to play dress up. Benjamin told her that if she tried to make him dress up, he would not show up. And we both knew he was serious.

Together, we picked out a Sean John stripe shirt, a navy blue blazer and some light linen wash jeans. I thought we were good to go, and although he contested a little, Kael seemed pretty happy with his purchase. We were going to be sharp come Friday.

Friday was magnificent. Not only was Darius not there with his baby's mama because he took Corey out for a farewell dinner, but the night itself was marvelous. Olesia cooked a scrumptious meal, which consisted of calamari and shrimp with sauce, mixed greens, and the white wine that Kael and I brought.

After dinner, we played Tonk and then a few hands of Spades. The night ended just after midnight, and we thanked them and promised to do it again real soon. I could tell Olesia and Benjamin liked Kael a lot better than Stan. Basically because Olesia told us that she liked Kael a lot better than she like Stan. And I knew that Benjamin liked him better because he actually stayed in the room with us the entire night. The last time I'd brought a guy around them was right before Stan got locked up. This had been our third attempt to hang out with the Tates and it turned out to be a disaster just like the other times. Benjamin and Stan almost got into a fistfight, and ended up breaking an expensive vase given to them by Olesia's mother before she died.

So the fact that me and the Tates could finally hang out together was a triumph in itself. It wasn't that event alone that made me decide to sleep with Kael that night, but it did contribute to my final decision. This guy was the only one for me and everyone knew it. So that night in his condo we made love in his king-size bed until the following morning. Kael was like the Energizer bunny, and kept going and going and going.

He was the perfect gentleman all night long, concerned with my feelings over his own. And for me it was all about him. He kept me moist and wanting more, all night. Even when he finally asked for a time out, I waited patiently for him to come back. This was a time when I didn't have to take the lead. I was his toy to play with, his student to teach things to, his queen to service him. And I did everything I could to repay him for my stupid mistakes and the idiotic decision that I had made.

I called him daddy as a way to say I'm sorry. And without him knowing it, he forgave me by saying those three magic words. *I love you.*

When I woke up the following afternoon, I finally admitted to myself that I was in love with Kael Franklin and I was determined to one day become Mrs. Kael Franklin. I was actually happy he hadn't proposed yet though. After my divorce from Stan was final, it would feel great to be single a while before jumping over another broom.

Coming From Where I'm From

When we pulled into his driveway and all of the lights were still off, we knew something was up. Corey just looked at me with eyes filled with confusion.

"I don't like this at all," he said.

"You don't like what?"

"My mom and this Kael-character. He's over here almost every day and I don't like it. She keeps telling me how great he is, and how I should get to know him. But I don't want to get to know that pretty-bastard because I don't need a new father in my life. The first one was bad enough. I bet that Kael talked her into sending me away so soon."

"You know your mother can't be told what to do."

"But she can be persuaded. That's why dad got away with so much. Do you know how many times he cheated on her? She'd always throw him out, but after some time he would sweet talk his way back into the house."

"This is different, I guess." I couldn't believe that I was actually defending her new beau. "She seems happier with him than she did with your father. No offense."

"She does look happier. But what if he turns out to be like my father I won't be here to protect her."

"I'm sure it won't come to that. Kael seems like a nice—"

"Seems like," he spat. "That's the problem. We don't know what he's really like. And if I find out he's sleeping with her." His eyes were bulging. "She's a married woman, Darius. She shouldn't be sleeping with anyone... period. That's my mother."

That's when it finally hit me. Corey had been the center of his mother's life for years, so it really didn't matter if she was married, divorced or widowed. The fact was, no matter who came into Mrs. Jone's life, he would be taking her away from her son.

Patting his shoulder, I insisted that we go inside and chill out. He was resistant, but after noticing that Kael's car was gone, Corey decided that it was cool to go inside. Checking his mother's room, Corey was devastated that she still hadn't returned home.

"It's almost three in the morning. Where the hell is she?"

I couldn't answer because I was getting pissed myself. By that time, my parents were definitely in bed fast asleep. Dad didn't work weekends and although the gathering would have lasted later than usual, it would have shut down by midnight at the latest if he had anything to do with it. This meant one thing. Mrs. Jones was staying the night out with Kael. If Corey had asked me to go out and look for him, I would have quickly jumped at the opportunity.

"This is the third time she's done this." He had me in shock.

"Really?" I asked trying not to show my true emotions.

Corey flipped on the television set in the living room, and set up the video game system. "Three times," he finally said. "If he tries to move in here while I'm gone, I'm going to beat the hell out of him."

"Come on now, Corey. Do you think your mother

would do something like that?"

"I never imagined her to cheat on her husband either, but look at her. Staying out with some man she met at work. What kind of wife would do something like that?"

"Look, isn't she divorcing your father?"

"Yeah, but it hasn't gone through yet. My father is contesting the divorce. Which means, she's still married. This is infidelity, my man. I don't care what she says."

After a few games, and a few drinks, Corey almost passed out. I slapped him across the face and told him that he needed to go to bed. I watched a few music videos and then fell asleep on the carpet in front of the couch. That afternoon, I woke up when the front door opened. Mrs. Jones walked in, hair out of place, clothes needing to be ironed and an apologetic look on her face. She hadn't even noticed me yet, but I couldn't take my eyes off of her.

She walked through the living room, straight into the kitchen and into her bedroom. It is hard to explain the feeling you get when your *ex* is deeply involved with another man. Not that she was cheating on me, and despite what Corey said, she wasn't cheating on Stan either. Mrs. Faith Jones was moving on to something that made more sense. It still didn't feel right though, and eventually we needed to talk.

I knocked on her door softly, knowing that Corey would not wake up until about four in the afternoon, which left me with about three hours to spare. She took her time opening the door, and stared at me suspiciously, wondering if I knew what had happened the night before. I knew, because it was written all over her face. Mrs. Jones didn't speak at all, she just let me into her room and shut the door behind me.

Before I could say a single word, she said, "I told Kael about the two of us."

My mouth dropped.

"What do you mean you told Kael?"

"He bought a house in New Hampshire and he wants me and Corey to move in with him."

"What about Corey? Did you talk to him about this?"

"No. I just found out last night... well this morning. Corey's not going to like the idea at all."

"So, what did you tell him?" I asked eagerly.

"I don't know what I'm going to do. I have to speak to Corey about it, and then I guess I'll make my final decision."

"What about Stan? Aren't you still married to him?" I had to pull whatever card I could to change her mind. I couldn't lose her and Corey all at the same time.

"My lawyers said that in a couple of weeks I should be able to go in front of a judge. Kael has actually offered to pay for the court fees."

I hated to ask the next question, because I was afraid of the answer. But I did it anyway. "Did he ask you to marry him?"

"No. Not yet. He's still dealing with what I told him about us. Kael is a great man, and I didn't want to take this relationship any further without being honest with him. If he decides to take back all of his offers, I guess I'll be fine with that too. He just dropped me off, because he said he had a lot of thinking to do."

"Mrs. Jones, what if he tells someone? What if he tells Corey?" I was paranoid and upset all at the same time. She broke our promise to keep this rendezvous a secret and now we were an open wound.

"He won't. He promised me that."

"Well, a lot of us don't know how to keep a promise." I looked at her one last time before leaving her bedroom. "Well, I hope *he* can make you happy."

■ ■ ■ ■ ■

Nathan met up with me, Corey, and Wilson at Good Times Emporium late that Saturday night. It was Corey's last Saturday in Boston, and we all wanted to have one last night out on the town. We shot a few games of pool, played Laser Tag and then challenged each other to air hockey, which none of us had played in years.

I got my butt whipped on that table by Nathan who seemed to have had some sort of chip on his shoulder. Half way through our match, he shot the puck at me so hard that it skinned my hand as it flew past me. It almost hit this big fat white dude playing a video game behind us. I apologized, prayed that the dude wouldn't step on my hand when I reached for it, and then brought it back to the table.

"What's your problem, man?" I asked as I shot it back towards him.

"Just play the game." He hit it back, hard as hell, and this time the plastic hit me. I threw down my paddle and rushed him. I threw a punch, which struck the side of his face. As fast as they could, Corey and Wilson were on their feet pulling us apart. Nathan kicked at me like a little girl, and I got up enough energy to get out of Corey's grip and then lunged for Nathan again. I grabbed him away from Wilson, and then dropped him on top of the table, hard. The next thing I knew, this dude threw a blow that caught me in the eye. Grabbing his throat, I started banging on him. It took both Corey and Wilson to pull me off of that mofo. Security finally got there, and even though the fight was over and done with, the four of us were kicked out.

Nathan decided to go his own way, and it was lucky for him because I wasn't done yet. If it hadn't been for him, half the stuff that Corey had been involved with wouldn't have happened. The issues that Corey and I had wouldn't have elevated to the level that it had. And I could tell that Wilson was ready to bash on him as well. Corey, on the other hand could care less. We were back to our old selves, and I guess Nathan just didn't fit anymore.

The three musketeers ended the night at Ricardo's. Although Wilson doesn't smoke those Black and Milds, he does smoke weed every once in a great while. We watched some flicks, ordered Chinese Food and drank so many Heinekens that I can't remember the count. It was a farewell bash, and something that all of us needed.

While Wilson and Ricardo slept, Corey and I sat on the back porch and smoked one last joint.

"You know this is our last Saturday night in Boston together. We graduate Thursday, and then I'm outta here on Friday."

"It's not. You'll be back in August, and we'll chill then. I'm also going to try to make a trip down there soon. I told you about that girl I was messing with, right."

"That Mya chick, yeah you told me." He took a hit. "Darius, I may not come back in August. If I get myself situated while I'm down there, I may just stay. I'll come back for my clothes and everything, but I can't come back here to stay."

"What's going on with you?"

"I'm not ready for this new relationship my mother has. And I'm still not over what those guys in Heath Street did to me. I want to go back in there, but I won't. Like you've been telling me all along, I have a future ahead of me and I shouldn't let a bunch of knuckleheads ruin that."

"I got your back, no matter what you decide."

"You've always had my back, but for a little while, I was too stupid to realize it. I was so busy thinking about revenge and listening to Nathan, that I could have gotten all of us killed. But you have always been there no matter what. You even came down there to handle business that night with me, but Nathan said something about picking up his little sister. I was so pissed at that mofo, that I told his scary-ass to take me to my cousin's house instead. I told my mother I with Wilson so she wouldn't come over there rashing on me."

"What are you going to do about a place to stay after the summer program ends?"

"Well, I'll be on campus for the month of July, but after that I'll need to find an apartment. That's where you come in."

"What do you mean, where I come in?"

"The offer for you to move to ATL still stands. We can both find jobs and like I told you before, the rent is much less than the rent in Boston."

"I don't know. I haven't even thought about that since the last time you asked me. I'll have to do a job search and an apartment search when I come to visit you."

"You can even have your little girlfriend help us out a little. Or at least help me find some women."

I grabbed him in the headlock and said, "Yeah, she'll help you find a girl that won't get you shot."

We both laughed hard, and went back inside. I gave Corey Mya's phone number so that he could have someone to talk to while he was down there. I called her the next day and told her all about Corey. She was happy that my boy was coming to Morehouse, but she was more excited that I was considering moving down in August. She said that she was going to make sure my first visit was very special, but when I moved down there she was gonna do some things that would make Lil' Kim blush.

That Tuesday before me and Corey both went to the prom stag, my MCAS scores arrived. I passed the math section so I would be graduating with my class after all. Mom and Dad were so excited that they bought me a new car. Well, a *used* Honda Accord, but to me it was new. With all that had been happening, I never got around to applying to any colleges out of state, so Corey talked me into applying to Atlanta Metropolitan College to get an Associate's Degree. I guess it would give me the opportunity to figure out what I wanted to do. He had already downloaded the application for me, and literally stood by me as I filled it out.

My parents offered to pay my tuition, although they were not altogether happy. Leaving them was one thing, but deserting my son was a whole other story. They understood why I wanted to go, but they didn't feel the need for me to have to go so far away. Somehow my father talked my mother into letting me leave and everything was set for me. I bought round trip tickets for me to go down for a few days after Corey was settled. I was going to stay with Mya because Corey wasn't allowed to have overnight guests on campus.

The day before graduation I went by to check on Corey and to see if he needed anything else before he left. I was also excited to tell him that I spoke with Nina and she was happy that I was moving forward in life. She promised to visit with Lil' Darius in the fall, and I promised to come back to Boston as often as possible. This was the first time I was truly happy with my life.

Mrs. Jones opened the front door and I could tell she had been crying because her eyes were beet red eyes and her cheeks were still moist. Something terrible had to have happened, because I knew all of those tears wouldn't have been because of Corey.

"Kael broke up with me," she said when we sat down in the living room. "He said that I was *sorry* and that I needed to see a therapist."

"Is he stupid? It took him this long to think about it and this is what he came up with?"

"That's not the only thing. Kael asked me if I was over you, and..." Tears started to pour out of her eyes again.

"You told him it was over, right? I mean, not that I am a threat or anything, but I am leaving."

"That's not the problem, Darius. He broke up with me because I told him that I wasn't over you."

No More Rain (In This Cloud)

Surprisingly, I wasn't at all upset that Kael had broken up with me after I told him about me and Darius. What was bothering me was the fact that I wasn't over Darius and the way it was looking, I probably never would be. I didn't appreciate it when Kael called me, *sorry*, but I had to understand. As special as Kael was to me, I just couldn't give my all to him or to any man at the time.

"So you're saying that you're still in love with this boy?" He spat after I gave him the answer to his question about my feelings towards Darius.

I said, "I don't know if its love or not, but I do still have feelings for him. It's sad, and I thought that loving you would be enough. It's not fair to you Kael, that's why I had to tell you. You are a great man and you deserve to have someone's heart, their mind and their soul. I just can't offer my all to you right now."

He was more pissed than I had ever seen him before. "You're really *sorry*, and you need to get your head together. Maybe you need a fucking shrink or something. You're in love with a teenager. Are you sure you're not pregnant by him?"

"Excuse me?" I said. "You need to watch where you are going with this."

"No. You need to watch yourself. Maybe I need to watch myself. You had better not have given me any STDs. Messing around with a character like that, you could have caught something and passed it on to me."

"Kael!"

"Listen to me, Faith. I have loved you more than I've loved anyone else in my entire life. Now you go and do some shit like this to me? Fuck you!" Tears swelled up in his eyes. "I bought a damn house for us. I was going to propose to you tonight. And now, I gotta sell the house and return the engagement ring. No, forget that, I'll just keep the house and get the hell out of here. I can't believe this." He punched the wall in my living room, right near the spot where we used to sit and watch Good Times, and listen to J-J wreak havoc throughout Cabrini Green.

"I would say lets talk about this, but I don't think there is much more to say," I said trying to maintain a little composure.

"There is nothing to say," he snapped as he headed out. "Oh, by the way. Tell your little boyfriend that my niece can't wait to see him again."

"Your niece?" What in the world was he talking about?

"Yeah, my niece, Mya. Remember she was in town a couple of weeks ago? Well, apparently she met some guy while she was here. A nice dark skinned guy with braids. Name's Darius or something like that. Apparently he's moving to Atlanta with a good friend of his."

I was in awe. Darius had been seeing Kael's niece and now he was going down to Atlanta to be with her. I just lost everything because of my feelings for him, and he was starting over to be with another woman. My concern had only been Nina, I never expected anyone else to come along.

Kael had nothing else to say as he wiped his final tears

from his eyes. He left me in the apartment all by myself, and then suddenly the rain shower began.

It was a good thing that Corey had already gone to see his bastard father in prison. We discussed it the night before and he wanted to go and have one final visit before he left. It would be good for the both of them, we decided. So I dropped him off that afternoon, and he said that he would make his own way back. At least he didn't have to see his mother crying.

When Darius stopped by not too long after Kael left, I wanted to grab him and beat the living hell out of him. But I controlled myself, and ended up giving him a strong hug after I explained what had happened between me and Kael. He was surprisingly receptive, and actually insisted that I call Kael and tell him that it was all a big joke. But it wasn't and we both knew it.

Instead of asking Darius about Mya, I figured I should let him lead his life without having me in tow. He *was* just a kid, and he needed to find his way. Darius did not need any old baggage to carry around.

And when I thought it was all over, he kissed me like he had done on the kitchen floor when we spilled the orange juice. Neither of us pulled away, as I envied Mya for the good man she was about to get her hands on. If it had been twenty years earlier, I would not have let this guy leave my side. But that tired old song was dead: *the woulda, coulda, shouldas.*

At least that was what I thought. Darius lifted my hand and lead me into my bedroom. After shutting the door, we kissed again as if it were our last night on the earth together. I ran my fingers through his braids that were in need of a touch up. He slid off my shirt with ease and caution, kissing my salty tears every chance he could get. I removed his pants with the tips of my fingers, slid them down past his knees and then began kissing his stomach.

Lying down on the bed, Darius made love to me for the last time. When he cried, I let the tears soak my chest and asked him not to stop. The thought of Corey coming home never crossed my mind, and we were lucky that by the time we were done, he still had not come home. We lay there knowing that after that night, we would never be able to be together again. I told him to have a great time in Atlanta and to enjoy his new girlfriend, Mya.

"She's a very lucky girl," I said.

He started to ask me a question, but caught himself before he did. He probably wanted to know how I found out about it. If he guessed Corey, he would have been wrong. And the idea that maybe Kael was the culprit would never have crossed his mind. If it did, then he would have said something about it.

Losing Kael was one thing, but losing my son would have been the most devastating thing in the world. Darius and I had to end things because there was no way I was going to allow Corey to find out about our relationship. It would be too traumatizing.

When Corey called, he was still at the prison, and he said he needed a ride home.

"Can you pick up Darius too?" He asked. "We were supposed to go to the Wal-Mart and buy a few more things."

Darius and I drove down to Sharon with very little to say. He tried to explain how he and Mya met, but I told him that it was fine and that no explanation was needed.

"Damn, what took you all so long," Corey pouted getting into the front seat after Darius crawled into the back.

I said, "Watch your mouth, Corey. I don't want to have to tell you again. You're a college man now. You should have a much better vocabulary."

"Oh, please, Ma. College students swear more than the average dude on the street."

I gave him that mother's look, and he quickly cut the discussion.

"So, how was Stan?" I reluctantly asked him.

"He's all right," he started. "Dad was congratulating me on getting into Morehouse and all that. He told me not to get any Spelman girls pregnant so that I wouldn't end up like him."

"What is *he* talking about? That man never went to college."

"Wait, Mom. Listen to this. He said that he was accepted to Howard, but he had fallen in love and gave that part of him up. Of course I didn't believe him, but he told me to ask Grandma and she would confirm it."

I couldn't believe all the crap this man was feeding my son.

"And who supposedly, did he fall in love with?"

"Dad said it was you. He said that he was registered and everything. Classes were set for fall, but then that night at the club he saw you again and that was it. You got pregnant, he was in love and nothing else mattered."

"So tell me this, Einstein, he had been out of high school for a year already, why was he just registering for his first year in college, shouldn't he have been a sophomore?"

"Right after he graduated from high school his father died. Howard allowed him to defer enrollment until the following year. Mom, this man had his facts straight. I still didn't believe him, so while I was waiting for you, I called Grandma from a pay phone and she said that if I want to see the acceptance letter I could stop by."

"Well, what do you want to do?"

"Darius," he called. "I know my Mom went out of her way to pick you up so that we could go to Wal-Mart, but do you think we could do that later. I really do need to see my Grandmother before I leave, and this might be the best chance I get."

"Sure, you can just drop me off and call me later. I may be with Lil' Darius, so just call my cell phone."

We dropped Darius off at his baby mamma's house, and then Corey and I went to see my mother-in-law. Her house still had that damp, moldy smell, which always made me want to hurl my lunch. Stan was raised in that house, and I remember back in junior high school, sometimes his clothes would have that same stench.

Carol, which is what I have called her since the day I met her, gave both of us bear hugs. She wasn't a heavy woman, but she wasn't petite either. Even at her age, she still had a shape I would die to have. Curvaceous with beautiful skin, and only a few streaks of gray. I bet Carol still turned a few heads when she walked through town. Her face was made up lightly, with a tint of mascara and a hint of eye shadow.

"Are you going out, Carol?" I asked standing near the living room couch.

"No, girl. I have a friend coming over for dinner. You know I have never been much of a cook, so I ordered some soul food from Bob the Chef's. It should be here any minute. You two can join us if you want." She did her usual and pinched Corey's cheeks. And as usual he scrunched up his face because he hated it. "I haven't seen my baby in too long. Now he's a man thinking he's too good to see his Grandma."

"That's not it, Grandma," he said massaging his aching cheeks. "I've been busy getting ready to move."

"And thanks for the invitation to dinner, but I still have to get Corey to the store so that he can buy a few things for his trip. He's leaving in two days you know."

"Yeah, Corey told me when he called. I'm so proud of

this boy. Just don't make the same mistakes that your daddy did. Can you promise me that?"

This wench was starting up again. Not only was she telling *my* son that Stan had made a mistake by getting involved with me, but she was actually telling him that he was a mistake right to his face. In the past, I was used to her coming out of her mouth, but never in front of Corey. Although she never mentioned anything about Stan and college to me, she was always talking about the mistake he made. Indirectly, blaming me.

"You could've done big things, if you had just gotten your priorities straight back then," she once told him. "I'm sure Faith would have understood if you needed to leave to better yourself. There would have been no reason for you to go down this path and end up in prison, right Faith?" That's what she said during our first and only visit to see him in prison together.

"Carol, could you show Corey that acceptance letter that Stan got from Howard. We really need to go soon. And since you're having company, I don't want us to be in your way."

"Nonsense, you're never in the way. Especially not this guy," she said pinching his cheeks again. Then she left to find what we had been looking for.

"I hate when she does that," he spat when she was gone. "Ma, why do you call her by her first name instead of Mom or something? She is your mother-in-law."

"I've known your father since middle school, and I've been calling her Carol since I met her. It just stuck, and even after we got married I couldn't get used to calling someone besides my own mother, Mom."

"Are you sure that it's not because you two can't stand each other?" He laughed.

I said, "It's not that we can't stand each other. It's more that we come from two different places and we were sharing your father. And then when you came along, we had another man in our life to share. Your grandmother has her way of doing things, and I have mine."

"Yeah, I know. I come over here and I get money. I go home and I get yelled at."

I popped him across the head softly and we both laughed. This boy... this young man was amazing and I wouldn't have changed one thing about the way I raised him. He had a tough shell when he needed to, and he was a little jokester that kept me on my toes. I'm sure there was much more going on in Corey's life that I didn't know about. His father was a prankster, and I'm sure he got more than his green eyes from his dad.

"Here is my little memory box from Stan's childhood," Carol said sitting on the couch with Corey.

She flashed a few baby pictures of Stan, and then some of Corey. There was even a wedding picture stuck at the bottom of the box. It was honestly, the first time I realized that there were no pictures of our wedding hanging around her house. School pictures of Stan, and similar ones of Corey graced her walls. But there was not a single picture of me anywhere. As soon as Corey moved to Atlanta, the one picture that I had of her in my living room, was going to be moved to Corey's bedroom. After all, she was *his* grandmother.

"Right here." She handed the letter to Corey who read it to himself.

He glanced at me a few times, before handing it to me, so I breezed through it and handed it back to Carol. The son-of-a-bitch had actually been accepted into Howard's music program. If it weren't for his *mistake* then he would have possibly become something in life, besides a crackhead. It was time to go, and I was seriously hoping that her comments and this letter wouldn't upset Corey too much.

"Can I get a copy of this?" Corey asked taking the letter back from me.

"I have never let that letter out of this house, and—"

"I'll make sure it gets back tonight. I can scan it at home and then bring it back on our way to the store. We can do that, right Ma?"

Carol cut her eyes at me, wanting me to disagree with him.

"Of course we can. I'm sure your grandmother doesn't mind. Do you, Carol?"

Fly Away

I'd been waiting for hours for Corey to call me back, and since he still didn't have a cell phone, I couldn't get in touch with him. There was no way I was calling Mrs. Jones after what we had just done. Holding my son in my arms, I thought about the reality of not being able to see him whenever I wanted. There would have to be scheduled visits to see my own flesh and blood. It was going to suck, but what choice did I have. I sure as hell didn't want to end up like Stan, giving up on my dreams and making not only myself, but also my family, very miserable.

It would be good to get away from Mrs. Jones too.

"I don't think I told you this, but I am really proud of you," Nina said.

Rocking Lil' Darius on my knee. "You told me already."

"No I didn't."

"You told me that you were happy..."

"No. I mean I am happy for you, but I'm more proud of you than anything else. Passing MCAS, college and the move to Atlanta. Lil' Darius and I are going to really miss you, but when you come back, or if we move there..."

"Move there?"

"Not to be with you, but to be close to you. Your son will need to be near his father. Maybe you don't think so, but I will end up dating again. I may even end up getting married one day, and I'm sure you do not want another man raising your son. We can share custody, and he'll have both parents in his life."

"I *would* like to have more contact with him. Atlanta isn't that far by plane, but you know I can't afford to fly back as much as I want to."

"I've already booked a flight to Atlanta for the first week in October."

"Damn, girl you work quick. How much were the tickets? Mine cost me an arm and a leg."

"They were close to three hundred each, but it was worth it. Lil' Darius will have a chance to see his father's apartment after its all set up."

I kissed Nina on the forehead.

"What was that for?"

"We've been together for years and after all that we've gone through, we're still cool. Most of my boys who have kids don't get along with their baby's mothers at all."

She asked, "Like your boy Nathan? Tammy said Nathan never comes to see his baby."

"Nathan is not my boy. I almost beat his ass the other night at Good Times Emporium for talking smack. That dude was in there talking a lot of trash and ended up hitting me with an air hockey puck. So I snatched him up and if it wasn't for Corey and Wilson, I would have ended up beating the mess out of him."

"I have to say, I'm really glad you did. Nathan is a straight up ass, and the way he treats Tammy and his daughter makes me want to beat the hell out of him myself. He was never a real friend to you or Corey. Look at all the trouble he caused the two of you. You and Corey have been tight for too long, and this guy comes along and almost destroys that."

I said, "At least things are back to normal. Somewhat."

"Yeah, you're leaving soon, so *things* won't really be that normal. But I have to say again, me and Lil' Darius are really proud of you."

Nina kissed me on the cheek, and then wiped her lipstick off of my face. Her mother's car had broken down, and since it was getting late I decided to call a cab to take me back to my house. I knew Wal-Mart was going to be closing around ten, and since it was almost nine-thirty by the time I got home, there was no way we were going to make it before then. As soon as I walked in the house, my father told me that Corey had called three times looking for me.

"I told him that you were at Nina's, and that he should try your cell phone," My father told me. "Corey said that he'd been calling you for hours but you wouldn't answer your phone."

I searched my pockets for my phone. "What is he talking about? My phone never rang." I checked for my belt clip next, but it was gone. Not again. Where in the world could that phone have been? Patting myself down again, I grew frustrated and angry.

"Lost your phone again?" Dad asked. "With you moving away like this, you're going to need to become a little more responsible."

"I know, Dad. I know."

The phone must have been at Nina's house, because I was sure I had it on me when I got there. I called Nina, but she couldn't find it. She said she didn't even remember me having the cell phone at all. I asked her to call my phone number, using three-way on her telephone. She listened for my Kanye West ring-tone.

"Unless it's on vibrate, I don't think your phone's here. Ooh, I hope you didn't leave it in the taxi," she said.

Damn. If I did I might as well forget about getting that back. I was going to have to buy a new one before I moved. My contract wasn't up yet, so I couldn't turn the service off for another year. Since Nina didn't remember me having my phone with me, it was possible that I left it up in my bedroom.

As soon as I got to my bedroom, the house phone rang so I picked it up hoping that it was Nina calling to tell me that she found the phone. It turned out to be Corey asking me why I hadn't been answering his calls.

"I lost my phone again, man," I said flatly.

"Not a-damn-gain. This is ridiculous. Do you have any idea where you left it?"

"Why the hell do people always ask that question? If I knew where I left it, it wouldn't be lost," I said jokingly.

"Don't let me bust your ass like you almost did Nathan."

"Oh please, Corey I'll drop you like a bag of stale Cheese Doodles."

He chuckled as he told me about his day, and his visit to his Grandmother's house. For some reason, I wasn't too impressed about his father's awards and achievements in high school. Corey told me about the medals he had gotten for ROTC, his Honor Roll and School Spirit awards, and his trophy from the track team. All that I could remember was hearing Stan and Mrs. Jones argue back and forth, when I stayed the night as a kid. That still bothers me to this day. Now Corey was praising his father's name after all the bruises he placed on Faith's neck, back and arms over the years.

"How could you be proud of that man after all the shit he did to your mother?"

He said, "You don't understand. You have a real good father and a strong home. Even though I've been fighting it, I guess, sometimes I feel like I need that father figure in my life. I know he'll spend the rest of his days behind bars, and I don't respect him one bit for what he did to my mother. But, Darius, he is still my father. If it wasn't for him I wouldn't be here. I've spent so many years hating him, and I'm tired of having all of that weight on my shoulders. At least I have some of his achievements to hold onto. So now I can be proud of my father for what he could have been instead of what he actually is."

"All right, brother. That was pretty deep." I sat at my window and lit a Black and Mild. "I still don't like the man and I probably never will. But you're my boy and I have to respect what you're shooting for."

After I exhaled the smoke out the window, Corey asked, "Are you smoking in the house? Your parents are going to beat the hell out of you."

"I've been smoking in my room for years now. They haven't caught me yet and they won't catch me anytime soon."

"I don't know, Darius. You're not that good at keeping secrets. Every secret that you've tried to keep has been exposed. Just remember that when your parents come knocking at your door while that Black and Mild is dangling on your lips."

I quickly put out the cigar in the ashtray that I keep underneath my bed and kept my eye on the door.

"Shut up, Corey," I said. "You got me all shook. I can't even enjoy my smoke."

He was laughing so hard that he dropped the phone. We laughed a little while longer, realizing that in less than forty-eight hours he was going to be taking off for his new home. Corey offered to spot me one more time at Ricardo's. This time, I told him, it was going to be on me just so I could see the expression of Ricardo's face when I paid for a dime bag.

"Cool," he agreed. "I'll take a shower and then call you

when I'm on my way."

"So you got the car again? Check out Mrs. Jones still hooking a brother up."

Then he brought up something we hadn't done in years. He asked me if I wanted to egg up the Burger King drive-thru one last time.

"You gotta be kidding," I laughed. "We haven't done that since we were like sixteen."

"We were out of control, weren't we?" He chuckled.

I said, "Yeah, we were until you took that piss in the woods that day."

"Forget you, man. I'll call you in a few."

I'm Going Down

It had been a long Friday, and all I wanted to do was take off all of my clothes and hop into bed for a nice long slumber. Instead, Corey talked me into renting a movie after we left Wal-Mart. Corey wanted a Brad Pitt film, but after he and Jennifer Aniston broke up, I refused to watch his movies. I was a huge *Friends* fan back in the day, and all I could think about was how he broke poor Rachel's heart. We settled on a new release from Bruce Willis, since he and Demi's decision to separate was mutual.

We tried to invite Darius over to watch it with us, but he didn't answer his cell phone. Corey even tried his house, but Benjamin said that he was still over at Nina's. After the movie ended, Corey finally got in touch with him and they made plans to go out. While Corey was in the shower, I decided to give Cynthia a call to see how things were going with her. Actually, I was calling to find out if Kael had said anything about the breakup.

I made the call in my bedroom from the house phone as I looked for something to wear to bed. I found a Victoria's Secret nightshirt and then searched for some batteries for my trusty blue friend. It was about time that we got reacquainted. I was, however, going to have to wait until Corey left for the night.

"Hey, girl," I called into the phone. "I haven't heard from you in a while. I haven't seen you at work all week."

"Oh, hi," she said flatly. "I've been real busy during the week. You know, with the semester coming to an end, I need to make sure that my staff is putting in supply orders for the fall."

She sounded a little peeved, but not unlike most Fridays after doing weekly supervisions for her staff and when she didn't have a date.

"I know. Mr. Hughes has been piling all kinds of stuff on my desk. I've been taking late lunches at my desk since Tuesday. He hardly left his office at all, except to give me more work. He's there when I get there and he's there when I leave."

"Ooh, girl. I heard that he might be losing his job." Cynthia was back to her old self.

"Gossip, girl, gossip." I was ready for the 4-1-1 on this guy. But it did make me kind of nervous. If Mr. Hughes was getting the boot, then who would replace him? The devil you know is usually better than the devil you don't know.

"Yeah, I heard it in the faculty lounge. Rita heard it too."

"Heard what?" I sure did miss a lot of new gossip by not having lunch with the ladies this week. "Don't leave me hanging."

"Mr. Hughes is just not working out. Other staff members have been complaining to the board for months now, I'm surprised you didn't know. A few students have even gone to the Vice President's office to complain. They called him a racist because he's been screwing with the financial packages of the minority students. You know about all the complications the Black and Latino students have been having with their account records.

And then I heard that a new student brought him up on sexual harassment charges." She took in a deep breath. "Didn't you tell me that he used to make inappropriate comments towards you?"

"That was a long time ago, before I put him in his place," I said. "I had been there three years before he started, so I think he was trying to make me so uncomfortable that I left on my own. But I can't say that I want to see him go."

"What?" She snapped. "Are you serious? Once he's out of the school, it'll make room for a much more qualified man and probably even young, attractive, and Black."

"How do you know it'll be a man?"

"Prayer, girl. It works," she laughed.

There was a brief pause as I gathered up enough nerve to ask her if she had heard from Kael. She must have been reading my mind, because she suddenly told me that she had.

"Kael called me earlier and told me that you two broke up," she said in one breath. She was disappointed because she had really been pushing for us.

Embarrassed, I asked, "What did he tell you?"

"He said that you were still in love with another guy. No matter how much I argued with him, he wouldn't listen to me. I told him that you hadn't seen Philip in years, and that you were done with him."

"Is that who he said it was?" I asked, now even more sorry because I could still trust Kael after what I had put him through.

"He didn't have to. I knew who it was. Kael didn't deny that it was him, that's how I knew for sure that it was Philip. I'm psychic like that." I just smiled at her comment. "Why don't you call him and tell him that you want to be with him."

I wished I could call him and tell him that, but my

heart wouldn't let me. Kael was a great man, and I am more than glad that I had been with him. But he, along with Philip, and Stan were all a part of my past. Hopefully, one day Darius would be too.

"You know he quit his job today, and he's moving to New Hampshire in a few weeks."

"What about school, he still has another year to go, doesn't he?"

"He'll just drive down a couple of nights a week, he told me." She hesitated for a second. "Kael wants to be with you, Faith. I'm not only saying this because he's my cousin, but Kael is a damn good man. Rita was just saying today that she wished she'd jumped on him when she had the opportunity. I told that crazy heifer that she never had the opportunity. Ever since the day he met you, Faith, you've been the only woman for him."

"I know, but... hold on." Corey knocked on the door to my room and then walked in with his hands covering his eyes. "Didn't I tell you to wait for me to say come in, boy?" I said to him.

"I can't see anything. I just need to borrow your cell phone so I can call Darius." He sighed. "Are you dressed?"

"Go ahead and uncover your eyes," I said. "Of course I'm dressed. You think I would leave my door unlocked if I was walking around here naked? I know you don't have any manners, you're always barging in here."

He lowered his hands slowly, and then laughed at my bare feet on the bed. The bottom of my feet was not that desirable, because of all the years I used to walk around the house barefoot.

"Put on some socks or something," he laughed grabbing my cell phone off of my bureau. He picked up the car keys too and said that he and Darius were going out for a spin.

"Don't get into any trouble either," I told him almost

forgetting that Cynthia was on the phone. "Oh, hello. I'm sorry. That's just my crazy son." I relayed the message from Cynthia to Corey, telling him to have a safe trip and to enjoy himself. "I'm not telling him that," I said after she asked me to tell him to keep his condom supply stocked.

I couldn't continue my conversation with Cynthia about her cousin, until Corey was out of the room. Corey didn't like Kael at all, and if he found out that we broke up, although he would have been happy, he would have started asking a lot of questions, which I was not prepared to answer. As Corey dialed the number, I watched with impatience. "Do you have to do that in here?"

"I'm just going to tell him that I'm on my way, and then I'll put the phone back. I don't want to leave the room with your precious Motorola and have you complaining about your minutes." He put the phone to his ear. "Ahh man, I just dialed his cell phone number. I'll just see if he found it or see if somebody else picked it up."

That's when my heart dropped into the basement. The popular Kanye West ring tone went off. And kept going off. Even after Corey placed my phone back on the bureau, leaving it on, Kanye West continued to haunt the atmosphere. I stared at Corey, as his eyes dropped from mine to the floor underneath my bed. And then the ringing stopped. Only one person we knew used that ring-tone.

It Don't Have To Change

There was never a reason for me to suspect anything when I heard the horn blowing outside. But when I saw that it was Nathan's car instead of Mrs. Jones', a red flag should have gone up. I almost changed my mind, but I decided to be the bigger man and go along for the ride anyway. The fellas dapped me up as I piled into the back seat and the car sped off down the road.

"So are we still hitting up Ricardo's?" I asked. "Or do you want to go and egg up Burger King like you said."

"Nah, we just need to make a quick stop on the way to Ricardo's," Corey said with an odd, almost frightening tone in his voice.

"Where're we going?" I asked trying to get past the awkward mood.

Nathan said, "You'll see."

We drove for a few minutes, and no one said a single word during the ride. Nathan brought us near Dudley Square, not too far from the school, and I hoped we were going to stop at Stash's so that I could get a sub. I hadn't eaten since earlier that day and I was starving.

"Mind if we stop at Stash's for a second?"

Neither of them responded, so I repeated the question loud enough so that they could hear me over the music. Corey looked back, grilling me, and told me to shut the

fuck up until we stopped the car.
"What the hell is wrong with you?" I asked totally confused. The night was supposed to have been another night of celebrating and it was turning into some craziness.
"Pull over here," Corey told Nathan when we got near the Heath Street Projects.
"I thought you were passed this, Corey," I said as he rushed out of the car. "Leave the dudes alone. We're moving to Atlanta, man. Let's leave this behind us."
Corey threw open the back door, grabbed my shirt and snatched me out of the car. Before I could protect myself, he punched me dead in my eye and then slammed me against the car. I fought to get free, but he was too quick and started punching me in the ribs. With the little energy that I had, I brought my knee between his legs and then pushed him away from me.
"Get that bitch," Nathan shouted from the other side of the car. I was about to run, until I noticed a group of guys piling out of one of the buildings. Nathan grabbed me from behind, just as Corey was getting to his feet.
"Let him go," he said. "I want this mofo to fight me like a man. Then we'll leave him here to finish getting his ass kicked by these dudes."
"What the hell is going on?" I shouted to him. "What the hell is wrong with you?"
When he dropped my cell phone by my feet, I knew that it was over. Somehow I must have left my phone in his house. Probably in Mrs. Jones' bedroom on the floor where I had thrown my pants. Now Corey knew about us, and whatever happened to me that night was well deserved.
I stood there and let him beat the hell out of me. When he told me to fight back, I couldn't. I apologized until my mouth was filled with so much blood that I

couldn't speak anymore. Until I couldn't see no more. And then I was out.

I remember hearing them argue, and Nathan saying, "We should have left him there." Then I remembered hearing the car pull off. I forced one eye open, hoping that the dudes from Heath Street would just pull out a gun and shoot me. But from what I could see, I was no longer in the projects. It looked like they had left me outside my brother's building. For a while, I just lied there wishing that Corey had left me by Heath Street so that I would have been put out of my misery. I didn't want to think about the long road ahead.

Finally getting to my feet, I dragged myself to the front door, put my key in and fell into the hallway. It took a while, but I got to the second level and was able to get down to Deon's door with my body in tremendous pain. I couldn't pull the energy together to knock, so I felt blessed to find the door unlocked. I would probably be alone in there anyway, because Deon and Terrell were supposed to be spending the night in Rhode Island.

The sight I saw inside the apartment was enough to send me into convulsions. My keys, my phone and my jaw all crashed to the floor at the same time. Deon's shameful eyes caught mine. I wanted to move, but I was stuck in the position, and immediately vomited everything I had inside of me.

Terrell was not even fazed. He looked at me with what I would consider a smirk, almost as if he was happy with my discovery. Deon, pulled himself out of his new partner, zipped his pants, and then tried to explain. Then Terrell got off of his knees and went straight for the bathroom.

"It's not what you thi..." When Deon saw my bruises he forgot about his own issues and focused in on me. "What happened to you? Who the hell did this to my brother? I'll kill him!" He searched the kitchen drawers and then pulled out his glock.

"No," I muttered. "I did this to myself."

We sat on the couch and I explained everything to him, starting with me and Mrs. Jones, all the drama we shared, the cell phone and then the fight with Corey. He agreed that we should let it go and try to move on. Terrell left without having to be asked, and I decided not to question Deon about my discovery. He would tell me about it in his own time so I wasn't going to pressure him.

My brother and I slept in late on Saturday, and then called my parents to tell them that I was going to stay the week with him. They liked the idea, especially since Corey had moved away and thought that I could use the company. Corey left for Atlanta the following day, but I had no contact with him. Months past before I heard, through Wilson, that Corey was doing well. Instead of coming back in August, Corey ended up staying with a girl he met from Spelman.

"You really fucked up bad," Wilson said when we finally got together at Stash's. "I never would have thought any of us would do something like that. If it were that fine-ass teacher, Ms. Jackson then I would understand. But your boys' mom? I'm surprised he didn't kill you."

"I thought he was going to." I tried to force all of the images out of my mind. I hadn't spoken to Mrs. Jones since the night I left my phone in her bedroom. It bothered me not to know how she was doing, but I wouldn't dare call her. We would just have to let things be.

"By the way, congratulations on getting accepted to Johnson and Wales. I hear you're registering for the Spring semester."

"How'd you know?"

"Corey," he said after downing his Coke. "He got your email and told me about it. The dude may front like he hates you, but he was happy to hear the news. I just don't expect him to call and tell you."

"I don't expect him to either." It did feel good knowing that Corey was actually opening my emails and not just deleting them. Believe me, if he decided never to speak to me again I would be willing to accept that. Like Wilson said, it was a surprise that Corey didn't shoot me that night. One thing I would hate to think about is what I would have done if the tables were turned. If it were Nathan, I would have probably shot him. Corey... I don't really know.

Nah, I wouldn't have shot him, I'll admit that. I just don't know if I would have ever forgiven him.

"So have you heard anything else about Nathan?" Wilson asked. It's not that he cared, but I guess he was just being courteous. Or it could have been out of fear of being snitched on. After all, it was partially his fault too. It was all of our faults.

Somehow, and it's still not clear to any of us, the jogger we held up in that park identified Nathan in a photo lineup. Nathan was arrested a few weeks after Corey left for Atlanta, and me and Wilson have been waiting anxiously for Nathan to spill the beans on us. But even if Nathan did dime us out, he was still the one who pulled out the weapon. Aggravated robbery.

I said, "I haven't heard anything."

"It's been over three months, do you think he'll ever sell us out?"

"He's been in too much trouble with the law for them to believe anything he says. Plus, the guy identified him as the gunman. I don't think they care about any of us or else there would have been a manhunt. Nathan put a gun to this poor guy's head, so now he's suffering the consequences."

"I guess what goes around comes around," Wilson said. "So when do you think we'll get what's coming to us?"

"I think we already did."

Flashes of Mrs. Jones ran through my mind again. We're all getting what we deserve in one way or another.

At least my parents didn't find out, but I'm sure that it was only a matter of time before they would. If Nathan was out on the streets, I'm sure he would have been spreading the story around. I know Wilson could be trusted with something this serious, that's just the type of guy he was. And Deon still hadn't come out to my father yet, so my secret was definitely safe with him.

"Can you keep me posted on how Corey's doing?" I asked Wilson, who had become my only link to my best friend.

"You know I will."

Before we left the restaurant, I asked him about the girl Corey was staying with.

"Some girl named Mya, or something. She's supposed to be real nice. Corey said that he told her everything and she stood by him. Maybe one day we can all meet her. It sounds serious."

"Maybe," I said as I gathered my trash. For some reason I was expecting to hear those very words from Wilson. Corey was like that, always out for vengeance. Hopefully he would grow out of it before he broke Mya's heart. She was a sweet girl and deserved a man who would give her his all. Maybe I wasn't that guy, but hopefully Corey would turn out to be the one.

They both deserved someone special in their lives. We all do.

Throwing my garbage away and following Wilson

outside, I asked, "So when is your first game as a high school senior?"

"This Saturday," he said. "So, you're gonna be there, right?"

"How can I not? This may be the last year I get a chance to see you play on a regular basis so I gotta make it to your games. By the way, have you decided on a college yet?"

"Not after everything went down. I guess Morehouse is still an option, but I've been checking out schools on the West Coast as well. So it'll end up being the school that offers me the best package."

We shared a half hug, and then went our separate ways. I didn't make it to his game after all. Foot Locker called me back for a job, and they wanted me to start that Saturday. Not that Wilson showed any resentment about it, but I only made it to three of his games that season. He had a whole new crew of followers from Quincy, so even when I did show up, he didn't have much time to chat.

The day before I left for Johnson and Wales, I picked up my telephone and dialed a number I hadn't used in months. It was a call to say hello and that's it. Although the feelings were still there, and I knew in my heart that it was a bad decision, I had to hear her voice one last time.

"Hello," a deep, almost sadistic voice greeted.

I waited a few seconds, and then apologized to whoever this guy was. "I must have the wrong number," I said and then hung up the phone.

A Change is Gonna Come

"Who was that?" I asked from the bathroom. Kael had been staying with me from time to time. The commute back and forth to New Hampshire was kind of a hassle on school nights, so we agreed that he could stay over two nights a week. We were not a couple anymore, we were simply friends *without* benefits. But like Cynthia said, you never know what will happen.

"Wrong number." Kael was cleaning up the living room after sleeping on the couch again.

I hadn't had a wrong number or a crank call since Corey moved to Atlanta. All of his friends and ex-girlfriends knew that he was gone, so I couldn't understand who would be calling the house like that. It seemed like something minor, but... I don't know. Maybe I was expecting that *wrong number* to be someone that I knew.

Going to my room to get dressed, the first thing I did was check the caller-ID on my cordless phone. The most recent call. It was a very familiar number and I was almost tempted to lock my bedroom door and return the call. And if Kael hadn't knocked on my door, I think I would have.

"Do you still want me to come to your session

tonight?" He asked.

I looked over at my clock and saw it was almost time for him to go to work. After this brief setback, which he was unaware of, I thought it would be better if I went to see my therapist alone.

"No," I called struggling to get a shirt on. "I think I need to go alone tonight, but thanks. I have another one on Thursday. We can go before your class."

I started seeing a therapist almost immediately after Corey left for school. Kael helped me out a lot and even offered to pay if my insurance didn't cover it. He insisted on coming a few times, and I accepted with open arms. The therapist agreed that it was a good idea. Kael was the best thing that could have ever happened to me, and I just hoped one day that my heart would realize it.

But that phone call was bringing me back to what started this whole mess. It reminded me that my son was still pissed at me, and sometimes wouldn't even accept my calls. Luckily Kael kept in touch with his niece, Mya, who Corey was now involved with. That was usually the only way I could get updates on Corey.

He never came back to Boston that summer after he went to Atlanta. Mya helped him find an apartment near campus, and I came to find out months later, that she moved in with him. Corey did contact me from time to time to say hello, or to say I love you. But he wouldn't carry on a conversation with me. I believe he was too ashamed and he had a right to be.

I continued to send him things from his room whenever he or Mya requested it. I still sent my baby money whenever I felt the need, and I still bought and shipped new outfits to him.

It took an entire school year before I saw him again. He didn't come to Boston, but he asked me to come to Atlanta. While I was there, I stayed in a hotel with Kael.

Corey and I both agreed that it would be more comfortable for everyone if Kael and I stayed in a hotel. So Mya found us a nice Bed and Breakfast a few miles away from their apartment.

I sat across from my grown-looking son, who was now growing his hair out and had a full beard and mustache. His skin was a little darker from those southern rays, and he was now speaking with a mild accent.

"Hey, Ma," he said offering me an uncomfortable hug.

I squeezed my boy tight as hell, but he reminded me that he still had pain from when he got shot in the stomach. I apologized and let him go with a kiss on the forehead.

"I missed you more than you know," I said as he offered me a seat in the living room.

His place was smaller than I imagined, but it was a nice size for the two of them. Books were in piles in the corner of the room. There was a notebook computer on their desk with more books and papers gathered around it.

For the most part, it looked pretty clean, and I assumed that Mya had a lot to do with that.

"I missed you too," he said lowering his eyes. "Do you want something to drink? We haven't gone shopping yet, but..."

I interrupted him. "No, I'm fine. Do you need some money for groceries? I hope you've been eating while you've been here, you look a little thinner."

"That's because I walk a lot. It helps me clear my thoughts, ya know. I haven't changed that much. I still eat like a mule."

We laughed just enough to get over that uncomfortable hump that was still dividing us. A tear ran down Corey's cheek and he allowed it to run its course.

The next thing I knew, water was running down my face as well, and I couldn't stop it.

"Why?" he asked me. "Why'd you do it...?"

And before I could respond.

"...Never mind. I don't want to know. Just tell me if it's over. Please, that's all I want to know. No details, nothing about your feelings for him. I just want to know that it's over."

It was over and it felt good to let him know that. I hadn't spoken to Darius since Corey found out about us, and it made me feel better about not returning that phone call that I received a few months before.

He smiled for the first time since I'd been there. "You were all I ever had, you know that, don't you?"

"And vice versa. Everything I did I did to make sure you were happy. I guess I forgot about myself for a while and ended up getting side tracked."

"Mom, Kael is a very good man. I know I gave you a hard time in the beginning about him, but the way he treats Mya and the way he's stood by you, proved to me that you deserved someone like him. I mean, I have someone special now, and you deserve to be with someone who makes you feel special."

We hugged again, but this time I was more careful. Something in that conversation changed me and changed my feelings towards Kael. Maybe what I'd been doing all this time was waiting for approval from Corey. Corey always loved Darius and maybe that was part of my attraction to him. I don't know. What I do know is that after his little speech, I felt something stronger about my relationship with Kael. Not that I was going to rush anything, but I was going to eventually stop resisting. It's the same thing my therapist had been saying to me.

"One more thing," he said with a sigh. "And I don't want you to get upset."

I wiped a few more tears from my eyes as I waited for the news.

"Mya's pregnant."

"What!" I had to catch myself before I imploded. I wasn't old enough to be a grandma.

"Only six weeks. That's why you didn't notice anything. We're happy about it and we're going to keep it."

"What about school?"

"We're not dropping out or anything like that. We're both working part-time. And since Mya will be out of school in two years, she'll be able to get a better job when we really start to need money."

"I don't know what to say," I told him. My son was going to be a father. I couldn't fathom the thought. He'd changed so much in the last year, maturely and physically. Maybe he was the one keeping the apartment clean, and maybe he was cooking the meals now too. I didn't know Corey anymore. It was time for me to get back into his life, even if it was a minor role.

"Congratulations, baby," I finally said giving him *another* hug. "Although I'm not happy about being a grandmother, I am so happy for you. Make sure you let me know what you need for the baby. I have to go shopping and get some diapers, some bottles... Wait, does Kael know? If you told him first, I'll—"

"Mya's out telling him right now. We wanted to tell you both in our own way and this was the best way I knew how."

I took Corey to the Underground Mall, and bought him gift cards for the baby, a few things for Mya and some underwear for him. That was all that my son wanted. He told me that he was trying to disconnect from the name brand, superficial style he had in Boston. It was going to be challenging, he said. But he knew that it was time to grow up.

My baby had grown so much and I loved who he was becoming. Now it was time for his mother to grow up as well. I excused myself and headed into the ladies room. Pulling out my cell phone, I scrolled down to the Ds and... Danielle...David...Darius. I deleted that name from my cell phone, and deleted the number from my mental Rolodex.

Although Darius was always going to be in my heart, as a son, a friend and a former lover, it was time to get my life in order. It had been a long time coming, but my life was finally headed in the right direction.

Back at the apartment, we celebrated new life and new endeavors. During dinner, I sat next to my grandbaby's mother, and hopefully my future daughter-in-law. While Corey sat near the man who had been there to help me weather the storm.

We were all going to be all right. For the first time in my life, I could feel it.

Coming Soon from

K. M. Thompson

**Ordinary People
(A Family Reunion)**

NEGLECTED SOULS
Richard Jeanty

Motherhood and the trials of loving too hard and not enough frame this story...
The realism of these characters will bring tears to your spirit as you discover the hero in the villain you never saw coming...

Neglected Souls is a gritty, honest and heart stirring story of hope and personal triumph set in the ghettos of Boston.

MEETING MRS. RIGHT'S WHIP APPEAL
Richard Jeanty

Malcolm is a wealthy virgin who decides to conceal his wealth from the world until he meets the right woman. His wealthy best friend, Dexter, hides his wealth from no one. Malcolm struggles to find love in an environment where vanity and materialism are rampant, while Dexter is getting more than enough of his share of women. Malcolm needs develop self-esteem and confidence to meet the right woman and Dexter's confidence is borderline arrogance.

> A NEW NOVEL FROM THE AUTHOR OF 'NEGLECTED SOULS' AND 'MEETING MS. RIGHT'
>
> # RICHARD JEANTY
>
> # SEXUAL
> *exploits of a*
> # NYMPHO
>
> "The book is hotter, steamier and sexier than the title suggests. Jeanty has done it again."
> —Treasure E. Blue Essence best selling author of *Harlem Girl Lost*

SEXUAL EXPLOITS OF A NYMPHO

Richard Jeanty

Tina develops an insatiable sexual appetite very early in life. She only loves her boyfriend, Darren, but he's too far away in college to satisfy her sexual needs.

Will her sexual trysts jeopardize the lives of the men in her life?

Coming Soon from

Richard Jeanty

The Forgotten Souls (Summer 2006)

Neglected No More
(The sequel to Neglected Souls)

Sexual Jeopardy

And

The Cleanup Man
by George S. Screws

Order these exciting novels from

RJ Publications

Available at bookstores everywhere.

Use this coupon to order by mail.

- ❏ NEGLECTED SOULS (0976053454 – $14.95)
- ❏ MEETING MS. RIGHT'S WHIP APPEAL (0976927705 – $14.95)
- ❏ SEXUAL EXPLOITS OF A NYMPHO (0976927721 – $14.95)
- ❏ ME AND MRS. JONES (097692773X – $14.95)

Name _____
Address _____
City _____ State _____ Zip Code _____

Please send me the novels I have checked above.

Free Shipping and Handling

Total Number of Books _____

Total Amount Due _____

This offer subject to change without notice.

Send check or money order (no cash or CODs) to:

RJ Publications
842 S. 18th Street, Suite 3
Newark, NJ 07108

For more information call 973-373-2445, or visit www.rjpublications.com.
Please allow 2 – 3 weeks for delivery.

Order these exciting novels from

RJ Publications

Available at bookstores everywhere.

Use this coupon to order by mail.

- ❑ NEGLECTED SOULS (0976053454 – $14.95)
- ❑ MEETING MS. RIGHT'S WHIP APPEAL (0976927705 – $14.95)
- ❑ SEXUAL EXPLOITS OF A NYMPHO (0976927721 – $14.95)
- ❑ ME AND MRS. JONES (097692773X – $14.95)

Name _____
Address _____
City _____ State _____ Zip Code _____

Please send me the novels I have checked above.

Free Shipping and Handling

Total Number of Books _____

Total Amount Due _____

This offer subject to change without notice.

Send check or money order (no cash or CODs) to:

RJ Publications
842 S. 18th Street, Suite 3
Newark, NJ 07108

For more information call 973-373-2445, or visit www.rjpublications.com.
Please allow 2 – 3 weeks for delivery.

Order these exciting novels from

RJ Publications

Available at bookstores everywhere.

Use this coupon to order by mail.

❑ NEGLECTED SOULS (0976053454 – $14.95)
❑ MEETING MS. RIGHT'S WHIP APPEAL (0976927705 – $14.95)
❑ SEXUAL EXPLOITS OF A NYMPHO (0976927721 – $14.95)
❑ ME AND MRS. JONES (097692773X – $14.95)

Name _____
Address _____
City _____ State _____ Zip Code _____

Please send me the novels I have checked above.

Free Shipping and Handling

Total Number of Books _____

Total Amount Due _____

This offer subject to change without notice.

Send check or money order (no cash or CODs) to:

RJ Publications
842 S. 18th Street, Suite 3
Newark, NJ 07108

For more information call 973-373-2445, or visit www.rjpublications.com.
Please allow 2 – 3 weeks for delivery.

Order these exciting novels from

RJ Publications

Available at bookstores everywhere.

Use this coupon to order by mail.

- ❑ NEGLECTED SOULS (0976053454 – $14.95)
- ❑ MEETING MS. RIGHT'S WHIP APPEAL (0976927705 – $14.95)
- ❑ SEXUAL EXPLOITS OF A NYMPHO (0976927721 – $14.95)
- ❑ ME AND MRS. JONES (097692773X – $14.95)

Name _____
Address _____
City _____ State _____ Zip Code _____

Please send me the novels I have checked above.

Free Shipping and Handling

Total Number of Books _____

Total Amount Due _____

This offer subject to change without notice.

Send check or money order (no cash or CODs) to:

RJ Publications
842 S. 18th Street, Suite 3
Newark, NJ 07108

For more information call 973-373-2445, or visit www.rjpublications.com.
Please allow 2 – 3 weeks for delivery.

Order these exciting novels from

RJ Publications

Available at bookstores everywhere.

Use this coupon to order by mail.

- ❏ NEGLECTED SOULS (0976053454 – $14.95)
- ❏ MEETING MS. RIGHT'S WHIP APPEAL (0976927705 – $14.95)
- ❏ SEXUAL EXPLOITS OF A NYMPHO (0976927721 – $14.95)
- ❏ ME AND MRS. JONES (097692773X – $14.95)

Name _____
Address _____
City _____ State _____ Zip Code _____

Please send me the novels I have checked above.

Free Shipping and Handling

Total Number of Books _____

Total Amount Due _____

This offer subject to change without notice.

Send check or money order (no cash or CODs) to:

RJ Publications
842 S. 18th Street, Suite 3
Newark, NJ 07108

For more information call 973-373-2445, or visit www.rjpublications.com.
Please allow 2 – 3 weeks for delivery.